Bruce Allen Powe was born and raised in Edmonton, Alberta. After serving overseas during the Second World War, he returned to Alberta, where he received his M.A. in Economics. Now living in Toronto, he and his wife, Alys, have two children.

Powe's first book, *Expresso '67*, a satire, was published in 1966. He is also the author of two other novels, *Killing Ground: the Canadian Civil War* and *The Last Days of the American Empire*.

THE ABERHART SUMMER

BRUCE ALLEN POWE

PENGUIN BOOKS

Penguin Books Ltd., Harmondsworth, Middlesex, England
Penguin Books, 40 West 23rd Street, New York, New York, 10010,
U.S.A.
Penguin Books Australia Ltd., Ringwood, Victoria, Australia
Penguin Books Canada Ltd., 2801 John Street, Markham,
Ontario, Canada L3R 1B4
Penguin Books (N.Z.) Ltd., 182-190 Wairau Road, Auckland 10,
New Zealand

First published by Lester & Orpen Dennys Ltd., 1983
Published in Penguin Books, 1984

Canadian Cataloguing in Publication Data

Powe, Bruce, 1925-
    The Aberhart summer

ISBN 0-14-007260-8

I. Title.

PS8581.093A72 1984   C813'.54   C84-098140-6
PR9199.3.P67A72 1984

Manufactured in Canada by Webcom Limited

To my parents, who were there.

Author's Note

Except for a number of political or historical figures who appear in actual events and are quoted from published accounts of the period, all the other characters in this book are fictitious. For instance, there never was an Albert Roothe nor, at the time, a constituency of Strathcona-White Mud.

The quotation on page 20 is from "O God Our Help in Ages Past" and the quotation on page 175 is from "Jack Frost" by Gabriel Seaton, in Olive Beaupré Miller, ed., The Latch-Key of My Bookhouse *(Chicago, Toronto: The Bookhouse for Children, 1921).*

So many people have contributed background for this book, it would take another volume to thank them all. My appreciation to those of you who took the time to dig up material, search your memories, and otherwise help out. Of course, the interpretation of this research is solely the responsibility of the author.

Primary documentary sources include the author's own research for his M.A. thesis in economics at the University of Alberta ("The Social Credit Interim Program and the Alberta Treasury Branches") and the Edmonton Journal *for 1935. However, among the published works used as background two should be mentioned: J.A. Irving,* The Social Credit Movement in Alberta *(Toronto: University of Toronto Press, 1974) and W.A. Mann,* Sect, Cult and Religion in Alberta *(Toronto: University of Toronto Press, 1972).*

Finally, I would like to thank the Ontario Arts Council for its support.
                                                                    BAP

CHAPTER ONE

YOU SHOULD HAVE BEEN THERE THAT DAY IN 1935, WHEN THE future was born in cool, drizzly twilight at a race track. Only then would you understand what this is all about.

In our prairie city, a place called Edmonton after a northern suburb of a distant London, the millennium was to arrive below the altar of a packed grandstand facing onto a race track, where there were the shabby trappings of carnival: concession stands, wood chips on the ground, games booths and barkers.

Even after they got up on the platform for the hymn-singing and speeches, there was all the horseplay, done with a kind of joy mixed with a simmering undercurrent of anger. Horseplay. Playing at horses, I mean. They took the presence of the race track and turned it into a tableau that had grown men galloping around in bright silks to portray the competing political parties.

Contrived maybe, but loads of laughs just the same. Devised to get the juices agitated for the final oration, when the horsing around merged into a wrenching religious-political revival.

For the thousands who came it was a reminder of the qualities the world had taken away from them: mirth, hope, decency, and the prospect of a returned prosperity. God knows they needed it. As they sat there on the hard seats, blankets over their shoulders against the chilly, damp night, I don't think they had any inkling that they were being prodded in a mass along vast chutes to a foggy arena.

Those of us who were too young to know didn't grasp the meaning: the slicing up of old-line politicians; the attacks on the Fifty Bigshots, betrayers of the people; the mystical economics that would bring an end to the terrible Depression. None of that we knew. But we felt the rebirth of energy, an end to despair, a sense of triumph about to be realized against the hazy forces of evil that had ruined so many.

All of this was wrapped up in the voice of one man: William Aberhart, who was to lead them forth to a glowing future, its vision rising through the aroma of hotdogs and sawdust and the sour smell of their own poverty. He would do it, and they believed. They really thought his election would bring forth a miracle; twenty-five dollars a month for every adult in Alberta.

It was strange, all right.

This took place on Saturday, July 6, 1935, at the Big Northern Alberta Social Credit picnic at the Exhibition Grounds. None of us was to be the same afterwards.

Forty-five years later, on a day in July, I closed up my mother's small bungalow on the South Side. There wasn't much left of any value. My sister Doris and her husband had already taken the few good pieces. But my wife insisted that we pack up all the rest to sell to the antique dealers.

"You can't throw out that stuff," Claire said, as she washed out the old medicine bottles, bundled up the fountain pens with encrusted gold nibs and the postcards showing another world of low buildings and small black cars. "They're collectibles."

"We don't need the money."

"That's not the point, Doug."

I closed the tailgate of the station-wagon we had loaded with bulging plastic bags, and stood on the sidewalk for a last look at the house. Except for its new aluminium siding and double-glazed windows, it was unchanged. My mother had been the last of the old-timers on the block, and the new people wouldn't even know enough to call it the Sayers' place. While Claire smoked a cigarette and wouldn't look at me, I walked along the sidewalk.

At the fourth house west of ours, I stopped. The Fetterman place, as I still thought of it, had been rebuilt into something with bright-blue siding and huge picture windows. My friend Norm had lived there. As I walked back towards the car, I passed the only brick house on the street where, at the back, old man Headley had kept horses in the barn. The barn was long gone. I could still picture it, though, an unpainted, grey clapboard shed with its stalls and loft, where all that had happened to us that summer of 1935 had been focused in one terrible night.

I stared at the last two houses. Beside ours was the Roothe place. Its front door was propped open as though those who lived there were letting the fresh air blow out an unexplainable heaviness. The house was so changed I had difficulty visualizing my friend Babe again, in his last summer, slouching out the door to take command of our endless days of idleness, or Albert, his older brother, leaping down the steps on his way to create the ideal new world of Social Credit at the side of William Aberhart.

Between the Roothe place and Headley's was the smallest of the houses, so tiny it had defied renovation. The Thorpe place was as I remembered it: set back from the sidewalk, as neat as a miniature white chapel amid the garish new colours of the street. Its glassed-in verandah was intact, and someone was sitting there in the shadows. Here the Thorpes had prayed and sought their salvation in a frenzied circuit of gospel lighthouses where they found only darkness.

Whoever was sitting on the porch moved, and I saw a glint of blond hair that made me think of Diane and how she had appeared to us as a kind of vision, unattainable and as perfect in her beauty as a movie star. And of Pete, her brother, missing all these years, whose only weapon against our torments was his talent for mimicry. I smiled. I could hear Pete running through the voices of radio and, finally, his exact rendering of Aberhart's voice.

When the radios on the street were echoing with one of Aberhart's broadcasts in shrill distortions of his actual voice, one could hear, in the Thorpes' yard, Pete repeating the words in resonant tones that were unsullied by the crackles of primitive broadcast, until his father wheezed at him to shut up, while the real Aberhart went on with a message of hope that would change our lives forever.

CHAPTER TWO

THAT VOICE OF WILLIAM ABERHART.

It came from the cavity of his chest, as though all the people had gathered in a deep cave and were crying out in a unified chorus for rescue; it was hi-fi in the days of squawky microphones and tinny radios; it was caring and sympathy when all others spoke meaninglessly of the need to work hard, as though the whole thing had been the fault of the people; it was rough and down-to-earth, ungrammatical at times, the way they talked in the shadows of the grain elevators; it was funny and raucous when others' were solemn and empty, combined even with the visual shock of him appearing on stage in a patched-up coat of many colours to show them, in images and voice, the chaos of the times; it was inventive and as good a show as anything on radio; the Man from Mars who arrives on earth and is stunned by the inability of the earthlings to solve their problems.

Above all, it was the voice of a plain preacher, a part-time one at that, whose fundamental beliefs shone through, whose con-science had reluctantly driven him to study economics in order to save them here on earth from the madness of the Depression. And it was understood and implied by many that perhaps—just possibly—William Aberhart had indeed been chosen by the Almighty to bring this message of rescue to a suffering world.

Until that night of the rally in July 1935, I had only heard Aberhart's voice at odd times, muffled and a bit shrill, on the radio. But his presence had become a focus of conflict in our household. My father's parents lived with us, driven from their farm like so many others, cramming our small bungalow with their bitter

4

defeat. My grandfather was an Aberhart supporter. His desire to hear Aberhart was matched by my father's contemptuous refusal to listen to "that drivel." Like many teachers, my father believed the answer would be found in a vague form of democratic socialism, and the two men would glare at each other while that tinny voice talked on, until my mother would finally get up and snap the dial with a placid and good-humoured grin.

"Can't you two get along?"

That Saturday morning, when I came into the kitchen to ask her for a quarter to go to the Big Northern Alberta Social Credit picnic away over town at the Exhibition Grounds, my mother found herself in a dilemma. Father was off at summer school, and she would have to make the decision herself.

"What makes you think I've got a quarter to spare?"

"And, uh, car tickets."

"Adult ones?"

"They don't take student tickets in the summer."

She crinkled through the cigarette smoke blowing into her faded blue eyes. In the breeze coming through the back door, the long grey ash wavered, about to topple onto her library book lying open on the kitchen table, where the breakfast dishes congealed. A lingering smell of burnt toast mixed with the tobacco and a hint of gas from a faulty pilot light in the stove.

"Can't you find anything else to do?"

"Well, Babe says Albert told him there's a carnival going on all day. Lots of things to see. It's an all-day picnic, see?"

"So you'll want some sandwiches, too."

"Guess so."

"Gee, this is quite an outing you've got cooked up. I don't know what your father'll say."

"Tell him I'm going as a spy."

She chuckled deeply, the wide freckles on her pale skin stretching around the two cheek dimples that must have endeared her to my father when they were young.

"It's Babe's doing, then, isn't it? Or Albert has talked Babe

5

into going because they want all the warm bodies they can get to hear Abie. Isn't that it?" She called Albert's younger brother Babe the way we did, not by his proper name, Hamilton.

"Nah, Albert hasn't a hold on Babe. He goes out of his way to kid Albert about being a holy roller. He keeps hitting him up for the twenty-five bucks Abie says he's going to hand out to everybody. Babe just figured it'd be something to do, good for a laugh. Norm's going. His mom's making sandwiches for him."

"I bet you Mrs. Fetterman doesn't have a quarter."

"We'll go dibs. I'll make sure Norm gets a pop."

I knew I had won when she took the yellow library card out of its pocket on the inside back cover and slipped it onto the open pages. She closed the book and got up slowly from the table. A loaf of bread, half open, was already hardening on the table. Her cotton dress wrinked around her large breasts as she slithered over to the icebox in carpet slippers. The ash finally fell onto the floor, but she didn't move the cigarette from the corner of her mouth.

"Mustard relish and cold ham?"

"That's fine."

As long as I can remember my mother seemed perpetually attached to a limp cigarette — a roll-your-own during the hard times — that drooped, unladylike, from the corner of her mouth. Our mashed potatoes were always sprinkled with grey ash, our milk speckled. Instead of Grace, our mealtime ritual was to dust off our plates, flicking away the bits of tobacco that showered from her inexpert makings.

Over the years my mother tended to let herself become sloppy. She was a big woman, blowzy, to use an archaic expression, and before she died, she had put on an enormous amount of weight, could hardly heave herself out of the deep chair where she sat reading all day in a halo of blue smoke. That's where I found her many years later.

How someone so immobile knew all that went on in our neighbourhood is difficult to fathom. . . . Yet she wasn't a gossip. By some arcane process she absorbed the daily lives and crises into her own retrieval system, and this combined with a total recall that enabled her to enliven our table-talk with accurate, sardonic vignettes about those who shared our street of little wooden bungalows. I have come to realize, too, that I have built my own success on the qualities inherited or acquired from her. If one has the skill to find out everything that's going on, one has access to power and can make what others call astute moves. I can thank her for that gift and my father for his incessant work habits, which rescued me from her sloth; although nowadays, I must say, I find myself fighting off a growing tendency to inaction. Like her, I smoke too much.

Well, at least she never ended in a nursing home. A victim of a cerebral haemorrhage, brought on no doubt by her incessant smoking and overweight, she died sitting up in the living-room of the same small frame bungalow, the inevitable library book on her lap. The neighbour who found her panicked at the sight of all those overdue library books. I had been busy and hadn't made it to see her for two weeks. The library books were a reproach to my neglect.

Yet, that day her intuition was grinding away. She came back to the table with the relish and some dried-out ham in waxed paper that hadn't been properly closed. I went over and shut the icebox door. We were always running out of ice before the next delivery because she left the door open.

"I can't see you boys sitting through all those speeches. What's Babe up to? He going to make fun of Albert?"

"Mr. and Mrs. Roothe are going too."

"Well, see that you behave yourselves. Don't make fun of Abie and his bunch. You could get into trouble."

"Naw."

"How late'll you be?"

"We won't stay long."

"Just don't do anything dumb."

"Aw, we won't, Mom."

She began slicing the bread, and her jiggling brought down another shower of cigarette ash. Her freckled hand brushed at the specks and left smudges on the porous white surface of the bread.

7

CHAPTER THREE

ALL DAY THAT SATURDAY THE UNGAINLY WOODEN STREETCARS marked "Special" unloaded their occupants at the gates of the Edmonton Exhibition Grounds.

Those who came had the appearance of coolies hauling earth in wicker baskets to build that dam for the glory of the revolution. They crab-walked heavily with baskets, sacks, and leaden Thermos bottles in the hope that what they had brought from home — the egg salad, the peanut butter with honey, the pink ham sandwiches in McGavin's polka-dot wax paper — would keep the kids going all day and away from the popcorn, candy-floss, and hotdog vendors who cynically wore "Official Delegate" badges.

No one had the money, even when it was for such a wonderful cause. Some laughed it off and gave the kids their nickels.

They said: Come the election — whenever the Farmers' government, scared out of its britches, gets up the nerve to call it — and Mr. Aberhart will see that they get the money. These weren't the ones who would call the Social Credit leader Abie. That was what the unbelievers named him, not those who understood.

They knew that the hostile newspapers, under the thumb of wealthy alien forces, would make fun of them. The papers would deliberately underestimate the attendance and call it a campaign kickoff. As if the Movement was just another political party.

No, their enemies would never see that this was not politics. It was a way of educating the people, of giving them renewed faith and confidence to cope with the terrible conditions under which they suffered.

What could they do when all the others, especially the United Farmers, which claimed to be a peoples' movement too, rejected all the answers that were so clearly set out?

Who was the enemy?

Those who had betrayed them? Or those who pretended to be on their side, but who wore blinkers and wouldn't accept Social Credit?

It was the only way to end poverty in the midst of plenty.

It was their only hope.

It was why they flocked in thousands to hear and see William Aberhart in person.

From his radio broadcasts, first as a fundamentalist preacher, then, when the slump devastated Alberta and the other western farm provinces, as he gradually swung to the Douglas answer, Mr. Aberhart was known to them. They basked in his compassion. They felt close to him. But until the day of the picnic, few had ever seen him.

As we three intruders, infidels who giggled and shoved and aped the serious purpose of the throng, came down from the streetcar, I knew we had made a mistake. It was going to be a bust. We shouldn't have come.

This sense of being adrift had come over me slowly. At first, when we got onto the streetcar at the corner, it was all familiar and comfortable — clumps of neighbours and pals together, off on a picnic, faces that were our daily reality along the dusty, gravelled streets. But as others crowded aboard and we were shuffled along to stand among the new ones, we slowly began to pick up the aura of purpose.

It was no ordinary picnic. These were pilgrims on their way to do worship. We had strayed into the wrong church, where the lingo was a rising, excited chatter of "dividends," "credit," "twenty-five dollars a month," "the minions of Satan," "the Fifty Bigshots," the way in which Aberhart himself must have been put here on earth by an Almighty who was using him as an instrument to save the people.

"You get what they're talking about?" I muttered to Babe.

"What? Nah, wasn't listening."

He also disturbed me. For he was the one who had insisted we go, had jeered at Norm Fetterman and me until we finally gave in and sneered back at him that he was caving in to his big brother, at which point he got really mad, the way Babe could, and snapped back: "It's not for him."

Then who was it for? Babe didn't seem to be enjoying himself particularly. He had kept after us until we were swept along by our curiosity at his own strange urgency, yet now that we were on our way, on this so-called great adventure of laughs, he stood swaying on the streetcar strap, his dark eyes hooded and lost in some inner communion, not seeming to notice the rising, agitated babble of the alien tongues around us.

"What's eating him?" Norm Fetterman whispered.

"Search me. He gets all keen, ropes us in, then can't give a darn less."

That was the beginning. We didn't know it then, but Babe's sullen and preoccupied silence was the first sign of an enigma that has stretched down all these years. Even now, my memory of it makes me wonder if indeed the answer I later thought I found is really the right one. At that time it was only another ingredient in our own discomfort, our realization that we were lurching along in this stuffy streetcar with neighbours who had become strangers, towards a destination they saw clearly but one we sensed we didn't want to reach.

"He looks sappy," Norm added.

I stretched to see past some chattering heads to the rear of the car, where Babe had been pushed or had edged himself. Norm was right. Now Babe seemed to be staring back into the row of seats by the window, and his glowering, heavy look, so untypical of him, had dissolved into a faint smile and what seemed silent enjoyment of something that had occurred to him. But it wasn't for us. He was still beyond reach.

What happened after we arrived at the Exhibition Grounds only confirmed his distance. His inner departure became a physical one, and we lost him — as it turned out, forever.

Oh, he stayed with us for awhile. We fooled around a bit, circled the booths at the carnival, and watched the games. But for once we were leading him, and instead of leaping ahead, popping up with new things to try or see, Babe dragged behind as if we hadn't invited him.

"Okay, we've seen all there is to see. Let's have our eats and go home," Norm said.

"Now you're talking," I said. "This place gives me the creeps."

When we turned back to relay our decision to Babe, he was nowhere to be seen. He had been there a few minutes before, but now he was gone, as though he had slipped back farther and farther into the crowd and had been swallowed up in the tide of hope and expectation that charged these believers. We retraced our steps, expecting him at any moment to come out of nowhere with some crazy thing. Maybe he'd tap us on the shoulders and sock a candy-floss into our mugs. Or maybe he'd have pinched one of those hats with "Alberta Needs Social Credit" on the band, and some "Official Delegate" badges, and he'd tell us we were off to louse up some of the racing events. That's the kind of thing we expected from Babe. And we slowly became puzzled, then angry and hurt, when he didn't appear and we couldn't find him anywhere.

"Aw, he'll show up," Norm said.

But he didn't.

Around the grandstand was the carnival. There were ring-toss games and even a large open area where people sat to play bingo, or housie-housie as it was called, all proceeds, or at least a good cut of them, to go to the Movement. The smell of hotdogs, candy-floss, and other substances made us so wobbly at the knees we sat down and gobbled up our sandwiches. Then I used the quarter to buy cones and pop for Norm and me, feeling an odd sense of gratitude to my mother, who had coughed up the quarter knowing that Norm would not have any money, but also sure that her son would share it with him.

In the crowds groups of men in high-crowned fedoras, adorned with paper hatbands with slogans on them, stood around and talked knowingly of the Regina riots, the Relief Marchers, and the torrential rains in the north. In our size of city at the time, they could talk as expertly as farmers about grain and livestock prices.

Familiar faces popped up now and again to brush past us, but nowhere could we find Babe.

"Where the heck is he, anyway?"

"Let's go find Albert. Maybe he knows," I said.

We ambled over in the direction of Borden Park, where we found Albert running around like an idiot, supervising the swelling flow of kids wanting to enter the egg-and-spoon, the wheelbarrow, the sack, and other races. We hung around while he dispatched yet another lot of grubby kids towards a rope held by two men.

"You boys want to help out?"

"Wondered if you'd seen Babe. We lost him."

"No, no. Haven't seen him. If I do, I'll tell him you were looking for him."

At that time Albert was about twenty-six, taller and skinnier than Babe, his dark hair cut like a farmer's with a white wall of skin showing about his ears. He didn't have Babe's easy ways, who was more like their father, the itinerant carpenter who took taxis to his jobs. Instead, Albert had the flitting, birdlike energy of their mother.

"Good to see you boys here. Stick around and maybe you'll learn something."

His clenched smile implied that he was bringing you good tidings and you'd better go along, a mask that gave him premature wrinkles around his eyes. Yet, even then, I felt there was an oddly unfocused look about him, as though, like the Shadow on radio, some nameless creature was stalking him. He seemed to be holding back an inner anger.

"Don't miss the big show at the grandstand," he went on.

That day Albert Roothe was sweating. His green-and-white badge with the ribbons of officialdom sagged on his soaked white shirt. The compulsion to do well oozed out of him — this, despite the coolness of the day and the shifting underside of a full-bellied cloud that might bring more rain and spoil the whole outing.

For there had been no drought that summer.

In our part of the country the rains had fallen and there was a glimmer of long-lost optimism for the crops. Low as prices were, it would at least be something. Elsewhere, the treacherous sky had turned on them again: The rain hadn't stopped, the fields were awash, roads disappeared, and as a supreme joke, wheat prices had started to edge upward. The word was, the Chicago and Winnipeg speculators were betting on a harvest that would be short, ruined by rust.

Yet, on this cool, menacing day, Albert Roothe was sweating.

"You don't know where he's gone? When'd you last see him?"

I couldn't resist the dig.

"Babe talked us into coming, so we can't figure out why he brought us all the way over here, then took off on us."

"You know Babe. He's always fooling," Albert told us through his fixed grin, then he was off to resolve some crisis in the eleven-to-thirteen relay races.

We went over to the track to watch the motorcycle races.

By late afternoon we were still there, leaderless and indecisive amid a thinning crowd on the golden carpet of sawdust and wood chips in front of the grandstand. They were starting to move up into the stands to claim good seats for the rally. We were getting hungry again.

"If we go home now, I'll miss supper anyway," Norm whined. Mrs. Fetterman's small rooms were filled with boarders, which meant punctual meals.

"Hey, look."

While making another sweep of the crowds filling up the grandstand, I could make out someone waving to us from just behind the box-seats. It was chirpy little Mrs. Roothe. Babe's mother crooked her arm and invited us up.

"They've got eats," I said.

She had stacked up sandwiches on a vacant seat, and asked us if we had eaten, and when somewhat untruthfully we declared we hadn't, she told us to dig in.

"We just have to save some for Albert and Hamilton," she said, using Babe's proper name.

"Have you seen him, Mrs. Roothe?"

"Why no, I thought he was with you boys."

"If there's eats, he'll show up," said Mr. Roothe.

For once not wearing his white coveralls, old man Roothe was staring at the milling scene below and shaking his head. He had obviously been dragged out, probably under pressure from Albert, and now he glared down at the strange carnival where people still wandered about with dazed smiles as they listened to the come-ons: "Step right up. It's all for the Cause." Their serenity, the trust and hope that exuded from the crowd, seemed to disturb Mr. Roothe. How Albert got his religion and public spirit from that household was something no one understood.

"They'll take in enough down there to pay their twenty-five bucks a month," Mr. Roothe said. His words were slurred and we could smell the booze on his breath.

I poked Norm and whispered: "He's got a flask on him."

Then Albert came bounding up the stairs, followed by Jean Cullen, his girl at the time. She didn't seem to be enjoying the occasion as much as she was supposed to. Albert had put on a jacket over his sopping shirt, but his face was still shiny.

"Nope, can't take the time to eat, Mom; we've got to get the toddlers ready now for the dances. No, haven't seen Babe. Have you, Jean?"

Jean, who didn't seem to have Albert's overheating problem, hugged herself inside a tan raincoat and shook her head. She seemed to walk a couple of paces behind him, like a squaw, either because she couldn't keep up or maybe because she felt a twinge of envy for Albert's energetic faith in a cause to which she didn't have the same commitment. She returned my curious stare with a slow smile that dissolved easily, like a hard lump of dye releasing a bright colour. Her dark hair was undone and stringy from the dampness unusual for July, her stockings were a bit wrinkled, and her dress hung unevenly under her coat. Yet there was a languor in the slightly oily face, a kind of implicit trust in the damp brown eyes that drew you in somehow.

"No, I haven't seen him. Maybe he found himself a girl," Jean said, in a soft, throaty voice that, to me anyway, seemed to imply a conspiracy between us.

That she was capable of passion I knew. We had sneaked up

on her and Albert a couple of times necking on the Roothes' glassed-in front porch when the screens were open. Judging from her stifled responses to Albert's pawings (we couldn't see, could only crouch and listen) they were always on the verge of going all the way, but apparently couldn't bring themselves to marry, possibly because they were fearful of the future or, more likely, because they didn't have the money. Jean, with her teaching certificate and business course in typing, was still unemployed.

"Can't stay and have a bite with you folks," Albert was saying. "Got to get going."

His mother, proud and happy, rattled away in her English accent about his keeping up his strength until Jean pointedly sat down and took an egg sandwich. Albert turned and bounded down the steps again, not even looking back to see if Jean was following him. She took time to eat, then, lazily stretching in a way that showed off her breasts, she got up and went down the steps.

Mr. Roothe doused us all with his breath of cheap rye.

"Why don't you boys trail along and see if you can give them a hand," he suggested slyly. He had sized us up and knew that we wouldn't want to hang around once we had eaten.

So off we went, under the race-track railing to the rear of the large temporary platform.

It seemed Albert was supervising Jean, who was helping out a Mrs. Roberts and her dancing-school troupe of some twenty kids. Foul-mouthed, heavily powdered, and chain-smoking, Mrs. Roberts had a thick foreign accent and was losing control of her midgets. The band was already warming up, and Jean brought some order to the chaos, getting the children ready for their dances and acrobatic displays. A couple of elves hung on Mrs. Roberts' skirts, either to drag her down or to impart dumb comfort.

Most of the other denizens of fairyland had abandoned their teacher and were now gathered around Jean, who loomed wearily over them, smiling as always in her slow, easy way. The realm of fantasy had opened its doors to let out a sampling of its dwarfs: puny soldiers in red or blue tunics with white webbing an X on every chest; tiny ballerinas in droopy skirts of pink and white; fairies in tattered wings that looked as if they had flown too close to coal-oil lamps; underdeveloped roués from the past in cutaway coats that made them look related to others portraying beetles and bees in similar outer skins; others in dyed long-johns, sweaty from previous acrobatics; and those simply in party dresses, but stooping to dust off the shiny square shoes with metal taps on toe and heel.

All now summoned, they pushed to gather around Jean. Albert's paternal smile froze as we came upon them, but he shrugged and at least didn't banish us from the backstage glamour. Clumps of people now gathered behind the stage and at the wings, mostly men in white collars and suits.

After awhile we heard the band open up with the hymn, "Tell Me the Old, Old Story." From the grandstand a ragged chorus echoed back, a few beats behind.

The rally had begun.

CHAPTER FOUR

THERE WAS A STATELY CADENCE, A SLOW BUILD-UP OF assurance, a ceremonial rhythm to bring them along amid familiar sounds, mixed with a few jolts and laughs along the way, towards the message.

Behind the stage, where Jean had charged us with keeping order amid the jumpy moppets, we had missed the arrival of William Aberhart. Dimly, we heard his voice uttering a reedy invocation, and beyond the stage we could see the white blobs of faces disappear from view as all heads were bowed. There was other business on the stage, then Jean, on a signal from Albert, released two of her female sugar plums with a basket of flowers for Mrs. Aberhart.

As the two girls came down off the stage, the band started up "The Good Ship Lollypop" and the first group of midgets was cut out of the herd to climb the steps. Busy as we were keeping the excited little wretches under control, we didn't see any of their performance, although, judging from the smiles and nods of those who watched from the wings, they were managing to get through it all.

After the shrieking little monsters had returned to earth, there was another downer, an awful baritone who sang "Old Man River." Jean gave us one of her melting smiles and thanked us for our help. Albert jerked his head in dismissal, but we didn't go away. Much to his irritation, we trailed after him and his girl as they moved over to the sidelines to get a better view of the platform. I wondered at the time why Albert didn't return to his parents in the stands, but he seemed jumpy and anxious, as though waiting for something to happen offstage.

Now came the political horse-race that was actually called by Aberhart himself.

Even today it is a bit unusual for a politician to allow himself to slip out of the public character he has created, or has assumed imperceptibly, in the grinding process of talking, always talking. For someone in those hard days to have the self-confidence to clown around was a delightful shock to the masses. Not that Aberhart looked any different from what I expected of a politician. He had one of those solidly bulging bellies that men don't sport any more, a heavy pale face with overflowing chins, small round spectacles, and a gleaming dome of a skull. He stood by a microphone to one side of the stage, near his wife, who wore a dark suit and white blouse with a slouched hat over silvery hair, her hands flicking her crochet work. Yet, here was this corpulent, middle-aged man in a grey suit and white shirt, calling out a horse-race in a singsong voice that made fun of sports announcers.

Onto the stage galloped the "horses," grown men dressed in satin colours, hamming it up and grinning at the stands. There were "oh's" from the distant audience as Aberhart called the Social Credit horse trailing. Then it began to sprint forward to come in first across the finish line in a burst of speed that brought loud cheers. There was much laughter as he reeled off the final order of the field: Liberals: place (boos); Conservatives: show (boos); and the UFA, the crumbling, hapless United Farmers of Alberta, the provincial government, the also-ran (jeers).

"You should've heard the arguments about how to fix the race," Albert told Jean. "Not who'd come first, but the rest of the field."

"A fixed race, Albert?" She shook her head in mock disapproval.

"It's all in fun," Albert said sharply.

But it was a prophetic "fix."

A hymn, "What a Friend We Have in Jesus," brought the throngs back to a state of reverence, setting the scene for Aberhart's major oration of the evening. He began with quiet instruction, the grandstand shrouded in dusk brought on early by low clouds. At times the voice dropped so low that those around the stage exchanged looks, wondering if the loudspeaker system had gone on the blink. But he was only teaching again.

"You must first decide that there must be a change and then be convinced that a change is possible. My heart is heavy over the treatment of the young unemployed men in their Ottawa march. All they asked was work and wages. But they must realize there can never be work for them. The technocrats have told us, and I earnestly believe it, that if machines were allowed to run at only seventy-five per cent efficiency, there would be enough work to engage the men between twenty-five and forty-five years of age for two hours a day, and no work for anyone else. And what kind of a system is it that creates scarcity amid plenty, that destroys food such as wheat, coffee, and pork, which God has provided to feed His people?"

There were tears on his flabby white cheeks; the pale dome of his head was like an egg in the twilight.

"You remain in the Depression because of a shortage of purchasing power, imposed by the banking system. Social Credit offers you the remedy. If you have not suffered enough, it is your God-given right to suffer more. But if you wish to elect your own representatives to implement the remedy, this is your only way out."

The only way out.

In the slowly fading light of a northern summer, I could see the stricken look on the face of the young Albert Roothe. He was swallowing with difficulty and held on tightly to Jean's hand. I remember noticing how unaffected she seemed by the speech, and that she even gave me a small smile when she saw me studying them. Out there in the stands there would be damp eyes and cheeks, a kind of moist union that permeated the threadbare clothes and released long-suppressed feelings. Now his final words screeched along the edges of the loudspeakers.

"Our struggle is like that of a deep-sea diver with a devil-fish. Our battle is a terrific, strangling combat with the money octopus. But we still have one hand free with which to strike: to mark our ballot on election day. Let us strike, then, with all our might at this hideous monster that is sucking the very life-blood from our people!"

There was a moment of stunned silence, then the distant roar of a tide coming in. The grandstand moved as one organism, rolling forward with a new, tearful purpose. Yet, even here they were reminded that this was not to be a mob howling down empty streets. The band crashed through the surge of voices with "O God Our Help in Ages Past." The hymn picked up the voices, one after the other, and never before or since have I heard it sung with such deep yearning. As the hymn boomed across the inner field, the motormen, having apparently heard it, began to move their streetcars. There was a distant squeal of wheels as the streetcars eased up along the side track where they had been waiting, nuzzled unevenly together in the long grass that covered the old spur line by the cow-barns, coming to take them home.

They stood and sang all six verses. For some reason I became aware of Albert's silence during the singing of the fifth verse. His arm had crept around Jean's waist, as if he had to squeeze her warmth to him, and his eyes were fixed upward on the platform. But somehow he couldn't bring himself to sing that passage of the hymn. After what happened later, I can tell you, I often wondered about that moment when something inside him prevented him from uttering these words:

> Time, like an ever-rolling stream,
> Bears all its sons away;
> They fly, forgotten, as a dream
> Dies at the opening day.

Right after that, when the programme was over and the platform party was descending the steps to the well-wishers who flocked around, Mr. Aberhart spoke to Albert Roothe and changed his life forever.

Someone recognized Albert, introduced him by name to the leader as the one who had organized the young people during the day. What impressed me was that Mr. Aberhart seemed to know him. He clasped his hand and spoke in an oddly soft voice, his blue eyes steady for that instant before they unloosened again and went on to the next one in line. He said only four words to Albert, which probably didn't mean anything to those crowded around; but they obviously did to the both of them.

William Aberhart said: "Maybe next time, Albert."

Now his voice, soft as the petals of a wild rose, engulfed Albert and swept him away.

When I told my parents about it, my father was the one who guessed what it meant. He was sort of a political activist himself (of the Left) and would debate with Albert on the streetcar that took them to the Normal School to mark the high-school exam papers.

"Albert was considered as a candidate, put up by the South Side zone captains in the first round of screening. They have a Central Committee that checks out their reputation, moral and religious background, and their doctrinal purity. They get interviewed and cross-examined. The Old Man himself really runs the show. Albert says the word came back that they felt he was still too young, but he got some encouraging words from the secretary, Manning, who's about Albert's age and is like a son to Abie. Remarkable that he would remember, could store up such details when he's got so much else on his mind. I don't support him in any way, but he is an extraordinary man. How did Albert react?"

"He seemed kind of stunned, swallowed hard, and gave a funny grin. Then he turned quickly, took Jean by the hand, and headed for the stands to catch up with his mom and dad. We all looked around again for Babe, but didn't find him."

The truth was, we didn't look very hard. The evening chill, held back by the warmth of emotions, now seemed to grip everyone. People moved quickly and there was the smell of rain in the air. We were dazed and uncomprehending of what we had just seen, and mad at Babe for having betrayed us, for bringing us to this place with all its strangeness, then leaving us on our own. We had had enough of Social Credit and Hamilton "Babe" Roothe.

CHAPTER FIVE

THERE WAS A THICKNESS TO THE SUMMERS THEN, A WEIGHTY mass through which we floated so we wouldn't sink into whatever it was. The second week of school holidays began with none of that sense of freedom and released energy we had briefly savoured. There were no jobs for us, no summer camp, and our parents never went anywhere on holidays, unless they were among the lucky few who worked for the railroad and had passes. There was a kind of fluid slackness that possibly made us more receptive, in a primitive way, to omens that something was drastically wrong.

We were young for our age, unformed, drifting, and ignored, and what we had to face up to had the effect of a hammer on soft metal. On the farms, in other parts of the city, or riding the rods, there were boys of our own age who were dark and lean, stringy tough and handling themselves in the vast migrations of men searching for jobs. But we were the offspring of the ruined middle class, our protection an achievement of our worried parents, our education the only weapon they had left.

That day, the Monday after the Social Credit rally at the Exhibition Grounds, became a turning point, a time when we thought we touched the fringes of maturity, a process that would wait for its completion until the second war took us along the same paths as our fathers.

It began at breakfast with the four of us, my parents and my sister Doris, two years younger than me, at what we called the first sitting. The second sitting was when my father's parents came out of their bedroom, to eat alone in a grumpy and subdued silence, ashamed at the charity they had to take.

Someone scratched at the screen door and we turned to see Mrs. Roothe on our back step. In her quick, flitting way she came into the kitchen, a tiny woman in a cotton print which always seemed to hang like a tent, her sharp nose and face, white as flour, framed in a cap of closely trimmed black hair without a touch of grey.

"He's gone," Mrs. Roothe said, leaving off the "h" in the Cockney accent we often mimicked. "Is he over here with you, Douglas?"

"Who?"

"Hamilton. When I went to knock him up, he'd gone out the window. Took the screen right off. His bed's been slept in. Not a word or anything. Now, why would he do a thing like that?"

"Gee, I don't know, Mrs. Roothe. Last time I saw him was on Saturday when he ditched us. And we never called for him yesterday."

"How come?" asked my father.

"Aw, we were mad at him for taking off on us. Never saw him yesterday at all."

"Well, he got in late on Saturday night, so I made him stay in all day yesterday and help his father with some work," Mrs. Roothe said, her normally cheery expression showing that there must have been some tensions between them. "But that was no cause for him to run off."

"I bet he's round somewhere," I said. "I can't see him taking a powder. Where'd he go?"

My mother pushed her library book aside and knocked over the marmalade jar.

"Did he say where he'd gone to during the rally?"

"Not a word," said Mrs. Roothe, moving around the kitchen with a restless energy that made me think of Albert. She eyed a pan of bacon starting to smoke and turned off the gas burner. My mother didn't get up. "Wouldn't talk about it. Was awfully quiet for him. That led to some words and I made him stay in."

At that moment Albert came through the back door. He was dressed for the Normal School and carrying a scuffed briefcase.

"I looked up and down the street and the alley," he said irritably. "Don't see any sign of him. Guess we'd better get going, John."

My father sighed, drank his coffee, and gave up on the bacon which my mother had forgotten on the stove.

"If you want to stay, I'll tell them you'll be late," he offered.

"No, no. He'll show up. I'll call you at noon, Mom." Albert waited at the door while my father put on his jacket and got his hat and briefcase from the front hall. "No point calling the police yet."

That was always one of Albert's problems. He was so transparent. I could see by my mother's grin she had noticed, too, that he was more concerned about not having any flat-feet appearing at the Roothe doorstep.

"Alley oop," said my father from the doorway.

The two men, tall and rangy in their loose, floppy suits and wide-brimmed fedoras, left by the front door.

"Why don't you round up a gang and go look for him?" my mother suggested.

"Would you, Dougie?" Mrs. Roothe looked grateful.

"Sure thing." I got up from the table. "Don't know where, but we'll take a gander."

At last there was something to do.

The gang my mother had conjured up — perhaps her library-book imagination had invoked a posse of boys — would be made up only of Norm Fetterman and me. I managed to convince Mrs. Fetterman, heaving and sweating over her washing in the base-ment, that Norm should be sprung for this essential work, but a couple of calls failed to dislodge any of our other pals. They were firmly shanghaied into Monday slavery, the toting around of leaden washtubs, the routine we were now, thankfully, about to escape.

"Oh, no," Norm said as we came back down the street and saw Pete Thorpe waiting for us.

When he wasn't doing his radio imitations, Pete's stutter and high squeaky voice forever kept him an outcast from our bunch. Now he tried to ingratiate himself with some dialogue from the Ed and Zeb show.

"You fellas doin' anything?"

"Naw."

Pete hobbled around like an old man, smacking his lips and doing his hayseed act. Then, as we edged away from him, the door of the Thorpes' porch opened and Diane stood there, her face flushed and worried.

"Pete, don't go," she called.

"What say?" He cupped a hand to an ear.

"Don't go, not with them."

"Aw, shucks, 'tain't ——"

At this point Mrs. Thorpe loomed behind Diane, gently put an arm around her, and drew her back into the shadows of the house. The door closed on its springs. Pete lurched along beside us, one foot on the wooden curb, mumbling away as Ed (or Zeb).

"What parts air you young whippersnappers headin'?"

"Oh, for chrissake, we're going down to the creek to see if we can find Babe."

Pete stopped short and stared after us. He forgot about his radio characters.

"W-what d-do you m-mean, look for him?"

"He's gone. Done a bunk," I said, using an expression from the English boys' papers we read.

"G-gone where?"

"If we knew we wouldn't be looking for him."

I was about to tell Pete to scram when he did just that. His mouth open, he tried to dribble out some words, changed his mind, and slunk back to his own yard.

"That settles his hash." Norm grinned.

The morning air was cool. Low-hanging clouds gave everything a muted, slate look. We moved quickly along the wooden sidewalk, past the vacant lots between the houses where potatoes had been planted. A couple of lots had unfinished basements scooped out and now crumbling, the remains of our wooden rafts strewn on the clay where we had fooled around in the spring in three feet of muddy water.

At that time I was like a dwarf on stilts, with long spidery legs attached to a short torso. My growth seemed to be edging upward from long feet that collided with everything. Norm Fetterman had not yet started to sprout. His light-brown hair was still baby silk, his face round and soft, and his body a bit pudgy as it awaited the genetic trigger that would, so everyone said, surely yield the six-foot frame of his father, or what we remembered of him. He had been gone since the previous fall, gone east, we were told by the adults, to ride the rods and look for work. Mrs. Fetterman refused to go on Relief and filled her small bungalow with boarders. Norm and his brother slept in the basement next to the root cellar. Now the loose soles of his shoes made a flapping sound on the boards.

"He must've snuck out during the night," I said. "You see him running away?"

"Old Babe? Naw, why'd he do that?"

Norm was right. If there was any reason to get out of that house it would be Albert and his insufferable prating about Social Credit; but he was more than balanced off by an amiable dad who, when he wasn't carpentering, would sit on the back steps, let us feel the shrapnel ridges in his skull from the war, and tell us yarns of muddy battles. Nor was there sufficient cause in Babe's mother who, although they had their spats and she insisted on calling him by the proper name he detested, was always ready with her sharp Cockney wit and flagons of lemonade when we came over to hang around. No, theirs was not a cruel household.

"That Albert'd get your goat, all right," Norm said.

"Yeah, but Babe can hand it back. He told me. When Albert kept after him about joining their young people's group, he told him to stuff it."

"Who, to holy old Albert? That I'd have to see."

"And he did sweet-talk us into going to the picnic."

"Not for Albert. For himself, I bet."

"So he fools us into going, then he ditches us. Maybe he was seeing someone, eh?"

"Maybe it's him and Di."

"Aw, come on. They never let her out of their sight. Look what happened just now. She pokes her head out the door and they haul her back. Pete told me she's going to the Bible Institute to board there for the rest of her schooling."

"You just watch old Babe get religion."

"Who, him? You figure that?"

"I guess not."

"Wonder what she was getting at, yelling at Pete not to go with us?"

"Search me."

About two blocks east of our place the street ended abruptly at the edge of a ravine. On the other side of the valley our street began again until it petered out in a dirt track in fields where you could still find fire hydrants, put in before the first war, during the land boom.

At the bottom of the ravine, below a railway track that was once to have been a major line to the northland and a row of Calgary Power pylons, there was the creek bed; it lived briefly during the spring run-off, then normally shrank into stagnant pools, edged by fragrant platelets of mud, cracked like jigsaw puzzles. That July unseasonal rains had revived the creek into a steady flow of rusty water. The stench came from the packing plant upstream, which, so it was said, dumped its offal into the stream, permeating the clay with its rich, bloody decay.

This was where we headed first, for it was the refuge of the young away from the prying eyes of adults on the heights, a sunken haven of open spaces, clay cliffs with caves, and thick brush. It was the place I thought of first. If Babe was on the lam, or wanted to be by himself, or was meeting someone he shouldn't, this was where he would head.

From the edge of the ravine, across the valley, I could see the pines and firs shadowed in heavy blues which bled onto the ground and into the rich greenery of bush and the grasses that were usually bleached at this time of year. Yet, for some reason I couldn't grasp, it seemed like strange territory.

Norm looked at me anxiously, waiting for direction. I stood there and could think only of what we used to do, as though a phase of life had passed by, as though Babe was already gone and I was trying to recapture pieces of his memory.

Nearby was the pylon that Babe had climbed on a dare, ignoring the sign that warned of instant frying or a fine that could bankrupt his family. He had climbed it to win Eddy Weir's BB-gun for a week, which he did, going all the way up to the crossbars where he tied his handkerchief onto the hanging insulators. Then, when he got the gun, he used it wildly, pinking at us from behind bushes or in the back alleys, until he wiped out three sparrows in Mrs. Weir's bird-bath and the gun was taken away from him.

"What're you grinning at?" Norm asked.

"Oh, nothing."

"Well, where're we going to start?"

I didn't know. There was the barn down by the creek, near the house where they kept chickens, where once again (how long ago?) Babe had led me into danger. We had been skulking around the place for some reason, and from the open barn door we heard a noise like a human gasp. Well versed in the stealthy approach, the games of stalking in the ravine, we crept to the door and peered around the edge.

There, on a pile of straw pushed up against one of the stalls, was a man in denim coveralls and a woman lying on his coat to avoid the prickles of the straw. The man had opened the front of her dress and was sucking on a breast. One gnarled hand blackened with work had taken the breast and clasped it so that it was a pointed cone, the nipple out of sight in his mouth. His swarthy unshaven face somehow seemed evil against the gleaming white of the breast, yet there was no force here, for her head was back and she was bubbling her pleasure, the sound we had heard. His other hand was a slowly crawling tarantula on a bare thigh that shone with an inner glow.

The odd thing was that the man still wore a floppy tweed hat while his coveralls, the top strap buttons undone, were slipping downward. He seemed like a tramp or one of those men, once respectable, who had been hardened by riding the rods. She was not young, with greyish hair sprouting loosely out of a bun at the back of her head and the kind of shapeless cotton house-dress our mothers wore.

"Cripes!" I said.

Babe hit me on the shoulder, but it was too late. The man rolled over and stood up, deep-set eyes ferocious. And, one hand holding up his coveralls, he chased us, across the dirt road and along the creek, until we outran him up the hill, skittering through the pines. We could see him far below, shaking one fist, then turning back, dejected and shambling towards the barn where his moment of pleasure and relief had been stolen by two dumb kids.

That was Babe, all right. His leadership was so natural that we only felt the vacuum of its absence. He was taller, more developed, and already perceived as good-looking to grown-ups and older teen-age girls alike. His wild but contained energy, lazy smile, the straight nose, square chin, and the curly ash-blond hair, lighter than Albert's, made for an obvious superiority over the rest of us, with our anarchy of gawky legs, odd-shaped heads and bodies. Going on fifteen, Babe didn't even have pimples or hickeys, as though he had decided to forgo the messiness of puberty and was on his way to an unstated but assumed promise, so obvious even to adults and teachers. Everyone said he would go even further than his brother Albert, already on the way up, for Babe had a kind of fluid charm about him that Albert's brittle piety and toothy charm somehow missed. How much did Albert envy him?

"Let's try the ruins," Norm said, making it plain that I hadn't replaced Babe's leadership.

"Jake with me," I shrugged, not yet ready to assume the role.

Down the hill, just above the tracks, we approached a relic, what was to have been a concrete mansion, the broken remnants of orange tile showing that whoever had started it had envisaged something Spanish. Now overgrown in the bush, its front wall, facing the tracks, had collapsed to expose the metal tendons that were to have held the cement together forever. There was no basement. Whoever the eccentric had been, he had had no idea of the need for a cellar to hold a furnace or a zinc cistern to drain off the soft rainwater; perhaps he'd had some romantic idea of a hacienda in the bush, next to the railway that would carry a steady flow of settlers to the north. It remained a local mystery, and we had taken over the ruins as a kind of clubhouse where we could build fires edged by chunks of cement and roast potatoes filched from the gardens up top.

We called out Babe's name and poked around in the pillboxes we had made from rubble.

"He ain't here," said Norm. "Now what?"

I thought of a way to take charge.

"Up there."

I pointed towards the brownish line of the clay ridge above us.

"You nuts?"

"Got anything else in mind?"

"No, but —— "

"Aw, we can take a look-see."

Norm trailed behind as I led the way up the hill from the ruins, through a jumble of rusty tin cans, faded cartons, and even a set of bedsprings. Behind the last bit of cover, a clump of chokecherry bushes, we squatted and studied the clay slope now rising steeply in front of us. The face of the cliff was scored with the grooves of spring run-off. Up near the top one could make out steps, wooden planks embedded into the clay and leading down from a chicken-wire fence to the dark opening of a cave dug out of the hillside. At the entrance there was a kind of wooden gate set back from the lip and supported by two railway ties propped vertically into the floor and roof. There seemed to be a padlock on the gate.

If we went any farther we'd be asking for it, all right, for it was the lore of the neighbourhood that the cliffs were out of bounds. They were the territory of the Cawner boys, who had built the elaborate cavern, complete with pit props made of railway ties hauled up the hill, carpets on the floor, and an old four-poster where the Cawners' two female cousins could be had for two bits a throw. Or so Babe said. While he was prone to exaggeration, we also understood that Babe knew the Cawner boys better than the rest of us, having taken on Billy, who was sixteen in Grade Eight, and cleaned his clock.

Of course, the Cawner boys didn't live in the cave. Their place, a shack with a series of unpainted additions sprawling into a mud yard that was mainly occupied by wire chicken coops, was on the brow of the ravine above the cave. There were about eight of them in the Cawner family at any one time, all on Relief, so there was always someone around to keep an eye on things. It was just known, no edicts or signs needed, that no one — not even adults — attempted to poke around the cave.

"You figure he might be up there?"

"He was hanging round them for awhile."

"Naw, it's too risky."

"You're right, kid. Smart kid."

Neil Cawner, about nineteen, grinned at us. He had slipped up behind and now stood in his slow relaxed way, his smile lopsided. His old tweed cap was pushed over one ear at an angle — Babe once said it must be thumbtacked to his head but a Cawner wouldn't know the difference. Neil was short with plenty of daylight showing between his misshapen legs, warped with rickets. He was carrying a twenty-two, a tube-feed, bolt-action Cooey, cradled on his arm the way they did in westerns.

"Couple of elephants coming through the bush," Neil said, friendly enough. "Where's your other pal, the tall one?" He knew Babe's name as well as we did.

"He's not with us today."

"You been told to watch our place, too?" Still smiling.

"No, not us."

"You sure about that?"

"No — I mean yes. We're sure. Honest."

"Make up your mind." Even in the coolness of that day he reeked of tobacco; he drummed on his rifle with fingers so brown he might have spent all his spare time throttling grasshoppers. His stubbled cheeks were deeply hollowed, his skin as brittle as scorched paper. He continued to study us. "Okay, then."

We left as fast as we could, down the hill to clatter through the garbage, through the concrete ruins, onto the blue cinder path beside the railway tracks, then back up the hill to the nearest back alley. But we weren't clear yet.

As we made our way along the deeply rutted back alley, we saw Billy Cawner, a Grade Eight threat who force-fed chocolate Ex-Lax to smaller kids. He was lounging against the door of the Simmonds' garage, picking out his initials with a large clasp knife.

His presence altered our course to a dash through the McBrides'
yard and out into the street towards our place. The sight of my
mother hanging up the washing prompted us to retrace our steps,
ducking behind the unkempt caragana hedge around old Headley's
place. There we paused, then slipped around the side of the house
and into the darkness of the barn at the back.

That's where we found Babe.

CHAPTER SIX

WITH THE DOOR CLOSED, THE BARN WAS ALMOST IN TOTAL darkness except for pin-holes of light and small beams of white from empty knot-holes. The horse stalls were empty, which meant that old man Headley was out with one of the three wagons he kept parked on the vacant lot across the back lane. The air was heavy, gamy, and fragrant, much warmer than outside, as though the horses had left behind their body heat.

A thin bar of light angled across the floor from the door I had left open a crack. While Norm wandered around the earthen floor kicking at the carpet of loose straw, I peered out the slit at the lane, watching for Billy Cawner. We should have known it would be a one-two deal, that Neil wouldn't let us off so casually without a follow-up, a clincher to make sure it was fully understood that one was never again to squat down in the bushes amid the rusty trash.

Something was bothering the Cawners enough to send out one of them to prowl on a Monday morning, a twenty-two crooked on his arm. What was it? What would have happened if we had more sucessfully crept up to the cave? In the familiar smells of our own cave — the barn — we could let our imaginations run free about unspeakable things.

Like the creek, the barn was a hideout for us, something that old Headley knew and didn't care about as long as we didn't smoke or tease the horses. It was the only barn on the street, a kind of throwback, where Headley kept the last remaining team in the area to run his three wagons: a wooden water wagon that supplied fresh water to outlying houses beyond Bonnie Doon; a honey wagon for clearing out the outhouses on dirt tracks where the shacks cluttered outside the city; and an earth-moving wagon with steel trapdoors, seldom used.

Perhaps he tolerated us because there were always complaints about the barn. During the infantile paralysis scares the health people would come around and spray the manure pile to keep down the flies. Or Thorpe, next door, would complain about the smell and threaten to bring down the weight of City Hall where he was a clerk. But Headley, his sweaty stetson riding low over his eyes, ignored Thorpe and sold gunny sacks of manure at a nickel apiece to the neighbours for their gardens. Sometimes he would let us feed the horses and tell us stories about the early days, when you could ride for days without seeing a fence.

Norm had been dreading the possible arrival of Billy Cawner.

"Let's go up top. If he comes in he won't see nothing."

To show his independence or to hide his cowardice, I'm not sure which, Norm scrambled first up the heavy wooden ladder into the loft. The pale light filtered through gaps in the siding in long slices. We stumbled on piles of old harness on the uneven floor and looked around for a place to sit. Our vision had not yet adjusted to the smelly gloom. One of us sneezed.

Then we heard the creaking. The squeaky rubbing of the weighted rope on the joist, like the sound of an old ship taking someone away, made us look up.

And it was there, our eyes widening in the dark, that we found Babe hanging.

He was not very far off the floor, only the height of the wooden butter-box he must have stood on. Now he twirled slightly, first to survey us with his blind stare, then to turn away, almost in embarrassment at what he had done.

And there were the flies.

As he turned again, we could see that his face was mottled with a pattern of flies, their soft buzzing like the whir of an oily, well-shined machine putting something in or, more likely, taking it away: the fluids of his open eyes, the blood from his nose, and the salts of his mouth and tongue. A fly crawled across his blank eyes.

The rope had been looped around an old anvil on the floor, then flung up over a beam, the knot expertly slipped to snap tight when the weight hit and the slow strangulation and kicking started, for we could see that his feet and hands were loose and free. Babe's feet, shod in grass-stained running shoes, were now on tiptoe, reaching for nowhere, and we could see that he was fully dressed in shirt and whoopee pants, the latter with a dark stain at the crotch. Nearby was a long-handled shovel which might have been used to knock the box out from under.

How long had he been there? Had Headley not seen him, or his collie dog Pal? Had the horses not made a fuss, howled, snorted, or pawed at the smell of death in the barn? In the early morning, when he had started out, had Headley not wondered about the sudden head-tossing or the clump of uneasy hooves as his two sway-backed mares shied away from their routine harnessing? Had he hushed up Pal's whining so that he wouldn't wake up the neighbours? Or had it happened after Headley left on his rounds?

We stood there, awesomely, silently nauseated, transfixed in silent panic that this could have happened to Babe, the best of us all.

We ran from the barn.

We tore into our back yard and blindly, almost like in a slapstick routine, got caught up in the two clothes-lines of washing. The wet garments slapped our faces, like ranks of dripping scarecrows detailed to frighten us back into our wits. I saw my mother, stretched up to peg a sopping sheet, turn and let her cigarette drop from her mouth.

I was the first one to shout out what we had found.

CHAPTER SEVEN

THAT MORNING, MY FATHER TOLD US LATER, HE HAD FELT disappointed at Albert Roothe's silence as they strode along the wooden sidewalk towards the streetcar stop.

"I was all gingered up," he said, "ready to give him a good ribbing about the rally and old Abie. But he wouldn't play ball. There was something wrong, all right."

"What'd he say?"

"That's it. Not a darned thing. You ever seen Albert at a loss for words?"

Every morning during the summer the two of them evoked a silent familial pride as they reached out their long legs, found their measure, and, tall men going to mark exam papers, clashed their worn heels on the planks of the sidewalk. Yet, they couldn't have been farther apart in thought, belief, and approach to life.

Someone once told me that if John Sayers had owned some decent clothes he could have been a dashing figure in the way you would conjure up a lancer or dragoon of the last century. True enough, if one saw his wartime photo, with the peaked cap angled low over one eye, the way he must have looked to attract my mother, a buxom redhead, when he became a "return man," still young and unscarred after a short stint of action in the last months of 1918.

When he wasn't too exhausted from teaching or too worried about the fate of the world, my father was still capable of rakish insouciance and a crooked grin I have apparently inherited. They tell me I look a lot like him. He had slim hips and stretched bones, a long straight nose, brown eyes that seemed to catch the light in pinpoints, droopy eyelashes, and dark hair slicked back in a peak from dead centre on his forehead, the verges already receding.

But all of this potential, the image of the lounging cavalryman, was lost in the wrinkled, olive-drab gabardine suit he wore all summer, his one and only "light" suit, a bulky size forty-two bought for fifteen bucks and never taken in. The trousers, wide and flappy, were already gathering the summer's stains.

So Albert and John Sayers would fall into their stride, my father faintly amused at his friend's brisk, wide-awake, clenched smile, his fine curled head upright, with nostrils sucking in the clean air like a badly adjusted manifold, joyfully saluting the morn in an optimism that belied the reality of his own condition, that he was no better off than we were. In fact, with only two years' teaching experience, Albert was worse off financially. Lucky to have a teaching job at all, and probably he wouldn't have without the discreet help of his minister, Reverend Marant, who knew that the school superintendent was a staunch Aberhart supporter. Even though he lived at home, Albert often told my parents that he didn't know how he'd ever save enough money to get married.

Usually you had to have a belly full of sticky rolled oats to put up with Albert in the mornings. He would invariably haul out a Social Credit pamphlet — one of the yellow or white ones that they seemed to grind off the presses in great quantities; it was proof, my father said, that they already had access to phony money — or one of those garbled tomes from their Scottish founder, Douglas, all required reading. Not that Albert was obnoxious about it. Even to me, later, when we took a trip to a rally together, he was friendly, low-key, apparently ready to nod in sympathy to any stupid question, but poised for his smiling, assured response. My father's rational socialism made no dent on Albert.

Just how awe-inspiring this new faith was, was described to us by my father one night at supper....

One day at the Normal School, where they worked for six weeks or so every summer, he came across Albert standing very still in front of the open door of one of the marking rooms. He was staring. The sound of the voices inside was nothing unusual, only the standard chatter, the odd voice rising above the others to read out a particularly stupid or funny answer. When he saw my father standing beside him looking puzzled, Albert started talking, half to himself.

"I didn't know. Isn't that odd? All the time I've spent in this building, just a few doors away, and I hadn't realized that this is where it began. Harry told me just today. He was actually here that summer three years ago, in this room where Mr. Aberhart was chairman of the Math table. And he told me how upset Mr. Aberhart had been over the suicide of one of his prize pupils at Crescent Heights in Calgary. He was principal, you know. And, Harry told me, they got so engrossed in talking about the economic wasteland, what it was doing to people, how even the best students would have no jobs, that the other one, who was at the Chemistry table, began to talk again about the books he'd been reading: how the system could be saved without the bondage of socialism."

Here my father said he was about to interrupt with a smart remark; but Albert squelched him with the beatific look of one posing for an icon.

"You know who I mean: Scarborough. Teaches math over at Vic now. Had to give up chemistry. Was gassed in the war and can't tolerate the fumes, the chlorines and acids. They tell me he sometimes has to wear flesh-coloured gloves because the chalk dust cracks open the creases in his hands, and they become slippery with a fine mixture of pus and blood.

"In that room, and during the breaks when they went for walks outside, the arguments went on. You can see Mr. Aberhart now. Just one of us, a teacher, well, a little more maybe, what with the Bible school and the radio. Yet, still one of us, together in an ordinary room marking papers, but different from others, with his deep concern about the bleak future ahead for his students, seeing all around him our system in collapse, the fields turning into deserts, as if an additional God-given plague had been sent to teach us humility for our past avarice and greed, the frontier lusts that brought our people here. And at the next table, that wheezing voice broken by racking coughs from the gas, was the man who kept bringing in the books and tracts for him to read. Finally, that long night in his small room in Saint Stephen's, where he devoured the messages in those books, and as the sun came up he had his revelation of an economic answer that could be built upon the foundations of his faith. Imagine how his thoughts must have swirled, his head swimming as he sat here, one moment glancing at the examiner's key, his thoughts wandering the next instant to that other key, the one that would bring forth hope to the people.

"And," Albert smiled, "to think that beyond those lockers dividing the rooms, some markers on the other side used to yell at them to shut up, to stop all their yapping about economics and get on with their job. Of course, they couldn't see the hand of the Almighty at work, creating another task for one of their numbers. You can almost see it now."

Together, my father and Albert formed their own images of what it must have been like: of Aberhart among the other teachers in the hot room, yet wearing dark suit and vest, the white shirt-collar sinking into the folds of his striated neck; the shining pale dome of his head; and the crystal blue eyes magnified behind the rimless glasses, looking across at the wheezing chemistry teacher; and that trained voice, deep and penetrating, asking, questioning, arguing, until the massive head finally nodded in comprehension or shook in dispute. Finally, from behind the green lockers, the amused protests from the philistines.

"Some day," Albert Roothe said, "this room will be a shrine."

"And we'll be the martyrs if we don't get to work."

But on that Monday morning, not knowing that Albert was preoccupied with something else entirely, his fellow markers were ready for him.

"Back to earth, Albert. The big show's over and it's downhill all the way."

They were somewhat puzzled when Albert was a bit slow to react. He seemed to have trouble focusing, but he didn't let them down. His white smile came through.

"Ah, it was wonderful. Won-der-ful."

Jim Stoaks, the head marker in the room, kept after him. "Fish or fowl, eh? You decided yet if you're politicians or holy rollers?"

But Albert didn't reply. He shrugged, grinned, and took his

place before the stack of exam papers that flowed in from all over the province. Just numbers on the top of each paper. The end of a production line that began in the most distant one-room school-house, the teachers whipped their pencils over the hopes and dreams of all those kids.

Sometimes, my father told us, he would sit back and try to picture the kid who had scribbled a passage revealing a talent that would probably remain undiscovered. Maybe, he thought, as he scanned the English papers, it was a girl who didn't have enough warm clothing to go outside at recess and the teacher had handed her a copy of *Little Women* with the print so small you could hardly read it in the fading afternoon light. Or maybe, far to the south in the real dust bowl, in a bleached farmhouse, the windows plugged shut and the blinds drawn to keep out the fine grey fog and heat, there would be some kid curled up on a lumpy sofa, reading a volume of Browning with a cracked leather cover and pages yellow at the edges, one of a pile of forgotten books brought over from the old country.

And what would happen to all those kids? There were far too many like them and only a few who ever had the solace of Alcott or Browning. More often the only book in the house would be the Bible, taken literally, word for word, in the way Aberhart now quoted it to bring hope and the dawn of economic salvation. Odd: The book most often read, the one book the settlers and their children knew best, was never on the exam papers.

If my father had been day-dreaming that Monday morning, it was broken when he noticed one of the university students from the checking department downstairs standing in the doorway. The student looked around and headed for the Math table, where he whispered to the chairman. The latter pointed at Albert Roothe. The student then went over to Albert and murmured a message. My father saw Albert turn white and close his eyes. He clasped his hands together over the exam papers, bowed his head in silent prayer, then got up to leave the room.

"What is it?" Jim Stoaks said.

By the time my father had pushed back his chair and gone out into the corridor, Albert Roothe had left and he couldn't seem to find the checker who had brought the message. He went back into the room and shrugged at Jim.

During the lunch hour he phoned my mother. After several tries on a busy line, he managed to get through, and only then did he find out why Albert Roothe had left for the day.

CHAPTER EIGHT

THE FIRST THING ALBERT ROOTHE DID WHEN HE GOT HOME was to throw the two reporters off the front porch.

Teapot in hand (for that was what a close friend did on such occasions: take over the kitchen and serve) my mother watched Albert leap out of a car, driven by one of the teachers who had offered to bring him home from the Normal School, onto the gravel road between the other cars that were lined up on both sides at the curb. He nodded to the group of neighbours who stood around on the sidewalk; they wouldn't venture into the yard, their intimacy with the Roothes not sufficient to do more than hang around for awhile and murmur condolences to any member of the family who passed. Others, who knew the Roothes better, would be inside.

Our district was peopled by immigrants from Ontario and Britain who called weekly bridge partners "Mr. and Mrs." for twenty years, who had a few close friends, a nodding acquaintanceship with many, and contempt for a few. Anyone on our street would have been mortified if anyone had said "Howdy" to them. Who do they think they are, and where did they come from? Mother and Mrs. Roothe were friends because they both read books and went to the library together, each lugging a string bag laden with the volumes they devoured every two weeks to the neglect of their housework.

The old iron gate squealed and the screen door on the verandah banged shut as Albert came into the house. Before he could pass through into the dark interior, towards the moving shadows of visitors and the sounds of his mother, he ran into the squabble between the two reporters, at the moment separated by an exasperated policeman in uniform. This imbroglio was what had brought my mother onto the porch.

The reporters were arguing over photographs. The one who held the photos was older, with cold grey eyes sunken in pouches. He wore a fedora wavy with sweat-stains. The other reporter was a kid, thin, with pallid hair and a wheedling high-pitched voice that was putting everyone's nerves on edge. The young one was trying to get the older one to share the photos, and the policeman was on the verge of throwing them both off the porch when Albert appeared.

"What's this?" Albert's voice had the kind of authority that made them stop.

There was a moment's silence on the porch. Some flies whirred where they were trapped inside the screens, between the sliding glass windows that were only partly open. The verandah had a dusty closed air; the tan filtering of dirt from the gravel road was piled up in the grooves where the sliding windows had been open since spring, and the crisp leaves of dying geraniums lay along the window sill.

The young reporter was blocking the older one, who was obviously in a hurry to get away from the house. The young one appealed to Albert: It wasn't fair; those photos belonged to the family, not to him, and he didn't need them all. The older reporter smiled with yellow teeth and said that that was the game, sonny; I got here first and finders keepers.

"The first one on the scene always gets all the photos from the family so the others won't get any. That's the trick," the policeman explained to Albert.

"I am a son of this family," Albert said, in the voice of a prophet.

He opened the older reporter's hand, took the photos and snapshots of Babe, and counted them out evenly. Then he dealt half to each. The older one started to argue, but the policeman put a hand on his shoulder. The two reporters left the porch in silence. The older one called to a photographer who had been taking pictures of Headley's barn and left in a waiting taxi. The younger one trotted up the street towards the streetcar line.

"Albert believes in a real hell, doesn't he? Isn't he a whatchamacallit?" my mother asked. The stress of recalling the scene on the porch had reduced her facial pinkness and made her freckles stand out in a flurry across her nose and cheeks.

"Pre-millennial? Yes, but not in one of their extreme sects. Not like Thorpe." Father was referring to our neighbours, whose frantic search for the right fundamentalist sect was an object of derision and local embarrassment.

"Albert must have felt he was entering the gate of hell when he got home."

"I'm sure he did."

That day the Roothes' living-room had a dark heavy air to it, as if a light had been switched off at dusk. Outside it was cool and cloudy, muted and dull. The brightness, one always felt in that household, came from Mrs. Roothe herself: the perky, sharp-eyed good humour she had passed on to Babe rather than her older son, whose perpetual smile seemed more like a design flaw. Now all that remained was the dark wood, the heavy brown wallpaper, and the few dusty antiques from home in England, shaming the furniture of the new land's cut-rate stores. Shadowy figures stood or sat, carefully distant from all that was fragile in the room.

When Albert came in, his father moved over on the worn chesterfield to let him sit beside his mother and put an arm around her. Albert flinched when he saw how her chipper strength had gone. His fingers played in wonder on her shoulder, feeling each bone as though counting a tiny bundle of kindling. As surely as if a yellow quarantine placard had been nailed to their door, something unspeakable now marked their household. His father sat at the end of the chesterfield, head down, the twisted paper of a roll-your-own burnt down to his fingers. He didn't offer to introduce Albert to any of the others, but the Reverend Marant, who had been standing to one side of the green-glazed gas fireplace, moved forward, shook Albert's hand, and placed his other on top, the way one holds a small furry bird. Edward Marant — "Ed" as he liked the young people to call him — caught and interpreted Albert's silent plea.

"Let us bow our heads in prayer," he said, as he slipped smoothly, from long memory, into a lower voice register and the words: "Grant, O Lord, that as we are baptized into the death of Thy blessed Son our Saviour Jesus Christ, so by continual mortifying of our corrupt affections, we may be buried with Him. . . ."

Jean Cullen, Albert's girl, who with my mother had been helping out in the kitchen, came through the small dining-room at that moment and saw Mr. Roothe jump to his feet, his usually placid, almost bland face mottled and lopsided.

"What're you doing? What the hell are you saying?" He seemed about to place his calloused carpenter's hands around the good reverend's throat when Albert jumped up between them, frantically signalled to Jean to remove his mother to the bedroom, and in one of those deft movements that seem almost intuitive to someone in training for public life, pointed his father towards the kitchen, propelling him along with a quick shove while at the same time placing a hand on the back of the ashen clergyman. The latter sank onto the sofa where he continued to mumble at the thing hidden in his hands. Albert swept past the others and followed his father out to the kitchen, brushing past my mother who, of course, was standing in the doorway taking note of it all.

"What is it? What is it?" Albert demanded of his father.

By this time Mr. Roothe was at a kitchen cupboard, where he removed a mickey of medicinal brandy and gulped down half a tumbler. Although he had taken off his white carpenter's coveralls, with all the loops and pockets for nails, he still carried the vanilla-like odour of freshly sawn wood. He had been building cupboards for someone a few streets over when he had been phoned about Babe. He had arrived by taxi, his theory being that it was cheaper to take a cab than to run a car, especially if he kept his job radius to a minimum fifty-cent ride. In this day and age, the neighbours snorted, imagine a carpenter going to work in his white coveralls in a cab.

Usually a quiet amused man, he was now enraged. And Albert was doubly embarrassed, for the Reverend Ed Marant was his friend and mentor, the one who relied on him so much for his guidance of the young people's clubs at the church, who kept hinting he should marry Jean and accept a call to the ministry himself instead of trying to bring his religious beliefs into politics. As a friend and counsellor, Ed Marant was enough of a realist to wonder if Albert could handle the mixture. And here he had been one of the first on the scene — phoned by Jean — to offer spiritual comfort and condolences, and Albert's father had turned on him like a snake.

"What the hell did he mean?"

"I don't——"

"What'd he mean by 'corruption'? What's he getting at? Aren't they going to bury Babe?" In the much brighter light of the kitchen an etched web of veins stood out on his father's fleshy cheeks.

"It was just a prayer. One suitable for. . . ."

Albert's voice trailed off. Perhaps it had now occurred to him that the passage was from the service for the burial of the dead. Was his father right? Was Ed signalling to him that there might be some problem getting sanction for a full service if they found that Babe had taken his own life? Albert would never accept that. Or was it merely the first thing that had occurred to him? In all charity Albert probably believed the latter, for theirs was not a cage of dogma like the Anglicans or the Catholics. Surely they would bury his brother. But there were too many people around for him to take up the argument with his father.

The Roothe house, like most others on the street, had a small kitchen, and it seemed there was some kind of contest to see how many visitors it could hold: women passing back and forth with tea and cookies, Albert and his father glaring at each other, and now two large men who saw their chance to squeeze through the doorway with the impatience of those eager to say something, yet anxious to get away from that touched place. The first man, well dressed in navy blue, won out and introduced himself with a sly deference. He moved far enough through the doorway to place a white card on the oil cloth covering the kitchen table.

"You may not remember me, Albert. Cliff Morton from the

church. The choir? If it is your wish, the boy's remains will be released to our house of rest, once the other formalities have been observed."

"Get out," said Mr. Roothe.

My mother, pouring water back and forth between kettle and teapot in billows of steam, wondered too how so many people sniff out tragedy so quickly. Albert told the funeral director he'd be in touch with him, then turned to the second man, who brushed past and leaned against the sink. His shiny ankle boots reached out to the middle of the floor. There was no doubt he was the police. Unlike in the movies, though, he had taken his hat off and now politely introduced himself as Detective Sergeant Ewens.

"Sorry, but I must have a word with you about what happened."

"Yeah, that's what I'd like to know. What happened? Who knows anything?" Mr. Roothe turned on him.

My mother said she had the feeling that the cop was basically an inarticulate man whose way of dealing with such situations, probably through long practice, was to rumble slowly in short bursts in the direction of his boots. He seemed to have developed a careful way of imparting bad news in the style of a chopped serial, drawing his listeners into an increasing tension as they waited to hear the next chapter. The timbre of his voice rattled a row of hanging saucepans.

"The boy is gone. I mean the ambulance took him before you got here. Mrs. Roothe gave us positive identification. As the senior police officer present, I authorized removal."

"But what happened to him?"

"He, ah, passed away from strangulation by rope. In the barn. Apparently self-inflicted. At least that's what it seems. The medical examiner will be able to tell us more."

"You're going to cut him up?"

"Not me, Mr. Roothe. But I've phoned the coroner."

"Go on."

"Well, I ought to tell you we've requested an autopsy."

"You mean you can cut him up without our say-so?"

47

"Strictly speaking, Mr. Roothe, your permission is not necessary."

"How's that? Come on."

"Well, we've got the authority to make the request if the deceased has died of anything other than natural causes."

"Such as?" Albert asked after another silence.

"Oh, negligence, violence, or what we call misadventure."

"And who does this?"

"The autopsy will be carried out by a medical practitioner engaged by the coroner. If you think about it, I'm sure you'd want it done. Under the circumstances. . . ." He stared down at his boots.

"Quite right," Albert said at last. "Yes."

Having brought them along this far, the detective cleared his throat and offered another snippet of information.

"Could affect the timing of the funeral."

"Go on," Mr. Roothe urged. "In what way?"

"Might be a couple of days. Up to three, maybe. A lot'll depend on the length of time required to do the autopsy. The kind of examination done and the tests required. That stuff."

"I see." Albert peered through steam at a calendar on the wall. "Is that all?"

"Nope."

"Well?"

"You see what happens is this: The doc doing the autopsy reports to the coroner in detail — he's got to do it in writing — once the, ah, examination is over. The coroner may then want to hold an inquest. At that time he's authorized to ask us to make further inquiries regarding the circumstances under which the deceased met his death. He'll do this only if he feels such an investigation is warranted."

Exhausted by his own loquacity, the large detective sighed and took a cookie offered by my mother. He waved off a cup of tea.

"What do you think?"

"Now, sir, I can't say for sure, but if I was the coroner I'd hold an inquest. Haven't had many of them around here. As family, though, I'd think you'd want to know everything there is to. . . ."

"Yes," said Albert, to make some kind of noise in the kitchen other than the singing of the kettle. "Does that mean further delay?"

Cop's eyes appraised Albert.

"Might."

"How long, for God's sake?" Mr. Roothe inquired.

"Not sure. If he does hold an inquest, the, ah, body mightn't be released to you for burial till after the inquest is over. On the other hand, if he don't feel any more investigation is needed, he could issue a warrant for the burial right after the autopsy."

"What's he likely to do?"

"Hard to say."

"Give us a guess."

"Without going on record or nothing, I'd reckon he might wait till after the inquest."

"Okay, then, how long does an inquest take?"

"See, there's the calling of the inquest. Then a jury has to be selected and they've got to view the, ah, body and the rest of it. Probably your family'd be called to testify and anybody else the coroner wants."

"But how long?"

"Few days, I'd say. I'm just telling you this so you'll be prepared. You should know that you mightn't be able to set a date for the funeral for a few days."

"We appreciate your telling us," Albert said.

"Yeah, but when do we see him again — if ever?" Mr. Roothe asked.

"When he's turned over to the funeral director," the police-man said. "I'm sorry." He shuffled his large rump against the kitchen sink and eyed Mr. Roothe's tumbler of brandy. "If you could take the time now, I'd like to review your son's movements and contacts over the past few days. It'd save us bothering you again for awhile. But you may not want to."

"If it'll help to find out," Mr. Roothe said.

The detective glanced through the fog at my mother.

"Is there somewhere . . . ?"

"Why don't the three of us go out in the back yard?" Albert offered. "The house seems a bit crowded."

"I want you to show me where it happened," Mr. Roothe said.

"Fine, sir," nodded Sergeant Ewens. "Then I'll be going next door to interview the two boys."

"What two boys?"

"The two boys who found your brother in the barn."

"Oh," said Albert, "I'd like to talk to them as well. Or at least hear what they have to say."

They moved towards the back door, leaving my mother alone in the kitchen.

But we weren't there for the cops, Albert, or anyone else to interview. By that time, Norm and I had taken off.

CHAPTER NINE

A THIEF, I HAD RIFLED MY MOTHER'S LEATHER PURSE, lifted a buck and four car tickets she could ill afford, and persuaded Norm that we must run.

Why?

There was a need to put distance between us and that image of the sacklike gargoyle in the barn. Death wasn't anything like it was on the screen. Imaginations tumbling over the arrival of reality brought fears that the cops would be out to frame us. We'd seen that too often at the movies, read it in the pulps, and heard it on the radio. The harness bulls and the dicks would be out to grill us about what we were doing in the barn. Were the three of you fooling around, and you decided to play at hanging, and then what?

Yet there was also a strain of romanticism in our flight. It was a last gesture in the same way the air aces dropped a dead flyer's boots onto an enemy field. If one of us had been found hanging, that's exactly what Babe would have done.

We fled the best way we knew, on a streetcar over town.

And where the streetcars passed each other on the level stretch of 99th Street, so close they almost brushed off their red paint, I was sure I had seen Norm's mother, Mrs. Fetterman, in the one going in the opposite direction, homeward. If it wasn't Mrs. Fetterman, it was another overweight lady snivelling into a handkerchief, the ends of cloth chewed in her mouth as though she had been pulling cotton from the depths of her innards.

Through the wire mesh over the screen I spotted her and poked Norm, who must have caught sight of her at the same time. He dropped his head down between his knees to avoid being seen.

As I found out later, it had not been an easy time for Mrs. Fetterman.

That Monday morning Norm's mother had dithered. She started the washing, then gave it up and braced herself to go over town for a mortifying interview with Mr. Thorpe at the Civic Block. She had to see him about a problem that was just one more cross she had to bear. Like so many others in those times, Mrs. Fetterman was behind on her property taxes and the fear of losing her home had brought her to approach our neighbour, Mr. Thorpe, who was the official she had to see.

"I don't know what I can do, but by all means come and see me," Mr. Thorpe had said, his face not giving anything away.

"Should I go?" Mrs. Fetterman had asked my mother.

"Of course you should, " my mother told her. "At least it's somebody you know. And Mr. Thorpe is a good Christian man."

Her sarcasm was lost on Mrs. Fetterman, for she was what my mother classified as a "poor soul." The poor soul had lost her husband, temporarily at least, while he rode the rods east for work; or, poor soul, maybe she had driven him out with her whining; or, poor soul, now she had to fill up every room in the house with boarders and put Norman and his younger brother Bobby onto camp cots in the cellar; or, poor soul, now she was on her way over town to plead for relief on the backlog of taxes her departed husband had failed to pay.

One could picture Mrs. Fetterman sitting across from ratty little Thorpe. Her round face, like Norm's, was seemingly on the verge of rearrangement, as if some inner worm was about to cause its collapse and the flabby cheeks, bulbous nose, and her sandy hair, with a scorched odour from the curling irons heated over the gas stove, about to slip forward into an ill-defined mass.

Thorpe was a supervisor in the City Assessor's and Tax Collector's office, one of those fortunates who were regarded with envy as working for "the City." His salary at that time must have been less than a thousand dollars a year, but he had job tenure because he was a returned man with seventeen years' seniority. War veterans got preference for government jobs, but my father said Thorpe had probably been promoted to supervisor because he had the spiritual fortitude to handle the inflow of shabby supplicants appealing for mercy on their back taxes. He must have known how to tread a fine line and adapt himself to pressure when certain cases would interest the assessor himself, the mayor, the aldermen, or one of the other commissioners. His probity was unquestioned upstairs, his humanity negotiable from the right quarters, his control of the half-dozen enforcers in that room, absolute.

Unlike one tax delinquent two weeks earlier, Mrs. Fetterman had not arrived with a shotgun. That episode had earned a squib in the papers both for Thorpe and a man in coveralls, who, after walking into Thorpe's office stiff-legged, had unhooked the straps that held up his bib to withdraw the weapon. In the paper it merely said that Mr. Thorpe had talked him out of whatever it was he intended to do and had turned the man over to the police. That was one time we had sought out his son, Pete, to get the inside dope.

"Just as it says. Dad talked him out of it."

"How, for chrissake?"

"All he'll say, it was p-prayer. He says the whole room j-joined in. I guess they s-spooked the poor b-bohunk."

Pete didn't pick this opportunity to brag about his father and ingratiate himself with our bunch. He always wanted to be closer to us, to be included, but not on that basis. And I think he resented the fact that his sister Diane was so sought after for entirely different reasons. Pete was ashamed of his parents. His mother, Velma, was stout and foreign and spoke with a heavy accent that made the neighbours blink and strain to make her out whenever they had their rare contacts with her.

Just where Thorpe had acquired his religious obsessions I never knew. I remember once, before Babe died, Mr. Roothe telling us about the revelation of the angel over the trenches. It was said she appeared in a glow out of an oily mushroom of smoke, a vision claimed by hundreds, even thousands, who looked up from under their helmet rims and saw her clearly, even to the details of her outstretched arms and flowing robe, gleaming like phosphorescent bones at night.

"Never saw her myself. Talked to lots who did," Mr. Roothe told us. "You know someone who did see her? Mr. Thorpe, that's who."

Maybe that's where it all began for William Thorpe and what set him off on his quest.

My parents always said he really didn't get frantic about it until after the Crash, when his children were growing up and he had to cope with the guilt of having a job and dealing with the feckless and bewildered taxpayers praying to him for an absolution he was not able to grant.

But, as I was to find out, there was something else. Not until a decade later did I begin to understand.

On a January day in 1945 two young men, who seem grey and much older, are pacing on a gravel path in what appears to be the grounds of a convent. Against the indrawn light of mid-afternoon they wear heavy greatcoats over hospital blues. One of them staggers and veers off until the other pulls him back by the arm. The wanderer has a loose, crafty look: eyes rolling one moment, hooded and shifty the next. He is Pete Thorpe and he is insane, or appears to be. He is taking me through his family's odyssey, week after week, to those places of worship, visits never to be repeated or brought back by popular demand: the Pentecostals, the Calvaries, the Gospel Houses, the Nazarenes, the Missions, the Disciples. There are friendly smiles and greetings at every door, something you don't get in the big brick or stone piles where the established religions practise their self-centred devotions behind Sunday masks, not applicable during the week.

Out of his head, Pete greets us at the door: "Welcome, friends. What is your name? My, what a handsome family. What's your name, child? Diane? My, my. We hope you'll come again."

Kitchen chairs, no pews, brassy tones of trumpet, reedy clarinet, scraping violin, a tiny girl with a tuba who sits behind the piano player and belches the word of Moses. Hobos on the run from the cold modernity of the other churches. Break-aways searching. The warm-up. Welcome, welcome, welcome, and I have a few announcements to make. Now some music by these fine young folks, then some floating prayer in words they can all understand, rising heat and ardour, more music, the sermon about the unshakable truths in the Good Book and the frightening but joyful words of prophecy. Pleading, threats of damnation, testifying (leaping up, some shouting), beat-beat-beat, the band and the voices. Now comes the altar call. Come forth and unburden yourself of your sin and your fears. Come to the Mercy Seat of God. Stand up and freely express your sins. Accept the salvation that only He can bestow upon you.

Dad, why can't we go? Why do we sit here? We're alone here at the back, all the others have gone forward. Why are you here, your lips moving, your head bent, your fingers digging grooves into your temples? Why can't we go with the others? Look at Mother, she's all red and crying. Diane's stroking her own thighs and has had her own awakening. I just want to get back and hide under the blankets and clamp myself to the headphones of my crystal set. That's my link to the outside, radio waves that come and go in space. Ether is real, not this.

"Brother Thorpe, we have been blessed by your presence these past few weeks. You have been faithful and good in your attendance. You have a fine family. My, what a pretty girl, the Lord's blessing. But, if you will forgive me, I cannot help wondering, prayerfully and earnestly, why you have not arisen to testify, nor come forward during the altar call at the Mercy Seat. Would you care to join me in prayer while we ask for the divine....."

"No, thanks. Thanks just the same."

On to another congregation in a basement that smells of stale soup.

We sing, we pray, but we won't answer the altar call. He won't be an RKO radio mast and flash out his sins for the world to hear. But you shouldn't misinterpret this as any doubt or crack in his faith, although it's plain to see there is something holding him back, all right, which prevents that final step forward and sends him on to the next place, perhaps in the eternal hope that the tide of devotion there will at last sweep over him and provide that overwhelming compulsion to confess and beg.

So, what is it?

I know, but you don't. . . .

The two men wend their lurching way back to the convent.

It's a bleak day, a long way from the Civic Block in the city on the distant prairie and the moment when the man in coveralls pointed a shotgun at the head of William Thorpe.

The head in question is a largish one, perched on a small frame dressed in a shiny black suit and the old type of collar with the stud in the back. The outraged taxpayer hesitates as he comes under a cool, intense stare from the unflinching greenish eyes, bulging as though from a thyroid condition and extending from deep sockets where the flesh has receded in wash-board folds.

The intruder begins to notice that there are slight dents on either side of Thorpe's temples and that the cheekbones are high, stretching the pale indoor skin over a V-shaped scar gotten during the war. The brown hair is thin and plastered down in streaks. The hypnotic effect of the eyes is reinforced by a whispering, wheezy voice, the result of chlorine gas in the trenches.

The angry citizen hadn't counted on this. Nor on William Thorpe's response.

"Let's pray for your soul," William Thorpe said to the taxpayer. Heedless of the shotgun, Thorpe rolled out of his swivel chair and onto the floor, where he knelt.

Around the room the other clerks followed suit, until the oily floorboards were covered with kneeling figures and voices washed over the gunman.

He stood there for a moment, his dark eyes adrift, then he placed his shotgun on the desk and knelt down with the others.

Maybe, all along, it was this dusty room of clerks, handling the woes of the poverty-stricken, that was William Thorpe's spiritual home — and he didn't realize it.

Unarmed, except for her damp eyes, Mrs. Fetterman sat across from Thorpe on the Monday morning we found Babe. Because she was a neighbour, he had taken it upon himself to review her file.

"If you were on Relief we could do something," he told her.

"No, I'd never do that," Mrs. Fetterman said, which may

have endeared her to Thorpe sufficiently to lead to the conversation that followed.

Just as they were about to consider her case, the phone rang and she sat tensely while Thorpe spoke abruptly.

"No, I don't want any. No, that won't help. No, we can't wait until you get your twenty-five dollars a month."

He hung up the phone and concentrated those sealike eyes on Mrs. Fetterman. Possibly he had been under a lot of pressure that day, or perhaps he felt the need to speak to someone harmless with whom he had some tenuous personal connection. Whatever it was, he began to talk to her.

"May the Lord Jesus help them," he said to her. "You know what that was? It was some poor fellow offering me a case of eggs from his brother's farm if we'd just hold off a little longer... if we'd just wait until they started getting their twenty-five dollars a month from Mr. Aberhart."

Mrs. Fetterman didn't admit that she had a similar plea in mind as a last resort—not eggs, but the twenty-five dollars a month. Thorpe went on.

"Are they so deluded they believe they can create a divine temporal power through politics or economics or whatever it is? Have they forgotten that all men are sinners and have no prospect, no hope or power of overcoming sin through political action, no matter how well intentioned? There can't now be a Kingdom of God upon earth through such means. Their leader, himself so well versed in prophecy, should know that. I wonder if he does?" He leaned across the blotter on the desk. "You know, Mrs. Fetterman, theirs may be the ultimate heresy, the most sinful, maybe even more dangerous than the atheists, the old-line corrupt politicians, or the Reds. For there at least you can identify evil when you see it. And is there any greater sin than building false hopes? I apologize. I didn't intend to get into that. But it really makes you wonder. Oh, take people like Albert Roothe. Chasing after illusions. That's not salvation. Twenty-five dollars a month, indeed!"

That's all Mrs. Fetterman got from him that morning.

He started to ask what she thought were some rather searching questions about the number of boarders she now had in the house when his phone rang again. This time he scarcely said a word, though he never took his gibbous eyes off her. Gently, he put down the receiver. She remembered looking up at the clock on the wall. It was close to noon.

"The young Roothe boy. He has apparently committed suicide in Mr. Headley's barn. Hung himself," Thorpe told her. "That was Mrs. Thorpe on the phone."

Because of his work he had a phone at home, but his wife, Velma, seldom used it. She had few friends or relatives to call and, in any case, she was almost impossible to understand on the phone.

Thorpe bowed his head in prayer, and Mrs. Fetterman joined him, tears shiny on her fleshy cheeks. She left then to rush home and, as though it were some kind of epidemic, to make sure Norm was all right and to join the other neighbours at the Roothes' in damp misery.

That was how Mrs. Fetterman and Mr. Thorpe heard that Babe's body had been found.

CHAPTER TEN

THE TWO MEN FOUGHT, SLIDING ON THE WET GRAVEL OUTSIDE the beer parlour. Norm, watching with the rest of us, tried to grope his way to an understanding.

"So the little guy there, he's the one for Abie, huh?"

"Who cares?"

It wasn't much of a fight, but it was enough to keep us from closing off our day of escape and going home to face whatever a mystified parental justice could dream up.

We'd seen fights before. Better ones, even in the movies, where men struck for a quick decision, a sharp rap of knuckles neatly on the jawbones, a precise fakery, but more interesting than this. Here, outside the beer parlour, in the gravel parking lot at the side of the hotel, the two men floundered at each other, their boots slipping in pools of water left by the chilly rain showers. They had the awkwardness of beached amphibians slapping away with loose flippers, kicking ponderously with double-jointed legs. They were trying to settle a political argument.

Except for the white globe of the "Drinks Ladies" sign over the door, the parking lot was now in early darkness, brought on by the low clouds. No ladies had emerged from their own drinking place, but a number of men who had hung around after closing time to watch the scrap belched and farted loudly, sated with the watery, greenish suds or the mixture of tomato juice and beer that was called red eye.

"Where do they get the money for beer?" Norm asked.

"Who knows? Relief, maybe. Come into town and sell some chickens. Odd jobs. How'd I know?"

Cold and tired as we were, we stayed to watch. I believe what held us that night was the sense that here were two human beings who could let their feelings bring them to this. They were pouring it out, circling each other in a rush of hatred they had to exorcise. And there was Norm and I, refugees from all that the death of Babe meant, finished with a day of flight on a dollar stolen from my mother's purse, and no closer to our own inner understanding of ourselves. Yet he was still with us, for it was Babe who had first shown me how to sneak into the back entrance of the beer parlour, a trick first revealed to him during that time when he hung around briefly with the Cawners.

Coming out of the Princess Theatre, where we had just seen *Clive of India*, I had taken Norm through the empty parking lot to the back alley and the fire-exit door. I led the way down a short dim hallway lined with wooden barrels to a green curtain. The curtain was a thin filter for the heavy fumes and voices rising as closing time approached. From either side of the curtain we took in the long, dimly lit room with its dark wood panelling and ornate ceiling, built in the days of wide-open bars and free lunches.

Now the floor was heavy brown linoleum, gleaming with pools of spilt beer, and the old bar was where the waiters, in short white jackets, picked up the draft and carried the orders to the tables. As the ten o'clock closing neared, there was frantic empty-ing of glasses, flurries of dimes and quarters, low-tide froth ebbing in the empties, receding from the scored measuring lines near the glass rims.

What kept us there wide-eyed was the primeval human roar that came from the room. We seemed to be outside a cage filled with a different species of being: dark, rough, sweaty, coveralled for the most part, except for a couple of old men nearby in stained suits, vests, and celluloid collars.

In that bemused moment I began to realize what my father was getting at in his controlled rage at "the system," and why Mr. Aberhart's face had glistened with tears the night of the rally. Here the anger was running loose, noisy and vocal, as they leaned into each other, hands whammed onto the wet tables, the beer thrown back like medicine to kill the pain. In this dingy green room, the smoke streaming out along the ceiling from slow autogyro fans, was the fury of a generation. It was scary.

Over at a table near us, one of the disputes, louder than the others, arose through the smoky heat. Here sat two old men with two younger men. The two old geezers were feeding the intense wrath of the younger ones, who were glaring at each other with mounting hate, chopping off their words with harsh, bitter laughs. When the lights were clicked and the waiters started yelling, the beer parlour emptied slowly, except for the one table where the argument was still going on. When the manager came over and said something, they gulped down their beers and stepped outside to settle the matter.

The two old men stood as seconds, out of range of the heavy splashing boots, while the combatants, sluggish and ballasted with beer, circled. The smaller one, black hair flicking over his eyes, struck suddenly, his right arm quick as a snake. There was a wet slap, not like the clean crack of knuckles in the movies, and the other stockier one let out an unheroic "Ow!"

"That for twenty-five dollars a month," grinned the old man nearest to us. He wore a stained Homburg and a crinkled suit with a heavy watch-chain across his vest. Across from him the other old man dug his cane into the gravel and flipped some stones across the parking lot towards him. The other one had a wide-brimmed stetson riding low to his eyebrows, and he too had a thick watch-chain across his vest, as though it was a device for holding the aged together.

"Seen better at school."

"What did he mean? Why're they fighting?"

Norm had a view of adults as boarders around his mother's table, quiet polite men who didn't take too much from the bowls. The only political talk was soft-voiced, joshing, and pleasant. Mrs. Fetterman's boarders didn't even smoke at the table. I inflicted my superior knowledge.

"The little guy and the old gaffer over there were talking against Social Credit. They said some things about Abie the others didn't like."

Norm shook his head as though he had made the leap in time

and was now a whining elder himself. Was the entire adult world doing battle over twenty-five dollars a month? I tried to figure out what twenty-five dollars would buy. Well, there was the dollar I had slipped out of my mother's purse that noon, and it had kept us going all day, far away from that moment when we had found Babe.

It had begun with our scrambling passage through the slimy tendrils of the washing on the line, those cold sleeves and sheets touching us as we ran towards my mother on the back stoop. Her torpor flew. She took charge in a way I was long to remember.

She sat us down in the kitchen and got us to repeat what we had found; then she phoned the police; then she got Grandpa Sayers and my sister Doris out of the basement where they had been doing my job helping with the wash; then she sent Grandpa off to check the barn with instructions to report back immediately; then she sent Doris to the front bedroom to make sure Grandma Sayers stayed there and didn't get in the way. She lit a cigarette and waited until the first police car arrived in the lane and a constable appeared on our back step. Only then did she take the constable and go next door to find Mrs. Roothe, who was in her own cellar doing her wash. When Norm said that his mother was over town on an errand at the Civic Block, she told him to stay with me in the house and don't goddamn well move, see?

I had never heard her swear before.

From behind the ordered haze of our back screen door, our view blocked by the lines of limp washing, we listened to the chaotic voices and Mrs. Roothe's sudden, long wail. There was clatter, the arrival of more cars, the slamming of doors, glimpses of legs in motion. A cop appeared in the kitchen to take statements from us. We were told once again to stay put and were shooed out of the kitchen into the living-room so that we couldn't watch from the back door.

Norm and I slumped at opposite ends of the chesterfield and waited. The only sound was the clock on the mantel of the gas fireplace.

"So we're going to get the third degree," I said to Norm. "I thought that's what we'd been through."

"Nah, that was nothing. That was just a harness bull taking notes. Wait'll the dicks get at us."

"What'll we say?" Norm was close to tears, choking a little, his fine hair damply stuck to his forehead, his pudgy face flushed.

"You figure it out, bud. Suppose they put two and two together, make the connection with the Cawners, that we were on the run from them?" I thought about it for awhile. "Let's get out of here," I said.

That was when I slipped through the empty house to my mother's bedside table in the dining-room, where I found the dollar in her purse. I almost had to drag Norm out of the side door of the house. A police car was still in the lane, but no one was in it. There was no sign of Billy Cawner. We pelted down the lane and caught the first streetcar over town.

On the lacquered yellow bench that circled the rear of the streetcar, we swayed and rolled in the plunge down the hill into the river valley. We were on a green-and-red car going over town. The colour didn't refer to the car itself, which was painted red, but to the plaque of colour on its prow that denoted its destination. Only strangers read the lettering on the roller above the front window.

We had decided to take the long way around while we thought about what we could do with our illicit wealth. The single track followed the road down the 99th Street hill, and the passengers stared down into the windows of tiny houses built along the edge. As it gained speed the back of the streetcar fishtailed wildly.

Norm began to swallow as though he was about to be sick, but he was strong enough to shout over the noise.

"Why'd he do it?"

"Who says he did?"

"What's that supposed to mean? You figure someone else did it to him?"

"How'd I know? I'm just saying. You got any ideas on who'd make Babe do himself in? Come on."

"Well...no."

"So shut up. I'm trying to think."

Think we did — at least I tried and maybe Norm did too, as we let our heads loll drunkenly, not unlike Saturday afternoon when we had stood in the same place with Babe in a streetcar full of people going to the Social Credit picnic. I closed my eyes and could see us all there in the same swaying dive down into the valley. . . .

For some reason Babe had been twitchy and anxious to get going; his fair curly hair was shiny with a fragrant oil, his face washed and his windbreaker damp with smudges where he had scrubbed off some stains. We had raced to the corner where a group of neighbours were already waiting to catch the streetcar over town. In no line-up or order, they stood in family clumps.

Mr. Roothe, who had no doubt been dragged along because of Albert, was one of the few who looked out of place, dressed in a brown rumpled suit instead of his white coveralls. He brooded off to one side while Mrs. Roothe chirped away about wonderful Albert. Mr. Roothe barely glanced at his other son, Babe, when we came panting up to the car stop.

Even the foreign Mrs. Thorpe had ventured out of her kitchen to accompany Diane and Pete who, when he saw us arrive, started to sidle towards us. When we moved down the sidewalk he got the message and stood by himself, kicking his foot against the curb until his mother told him to stop, that they couldn't afford to get his shoes fixed if he knocked off a heel. Her thick accent somehow stiffened the group, not just because of its alien intonation, but more for the strangeness that the Thorpes implied, his irritable tyranny that drove them on their bizarre quest for the perfect church. Yet his dominance of his family was perhaps not so complete as the gossips liked to make out, for he must have grudgingly allowed Velma some silver to pay for carfare, not much else, judging from the large flour sack she carried, bulging with outlines of Thermos bottles. No nickels for drinks, but he had let them go on their own to seek a form of salvation that he had already rejected.

For me, their presence aroused another kind of curiosity. Had Babe in some way found out that Diane was going? Was this the reason for all the aromatic goo, including, I noticed at close range, a couple of razor nicks where he had whipped off his darkening peach fuzz? I kept alert for signs, for an exchanged glance or touch, but neither of them was giving anything away, if indeed they had anything to conceal. Diane sat with her mother and stared out of the window, her platinum-blonde ponytail, not at all typical of those times when ringlets were the thing for girls, jiggling in the breeze.

On the streetcar we found ourselves pushed to the rear, where we hung on straps and poked at each other, much to the annoyance of other passengers. It was when we were creeping up the long hill past the Legislative Building, its dome a brown-sugar nipple pointed upward, that we heard Mr. Aberhart's voice boom through the car.

"Now my friends, you're all here to be saved. And I want you to see my new house over there on the left. That's where you can drop in and see me any time. Just come on in and get your twenty-five bucks."

There was a gasp throughout the car. All talking stopped and heads swung around. There was no mistaking the voice they had heard so many times on the radio. When we looked around, we saw Peter Thorpe, pimply, thin, and trembling, swinging loosely on a strap. He grinned at us.

"Peter!" his mother's voice called out from nearby. Diane didn't move her silvery-blonde head, but her neck was red.

Babe turned to Pete, suddenly friendly, and moved aside to allow him a strap near us. Pete swayed and stammered: "Wha-what should I d-do next?"

We couldn't help smirking with him, but we hoped this didn't mean we'd be stuck with him all day.

At the Exhibition Grounds, out in the north-eastern part of the city, we ran from the streetcar (by this time a blue-and-white "Special") to ditch Pete Thorpe. He called after us again in his Abie voice: "No twenty-five bucks for you guys." But it no longer amused us, although it had a dramatic effect on the arriving crowds, enough to make one old lady swing at Pete with her purse.

And later, when we were looking for Babe in front of the

grandstand among the barkers spieling for Social Credit, we were almost run over by Pete Thorpe, who was being chased by two men in cloth caps and baggy suits. No doubt he had been doing more of his Abie impersonations, this time to the wrong audience. We watched their clumsy progress up the tiers of the almost empty stand, to a lonely, shapeless figure seated by herself. Pete sat down beside his mother, who stood up, an alien tent in her old raincoat. The two men in cloth caps waved their arms a lot, then retreated.

It occurred to me then, a thought that stayed with me afterwards, that Diane was not there. If their father had been around there wouldn't have been all this chasing about, nor would Diane have been permitted to wander off. I remember wondering if she had slipped away to meet Babe somewhere, but at that time it was only a suspicion, a possible excuse for a kind of distracted air, not typical of him, that we had noticed lately. It may have been something else entirely (the Cawners had sought him out after he had cleaned Billy's clock) and that was an invitation to get involved in God knows what. Hadn't Neil Cawner asked about him?

When it came to Diane we all knew one thing: She was unapproachable. Her beauty was already in place, her complexion without hickeys, her breasts full and pointed in the cheap blouses she wore like a fashion model. You could see that she would some day be a bit heavy in the tail-end and thighs, but she was now a stamp of what her mother must have been. In Diane there seemed little of Mr. Thorpe's seamed, ravaged features; the only similarity was in her eyes, which were a deep, hypnotic green. So, in a sense, she was not unlike Babe in the early perfection one sometimes notices in certain young people, as though the Creator has indeed touched them lightly and with love as a kind of rebuke to the ugliness the rest of us have to suffer.

Diane walked to school with her one friend, Mabel, a despondent fat girl whose parents were also fundamentalists and members of one of the many congregations the Thorpes had briefly joined. We had long given up any attempt to walk with Diane. She handled us by keeping her head down, mouth twitching at some momentous joke, while she elbowed her fat companion into gusts of devastating giggles. Unlike most of the other girls at school, she

66

had sent no signal that she would welcome attention from Babe.

Several paces behind, we had watched while Babe finally decided to take up our dare to get Diane to talk to him. Like his brother, always sound on tactics, Babe had moved into step beside her, trying to outdo her aloofness by faking a shy reserve, his head also lowered and not saying a word, so that even Mabel stopped snickering and trudged along in silence. Diane hadn't said a thing. It seemed almost as if they were skating along, languorously, heads bent, looking for fallen coins. But now I began to wonder if some contact had been made between the two of them.

Their eyes veiled, had they somehow achieved a silent understanding, flowing one to the other?

On that Monday Norm and I didn't stay in the streetcar for the long haul past the Legislature, not yet Abie's home. Instead, we got off at the bottom of the McDougall steps and took the wooden stairs up the steep bank, pausing for breath twice on the platforms, until we reached the top and stood far above the valley.

The stolen dollar had brought us this far, to the centre of the city, with its brick buildings of four or five storeys, wide streets echoing with the clatter of streetcars and sticky with the smell of automobile exhaust. Low dark clouds whipped along overhead, a canopy threatening more rain. Whatever impulse had brought us across the valley now began to play tricks with any ideas we might have had about dodging the reality we had found that day. It was a bust.

To begin with, we couldn't find a show where we could lose ourselves for awhile in the white reflections of somewhere else. The four downtown theatres had nothing we wanted to see. We grew angrier as we slunk from the stills of Shirley Temple at the Capitol, to Mae West at the Empress and Nell Gwyn at the Rialto.

"All soupy stuff," Norm whined.

We slouched around in the stores and tried to keep up a wise patter as we grew tired and the guilt dogged us. Among the guns in the window at Uncle Ben's there was a sign and a big coil that said "Rope Sale." We exchanged stricken looks and jay-walked across the middle of 101st Street to the Metropolitan store, downstairs, where the sounds of the lady playing sheet music on the piano had drawn us. And after a thumping rendition of a Mozart minuet, someone, perhaps a Bible-pounding Abie adherent, asked her to play "O God Our Help in Ages Past." We got out of there and ran up the down wooden escalator in Woodward's, until we were approached by a floorwalker with thin hair and ridges in his skull who reminded me of Babe's father. In the basement of the Bay we sat for awhile and had frosted malteds, silent, neither of us daring to break the code and be the first to say "Let's go back."

During a light drizzle we took cover in Mike's Newsstand, where I used up another nickel to buy one of those boys' papers from England. It had "2d" on the cover and an aerial dogfight between an SE 5 and a Pfalz. The purchase bought some time, peeking rights to the other magazines. Up to a point. The old guy in the grey jacket with "Mike's" stitched on the pocket didn't seem to mind until I made the mistake of guffawing at a picture of Billy Bunter on *The Magnet*.

"He looks just like Aberhart."

This seemed to incense the man behind the counter and he threw us out.

By this time it was getting on towards supper, and the wet streets began to fill with people starting for home. We loaded up on chocolate bars and blew another nickel for Turrets, my height being sufficient for the guy behind the counter, though suspicious, to hand over the pack. I then suggested that we go back over to our side of the river and see *Clive of India* at the Princess, where the first show would begin at six-thirty, as always starting half-way through. Norm began to fuss about being home for supper, not from any fear of punishment, but his concern about making his mother have yet another worry and an excuse for one more torrent of weeping.

"It's not going to make any diff now. We're going to get it any way."

"I'll have to stay in for the rest of the summer."

"Not a bad idea. We'd better stay on ice till the Cawners cool off. They'll want to know if Babe told us anything."

"Jeez, you don't think they —— "

"Let's not talk about it. Okay?"

A red-and-white streetcar carried us over the High Level Bridge, a narrow structure that stretched all the way across the river valley from one high bank to another. The line was laid precariously along the edge of the bridge with the CPR tracks running down the middle. Before going up top onto the deck, each streetcar crossed over on a switch so that its exit doors faced inward. Local wits said that if the streetcar got into trouble, you therefore would not step out into space, you'd merely step out into the path of an oncoming train.

At the Princess, where we sat through *Clive of India* one and a half times, I felt a lump in my throat as Ronald Colman slowly put the pistol to his head. Even then we couldn't get away from the images of death that had trailed us all day. But we stayed on to see the battle scenes again with the elephants.

Now, like two lumbering elephants, these lesser mortals outside the beer parlour circled each other in the dim light of the parking lot.

The fight began to heat up.

The smaller of the brawlers, the one who had already struck like a cobra, moved forward again, linked one leg behind the other's knees, then flipped him over onto his back and into a puddle. The watchers moved closer, suddenly quiet, suspecting that a decision was near.

Straddling the bigger man in the way a farmer bulls a heavy sack, the little one hauled him head first to the doorstep under the "Drinks Ladies" bulb. There he fastened his hand around the other's throat. He then used the leverage to lift the man's head and bring it down onto the footscraper imbedded in the cement doorstep. The footscraper had the shape of a miniature goal-post, with a sharp metal crossbar for peeling off the mud.

The man on the ground began to yell in pain. From out of the greasy shreds of his hair came a bright red flow. His blood showered into the muddy pool beside the concrete slab. A few spectators made noises of intervention, a rising, low growl that frightened me to the extent that I actually pulled Norm back from his hypnotic shuffle towards the bloody pool. It was perhaps my first intimation that soft doughy Norm might end up showing more courage than all the rest of us.

One of the old men who had started the whole thing did a little jig, using his cane as a maypole. Old men, I realized that night, relish the battles of others. Then the word was that a cop was coming down the street, and we all began to run from the parking lot, leaving only the groaning man curled up in foetal defence on the doorstep.

Other heavily breathing shapes pelted past us, down the dark alleyway to the end of the street near the CPR station. A long freight was clanking out of the yards, and we could see figures moving out of the shadows of the freight sheds south of the station to grab onto the ladders of the box cars.

"That's what we ought to do," I said.

For an instant the gullible Norm thought I meant it, but I had to reassure myself that his brief flash of spunk in approaching the thrashing men had only been a lapse, curiosity rather than valour. A familiar look of panic crossed his face, then he sighed in relief as the glowing yellow dome of the caboose faded into the thundering darkness.

We crossed the railway tracks and started home. For most of the way we were silent, thinking about what awaited us.

CHAPTER ELEVEN

IF WE HAD BEEN RELIGIOUS, LIKE THE THORPES OR EVEN Babe's brother Albert, I might at least have had some spiritual insight to cope with a death that raised so many moral questions. What right did Babe have to destroy his own gifts before they had been shared with others? Did he not know that through him his parents and others could see a hope for the future that was denied them? My parents were unable to provide comfort by invoking any kind of divine scheme within which his death could be accepted. There are certain disadvantages to being raised a religious illiterate. My mother had grown up in a household where the only deity was the Grand Trunk Pacific Railroad, and my father was engrossed in grand secular visions of equality for all.

I searched for clues to some kind of purpose.

The only thing that came to mind was a sermon one of our teachers had unloaded on us in our Grade Nine civics class. The teacher, Mr. Grapstra, kept us awake by jumping from one part of the blackboard to another, furiously sketching in arrows and diagrams as far as his wizened frame could reach.

"You live now in a depression, but it wasn't always like that," he shouted at us. "You know that twenty-two years ago lots over town were going at a hundred thousand dollars, that everybody was frantically dealing in land—what we call real estate? Some tradesmen were making ninety cents an hour. Can you picture that? It was called a boom, the opposite of what we have now. Can anyone tell me why it was all brought down?" No one could, but we were listening, we were beginning to take an interest. "Greed, that's what it was. Every man, woman, and child was after the fast buck. Here, I'll show you."

Suddenly, he threw handfuls of wrapped toffee candies at us, and for a moment there was chaos in the classroom as grubby hands snatched at the air.

"There, that's what it was. A scramble. Save your candy for recess; don't gobble it now. Too late, eh? You didn't see that, how to put aside for later. So it came to an end because it had to. The golden calf all over again, a visitation to bring sanity back to a people who had lost all restraint, all sense of value. Otherwise, how else can we explain it: the collapse of markets, the huge unemployment, the poverty and need, and—get this—the coming of drought and plagues all at the same time? Do you not believe it is a punishment, a warning and a lesson to all of humanity? The hangover after the big toot, eh? So it is your fate, as innocents, to be the victims of this massive global headache. That is your destiny."

When I told my father of these unorthodox teaching methods, he grinned and nodded.

"That's old Grapstra, all right. Lost his shirt in the land boom and had to take up teaching. He may be right, you know, perhaps it is all a visitation."

That was the closest we ever got to religious discussion in our household. I wanted to go on and ask someone if such sweeping divine rules applied to individuals too; if it was possible that Babe had taken the ultimate punishment for having such a good time, for his mischief and bubbling ideas, for his irreverence, for being liked maybe too much? Did this kind of careless, slouching joy in life also bring down wrath and visitations from on high? It gave one pause, and I vowed to be careful, not to enjoy life too much, or at least not to be too blatant and attract attention from Upstairs. It seemed unfair, somehow, but Grapstra had told us we were victims. And sometimes victims were sacrificed, weren't they?

On our way home from the Princess and the fight outside the beer parlour we had been silent, our pace slowing to a shuffle, heels catching on the planks of the sidewalk that ran along the darkened hedges of our own street. It was more shame than fear that made us drag our feet, for in reality what could our parents do to us?

They were up, all right, waiting in the living-room. Grandpa, his braces drooping over his upper arms, snored in a deep chair. Mrs. Fetterman and my grandmother sniffled together as their fingers whipped through mending. I realized how worried my mother must have been when I noticed the little triangle pencilled around the page number in the library book that lay open on her lap. Her addiction was such that she couldn't possibly remember all the books she gobbled up, so she devised her own coding system, a small triangle on every page fifteen, I think it was. She could flip through the pages in the library and her code would tell her that the book had been read. Possibly she had just marked the book open on her lap, or maybe she had not devoured all the library's supply and was forced into repeating the whole works. Whatever it was, she was not reading, just staring at the page when we slunk in the door to face the music.

It was soon apparent there was other music to contend with. After the predictable babble of outrage, they cooled down suffi-ciently for my mother, with a wry grin, to pinch the last of the Turret's in my shirt pocket and announce that we were to go next door to appear before Albert and my father. There had been, we were told sarcastically, a posse out looking for us. My first reaction to this news was to feel a bit flattered that we were worthy of such attention, but this fleeting sense of puffery soon fled when I began to realize the full consequences of our dumb tribute to Babe, paid for with my mother's dollar.

I began to sense something hidden, beyond our grasp, when our bedraggled entourage arrived on the Roothes' porch to wait amid a clump of neighbours. The first thing we could hear was Thorpe's nasal voice going on about how something should be done about the Cawners. What did that have to do with us? The Cawners were, he was saying, the source of corruption in the community. Why, they might have seduced poor young Hamilton into ways that led to his own self-destruction.

"You of all people should know," Thorpe was going on, stabbing a finger at a ghastly, ashen Albert. "They must be excised, removed. Those boys have been —— "

Our arrival stopped him. Attention focused on us. Albert waved at Mr. Thorpe and one or two others who were sitting with teacups on the verandah, all of whom glared at us and, with obvious feelings of relief, murmured further condolences to Albert and slipped away. Thorpe paused at the screen door to rake us with his slightly bulging hypnotic eyes, fought with himself to avoid what probably would have been a scriptural reference of some kind, shook his head, and faded away into the night. Albert, his nerves raw, turned on us angrily, but my father came across the porch like a defence lawyer to cut him off with a chop of his hand.

"I want to know, John, why they ran away."

"Albert, you have all our sympathy, but the boys are tired. Another time, tomorrow, or —— "

"Now!"

If the feeling, the silent contending of wills between my father and Albert, could at that moment have been harnessed, squeezed into a hot wire, and dipped into rubber, it could have lit a house. But the arrival of another visitor saved us, temporarily, from Albert's wrath.

A car door slammed. A big man in suit and vest tapped on the screen door and let himself in. He took off his large felt fedora and silently reached across our skirmish line to shake hands with Albert. He had thinning, slicked-back hair, a prominent chin, and exceptionally large teeth, designed for quick smiles but now partly covered by a fleshy curtain that kept receding as though the teeth would not accept expressions of sorrow. All of this conveyed a first impression of insincerity, but there was nothing false in the quaver of this deep voice and the steady fix of his gaze on Albert's face, intent on reading teacup leaves or searching for other omens. Later, as we sat together on the porch while Albert and the other man talked in the front room, my father confirmed the salesman image.

"That was Vic Bell, one of their city organizers," he whispered to my mother.

She then whispered back the inevitable question: "What's he do?"

"Insurance agency in the west end. Fire and car, some life. Used to be big in the Tories, a Bennett cohort. Still may support him federally, I suppose."

The arrival of Mr. Bell had prompted my father to make herding gestures to get us off that porch and home to punishment and bed.

"If you don't mind, John, I'd still like to have a word with the boys."

What could he say? Albert was the aggrieved one and had certain rights to claim. While the other man and Albert went into the front room, we were seated on the wicker chairs and couch to await our third degree, postponed once again. There was no sign of Jean, Albert's girl. I assumed she was probably still at bedside with Mrs. Roothe, seated in her placid way, staring into space. Although there was no sign of Mr. Roothe, a distant sound of juicy snoring somewhere in the house indicated that he had probably anaesthetized himself with a bottle and finally had gone to bed.

The foreboding stillness on the front porch enabled us to eavesdrop on Albert and Mr. Bell, who now sat together in the gloom of the living-room, its yellow reflection through the front window cast by only one lamp.

"Our prayers go with you, Albert."

"Thank you, Vic. It's a terrible thing."

"Does anyone know why? You know I couldn't help thinking of the boy that Mr. Aberhart sometimes mentioned, the lad who was one of his pupils who couldn't take what economic conditions had done to his family."

"I doubt that, Vic. We're not well-off, but we manage. He didn't leave a note or anything. Those boys waiting out there on the porch may know something."

"You know, Albert, I've just come from the Cameron place. This has been a sorrowful day. I guess you hadn't heard."

"No. What?"

"Walter died of a heart attack at noon today. He walked home from his store as usual, had dinner with his wife, and was getting up from the table to have his afternoon nap when he keeled over. Just like that."

"I'll say a prayer for him too."

"These times require great strength. Just when we see the unfolding of a divine plan, these matters come to try us." They thought about it for a moment, then Mr. Bell went on. "A very bad thing for us. You know, when we met with Mr. Aberhart at the Sunnydale Pavilion last Saturday, I was at Mr. Cameron's side when Mr. Aberhart spoke to him and hinted pretty strongly he'd be on the slate for the city. Walter was really bucked up by that. Now, of course, they'll have to come up with another name."

"I wouldn't know. I wasn't invited."

"Now, Albert, you had generously offered to take on important chores for the picnic. We knew you'd want to devote all your energies to that. The picnic had to be a success, and thanks to you and others, it was."

"The meeting at the Pavilion was at noon. I could've been there."

"May God forgive us if we made an error in judgement. It was not intentional, Albert. You know our high regard for you. Your appearance before the Central Committee was very favourably noted. It was just one of those things."

"Like Babe's death?"

"Albert, I can imagine how you feel. My heavens, I've just come from a widow, a fine church-going woman who's cursing the fates for what happened to her husband. I don't mean profanity. Mrs. Cameron never takes the Lord's name in vain. I mean the spiritual shock that has shaken her soul. Do you know that I had seen Walter just three weeks ago to try and get him to take out a life policy? He'd surrendered the only one he had back in 1931, and he told me he still couldn't afford to do it. All she has is the store, and you know how little that's going to bring in these days. Indeed, her faith will be tested, at least till we achieve power and she gets her dividend. But surely not yours, Albert!"

"Sorry, no, Vic. Forgive my bitterness."

"We all understand. What happens now?"

"How do you mean?"

"Will there be an inquiry of some kind?"

"I expect so, yes. An inquest."

"I see."

"There may be a lot of publicity, Vic."

"Publicity is a two-edged sword, not all bad. You'll need to be strong. When is it?"

"When is what? Oh, we're not sure yet. Very shortly. I gather later this week or the first of next."

"That soon? Well, well."

The conversation, muffled slightly, went on behind us in the living-room. I kept myself taut to avoid falling asleep, which Norm had already done, his head drooping onto his chest. I forced myself into an uncomfortable posture, knees primly together and back upright on the edge of the couch. I began to realize that we were listening in on the hushed backroom, where things are hinted and the participants understand each other even if no one else does.

"We had in mind you might consider taking some meetings outside the city."

"I appreciate that, but there are so many others."

"You're one of the best, Albert. You've mastered the principles, the readings. You know what you're talking about."

"I don't have a car."

"We might get someone to drive you. The collections usually cover car expenses, and our friends will always put you up overnight."

"Come to think of it, I'm sure Jean's father has a car he doesn't use very much."

"Is he one of our supporters?"

"No, but I think she could get it."

"When this is all over, we'd like you to consider it."

"Oh, it's Jake with me. Probably good medicine. I—we—must keep going."

My father jabbed an elbow into my ribs. I had been slowly tipping forward as though demonstrating a new gym stunt, the free-fall kneebend usually performed on someone else's front verandah. When I snapped open my eyes and looked into my father's, I could see his face was tightened in anger, not at me I suddenly realized, after he gave me a quick smile, but at the import of the conversation murmuring on behind us. He understood its implications, all right.

Now it seemed Mr. Bell had gotten up to leave.

"Our deepest condolences, Albert. If there is anything we can do. . . . You will keep us advised when the funeral will be held?"

"We don't know yet when the — his body will be released."

"I see. Well."

After another seemingly awkward pause, Mr. Bell clumped out, stopping long enough on the porch to look us over again, to say good-night to mother and Mrs. Fetterman in his mellow voice before easing himself out, gently holding onto the screen door so it wouldn't slam. My father glared at Albert, who was standing in the hall doorway, reluctant to turn back into that dark house. He seemed to have forgotten we were there.

"Albert, we've all been through too much today. I'm taking the boys home now."

Eyes glazed, Albert didn't give any sign that he had heard. We awakened Norm and shuffled off. The next day Albert went back to mark papers at the Normal School.

If the rest of us were puzzled and empty and hurt that such a thing could happen to our Babe, his own brother's reaction, as it unfolded during the summer, followed the same strange pattern I first noticed that night. Albert built up an inner rage, visible to me because of the time I spent later in their kitchen as a kind of surrogate son, half adopted by Mrs. Roothe. He seeped a clenched, bitter anger that made his smile a form of steely lock-jaw. You expected to see the steam coming out of his ears. Whenever Mrs. Roothe mentioned Babe's name, as she often did, Albert would turn away or stomp out of the kitchen. He became more of a mystery than Babe, for at no time would he admit to any memory of him. Not once did Albert allow himself to speak warmly of his dead brother. I began to notice this strange pattern and, unknown to me, let the seeds of malice grow. I would dream up a pretext to make a passing reference to Babe, something that would make Mrs. Roothe feel better, but leave Albert tight-lipped and cold.

Slowly it began to dawn on me that Albert's rage at his brother was for letting *him* down, for lousing up his own future, for stirring up doubts about the stability of the Roothe blood-line, possibly for creating scepticism about his own faith in the demanding political struggles to come and for taking the ultimate step without leaving any hint as to why. For I became convinced that Albert was sure all along that Hamilton Roothe had indeed committed suicide.

I wasn't so sure.

Nor, it appears, were the police.

The day after Babe had been found, a Tuesday, we sat in our living-room with the same big detective sergeant who had been at the Roothes', his heavy tweeds redolent with sweat and carbolic soap.

Mother made sure she was in attendance, and although it wasn't hot, the front room was airless and stale with her cigarette smoke, past and present. The detective first undid the little button inside his jacket, then the outer buttons and, probably to make an impression on us, let his shoulder holster show. We stared at it in fascination. He was friendly enough and there were long pauses while he wrote in his black-covered notebook. At last he came to the question we feared most.

"What were you two doing in the barn?"

"We go in there to fool around. Mr. Headley doesn't mind."

"Such as?"

"Just fool around. Like a clubhouse."

The detective turned to Norm, who hadn't said anything yet except to shake or nod his head after I answered a question.

"You do bad things in there?" Norm blushed. "Had you expected young Roothe to be in there?"

"No."

"Let's go back a bit. What about Sunday?"

I was still answering. "We didn't call on him."

"Why not?"

"We weren't sure that he hadn't told his mother to put us off by saying he had to stay in."

"So you were mad at him?"

"Naw, I wouldn't say that. We were a bit peeved because he'd ditched us at the fair. I guess we just thought we'd wait till he came around and told us all about it."

"You always do the talking?" the detective asked me in a cold flat voice.

I glanced at my mother, but saw no support in her contemplative stare, screened behind a blue haze.

"You tell me, Norm. Why'd you boys go into that barn at that particular time? Now come on."

Norm, on the verge of sniffling, told him we were trying to ditch one of the guys who was after us.

"Why was he after you?"

"We'd kind of gotten too near a place where they didn't want us to be. That's all."

"Oh? And who was this other kid?"

"Name's Billy: Billy Cawner."

The detective whistled. "A Cawner, eh? Well, well."

Whether we had provided the dick with anything useful, I didn't know, but he did tell me something: that he was aware of the existence of the Cawners in the way that names become familiar to minions of the law. And I thought of ratty Thorpe on the Roothes' porch the night before as he raved on about the evil influence of the Cawners.

Why had he suddenly become interested in them at a time when the entire neighbourhood was out looking for us?

CHAPTER TWELVE

A HEAT WAVE BROUGHT A SHIMMERING UNREALITY.

The weekend after Babe's death a red ball of sun dissolved the familiar shapes of trees and houses into the wobbly outlines of mirages. Until then it had been cool and damp, our thickened blood not ready for the reputed 136 degrees in the sun on Friday nor the 143 degrees reached by Sunday. The moisture squeezed from the dampened earth added a humidity that drove some of us into our cellars and the more fortunate ones, such as my sister Doris, who wasn't under punishment for pinching a dollar, to the South Side swimming pool. There they jammed together in a steam of strong chlorine added to prevent infection among the thousands who used the place as an outhouse.

We could smell Doris coming in the back door.

Old folks like my grandparents relished the heat to thaw out scraping joints and stayed upstairs, but my parents joined me in exile in the basement, where they had set up a card-table for my father's university homework. Across from him my mother sat bowed over a library book; her ample breasts, streaked carelessly with white baby powder, were almost popping out of a loose wrapper that distracted my father and led to exchanged glances akin to newlyweds'.

My head buried in the Doc Savage and Shadow pulps which, taking pity on my punishment, Mr. Roothe had taken from Babe's collection and lent to me, I averted my gaze from my parents' lust, rising as the heat leaked down the cellar stairs. All of their silent glances and secret signals told me how desperately they wanted to slip upstairs for a quick one, but how could they, with me around and the elder Sayers positioned at key vantage points on the main floor?

In the wicker chair brought down from the porch I squirmed and whistled tunelessly, rattled my long toenails against the zinc cistern, and generally put on a restless act that might bring my parents to change their minds and let me go to the pool. With me out of the way, the poor saps could've had their quick screw on the old cot behind the ancient steamer trunks, where we used to put up any wandering relative who came by for a handout and a night's bed. Old enough to appreciate their horniness, I couldn't quite escape an odd sense of shame that one's own parents still did it, had urges that were only now beginning to build up in my own body like the hot sweep of the grippe.

As I turned a page I came upon a brownish smear, what seemed to be a streak of chocolate. Farther down were the whorls of a partial fingerprint. I sat transfixed, suddenly still. It was as if Babe had appeared on the cellar steps, leaping the last few to the cement floor, grinning and ready with a new idea, something to do. And during one of his quieter moments, although not a great reader, he must have sat in his bedroom, maybe last Sunday, a mushy bar or a candy seeping through his fingers onto the page while he read.

What had he been thinking about then?

So much had happened that week, so many things piled up against the unseeing walls of our soggy minds—now, as the coolness of the basement slowly gave way to the enveloping heat, I tried to think it out. Even the fact that Norm and I had run off that Monday had set off other reactions that were already complicating our lives with real and imagined fears.

It was too much. It had to end.

But where?

By this time we had found out that our disappearance the day Babe was found had set off an aftershock that had rocked the neighbourhood. Or rather, it was Albert Roothe's twitchy need to do something, the death of his younger brother releasing in him a frantic search for action. By running away we handed it to him on a platter, for it was Albert who had decided that the whole neighbourhood should be organized into a posse to track us down.

The search for us that Monday night had led to dire consequences for the Cawners. And now the fear of what steps those members of the clan still at large might wreak upon us meant that I wasn't all that unhappy to hole up in our cellar in the heat.

Wednesday night the police had raided the Cawner place.

It was something long overdue, and certainly the neighbours were not too surprised at what was found. Such was the reputation of the Cawners that they were blamed for any theft that occurred anywhere near us.

When Mr. Taylor down the street, for instance, got into his Ford coupe one morning, turned on the motor, then found that the car wouldn't move, he lifted the hood, peered underneath, and saw that the driveshaft had been removed. There was never any proof who had done it, but Mr. Taylor made it plain that it must have been the Cawners who had probably been filling an order for a driveshaft from someone who needed one in a hurry.

That the squalid Cawners might have their own code of ethics never occurred to anyone until long after the police raid. Oddly enough, the clan's stock then rose in the neighbourhood.

Falling all over themselves in the best tradition of the Keystone Cops, our city police had broken into the Cawners' cave, where they found a cache of stolen goods harvested from far and wide on the South Side and over town. Later, when it was tallied up, the amazing discovery was made and the word flashed around over the back-yard fences: None of the loot was from our own area. With some kind of crafty acumen for local feelings, the Cawners had drawn an invisible Pale around our own neighbourhood and, with the possible exception of Mr. Taylor, had confined their depredations to those beyond. We were dumbfounded by this display of neighbourhood loyalty. But it didn't ease our fears any.

Motors off, their cars complete with properly operating driveshafts, two loads of police had coasted in for the raid. There were four — three uniformed men and one detective — in each car.

One patrol car crunched down the incline of the back lane while the other crept along the mud road to the front of the enlarged shack. The cops stepped out into deep puddles that always seemed to be there, as if the Cawners kept topping them up as a kind of moat. That part of the street was not gravelled, and there were deep ruts that merged into a stand of high weeds growing up through the boards of a raised wooden sidewalk.

The lopsided chicken-wire gate squealed on rusty hinges as the raiding party piled up in a clump, finally figured out how to work the latches, and rushed into the yard.

The raiding party that came in from the back lane found itself confronted by Jocko, the Cawners' mongrel dog, part Lab, part St. Bernard, and about the size of one of Clive's elephants. Not accustomed to visitors at that hour, Jocko, who was well known to us, must have greeted them the way he did everyone else: a kind of ambivalent dance, then a leap with fangs bared in a grin, but his tail wagging.

Not taking any chances on the nature of Jocko's welcome, one of the detectives smashed in the dog's skull with the hook end of a crowbar.

They were all armed with crowbars which they now put to good use. The group at the front of the house, not finding a doorbell, broke a pane of glass in the Cawners' porch door and plunged through to knock out the glass in the inner door.

The details of the raid soon became local folklore. It was said that the cops were astounded to find the Cawner household deep in dual layers of thick carpet pillaged from various homes, a luxury treated somewhat casually by the clan, for it was told that the expensive rugs were ruined with cigarette burns, mud, and crumbs.

"They might at least have pinched a Hoover vacuum cleaner while they were at it," my mother said.

After they had smashed in the front and back doors to gain entry, the cops stood around in the smelly shack while the Cawners began to appear in various stages of undress. Again according to legend, the first to appear was Mrs. Cawner herself, who wore a sealskin coat over her nightgown.

A women seldom seen by anyone else, she was thought to have "a touch of the squaw," a rumour that now seemed confirmed when she rushed out into the yard to cradle Jocko's bloody head on the rich sealskin fur and set up a toneless wailing that made her neighbours' flesh crawl. Mr. Cawner, said to be a worthless English navvy who had been on Relief ever since it was invented, made one of his rare public appearances and apparently put on an impressive display about "a man's 'ome bein' 'is castle." This slowed the police down a bit, who now went over their search warrant clause by clause, the other five sons gathering around in sullen menace.

At this point Neil, either to create a diversion or to make sure someone would be left to enforce the necessary revenge, leapt out of an open window and ran for the ravine. One of the cops, too fat or careful to venture on a night pursuit into the bush, fired his thirty-eight into the sky. Restlessly turning in my own bed, soaked with bad dreams about Babe, I jumped up at the sound of the shots and padded out to where my parents, grandparents, and sister were standing on the verandah.

The shock effect of the two explosions was immediate.

The threatening stance of the big Cawner boys wilted. They trailed along with the cops, the beams of flashlights picking out the wooden steps down the clay bank to the cave. The cave was found to be of magnificent construction, with raised flooring, the inside dry-walls built of two-by-four studding and stolen siding, the roof shored up by railway ties taken from a pile down by the creek. Our dirty little minds had always held to the myth that the place was an underground whorehouse — at least that's what Babe had always told us. He had been leading us on, all right, but then we began to wonder if he had in fact known all along that the place was a cache for stolen goods, or if indeed he had been part of the gang.

And what a haul it was!

The police had to post guards overnight until the next morning when the entire neighbourhood gathered to see radios, tires, cameras, silverware, gramophones, clothing, kitchen appliances — a whole department store — loaded into a moving van. Just why they had allowed such an inventory to pile up was a source of amazement to us.

"Not too bright," Father said.

"No fences," said my mother, exhaling smoke over the top of

85

yet another mystery novel. "Where'd they get rid of it all in this burg? They probably intended to rent a van to peddle the stuff in all the towns between here and Calgary. Or maybe they were going to head over the line."

It was not too long afterwards that our anxieties were confirmed by the word that the peculiar timing of the raid on the Cawners was a direct outcome of our own disappearance on the Monday before. We learned all this from Pete Thorpe and one of our pals, Sid Warren, both of whom had been pressed into a search party as sort of tracking dogs who could sniff out our haunts. . . .

Early in the evening, after supper and while it was still light, they had been assigned to the search party dispatched to comb the ravine. My father didn't accompany that group. Reluctantly, resentful at Albert for making such a fuss over our absence, yet going along because he appreciated that Albert had to handle his grief in this way, my father had joined a friend with a car whose task was to comb the back alleys in the area. He told me later that both he and my mother had come across her open purse, noted the missing dollar, and figured we'd be back in due course — when the money ran out and we had wound down from the shock.

"They can't go far on that," Mother said.

Albert's press gang, members of his youth group from the church, had gone knocking on doors after six-thirty, when most neighbours would be finished supper, to organize the search. I think it was Mrs. Fetterman's unabated weeping that had probably set Albert off, anything to get her out of the Roothe kitchen where she was lacing the tea with her dripping salt.

A call to the youth leader at the church and the dragnet was out for us. The presence of one of those clean-cut young men at the door was sufficient to bring out Mr. Thorpe (not noted for his community spirit), who in turn pressed Pete into service.

So the Warrens and the Thorpes ended up in the clump of searchers sent off to look for us in the ravine, Mr. Thorpe trotting ahead eagerly, while Pete and Sid dragged their feet behind three or four other men who seemed embarrassed by the whole exercise but felt it was a kind of neighbourhood debt to Albert for the terrible loss he had suffered that day. Sid told us Pete was particularly morose and silent, shuffling along as far away from his father as he could get and passing up the chance to try out any new impressions on this captive audience. Mr. Thorpe had turned around and made the two boys join him at this point.

"They're down there, aren't they? You know where they are, don't you?"

After the party had scoured our usual stomping grounds by the creek, they straggled along the railway tracks, checked out the ruins of the old concrete hacienda, and headed uphill towards the forbidden territory of the Cawners. Sid told us Mr. Thorpe got very excited when, apparently for the first time, he got a glimpse of the entrance to the cave in the clay cliffs above them.

"What's that?"

Sid told him, carefully avoiding our local folklore about the unspeakable things we all assumed went on there. But Thorpe was quick to infer the worst.

"Cave of corruption," Thorpe announced to the group of puzzled adults, most of whom had probably never roamed beyond the ruins into this part of the bush. What frightened Sid was the next possible step. Would Thorpe insist on going right up to have a look?

"That's the last place they'd be, Mr. Thorpe. Nobody ever goes near that place."

Mumbling to himself about vile cesspools and the like, Thorpe stared up at the cave for a long time. Sid uneasily suspected they were being watched by the Cawners, but the arrival of such a group had apparently kept them under cover. He wondered if Neil or one of them was out there somewhere with a twenty-two trained on them. Shadowy fingers began to stretch down the slope into the hollow, and the silence, except for Thorpe's wheezy breathing, began to affect the others; finally, in an exchange of glances and raised eyebrows, they drifted away to continue the search along the railway tracks. Thorpe remained, gazing up at the filthy temple of sin.

As Sid and Pete moved off with the rest of the party, they

heard him grumbling to himself: "You're wasting your time. They're up there, all right."

And that was why, when we had been dragged over to the Roothes' porch on our return, Thorpe had been wheezing away to Albert about the Cawners. To some of us, too, it was obvious that Thorpe must have been the one who phoned the police about the cave and gave them the tipoff about something they had probably long suspected. But there was no way the Cawners would know Thorpe's connection for awhile, and we had visions of the remaining members of the clan still at large, sitting around in their wrecked shack and brooding about who had ratted on them.

Those remaining consisted of Neil, Billy, and the mother. The rest of them had been hauled off to fill out a police blotter and await trial. And I could see Neil's slow mental processes grinding away on the fact that he had found Norm Fetterman and Doug Sayers hiding in the bush and spying on the cave just two days before the raid.

That was what was eating Norm and me as we lurked, separated and forbidden to see each other for the weekend, in our own cellars, waiting out the heat wave. If the Cawners had anything to do with Babe's death, what would they do to us? To add to our heebie-jeebies, our parents had received official notices requesting that Norm and I be duly hauled to the inquest that would be held the following Wednesday to examine the circumstances leading to the death of one Hamilton Roothe.

I had never been so scared.

Mother came down the basement steps with a fresh pitcher of lemonade afloat with slivers of ice.

"I got two blocks this week, but I bet they won't last till Monday."

"Aren't they going to have an extra delivery?" my father asked. "What'd Mr. Shewchuck say?"

"He didn't say. Didn't know."

"Guess they don't want to make money."

They were talking about our iceman, a stocky little man with squinty eyes. He always looked faintly sinister in the shiny rubber cape he wore while lugging in the blocks of ice slung over his shoulder and held by tongs. His horse-drawn red wagon, with "Arctic Ice" printed on the sides, dribbled a fine stream of water into the dust wherever it went. I thought of Norm a couple of doors away, where they didn't have an icebox. His basement would be cooler than ours because at one end was a raw clay wall with wooden shelves dug into the earth where they kept their perishables. I wondered if he was staring at the dugout and thinking about what had happened to the Cawners' cave, now just a raw gash of yellow clay at the top of the hill.

The Saturday paper came. A reporter had fried some eggs on a manhole cover. There would be a lunar eclipse on Monday night. There was a brief announcement of Babe's inquest.

We let the heat flow over us and waited.

CHAPTER THIRTEEN

THEY PUT OFF BABE'S INQUEST UNTIL WEDNESDAY, THE DAY after the exhibition parade. In the meantime, the six jurors were called in on Monday to view Babe's corpse and hear some long words from the medical examiner.

Imagine, though, how the Roothes must have felt when they learned that Babe's body would not be released for burial until after the inquest and that the inquest itself could not conflict with another spectator sport, the Mammoth Prosperity Parade along Jasper Avenue. Officialdom itself had been caught up in the illusion that prosperity could be coaxed back with a parade.

Mind you, there were some hopeful signs. For the first time since 1930 the price of wheat had broken through the sixty-cent barrier. In central Alberta, at least, there had been little trace of the rust that elsewhere was causing the price rise. Throughout our region there were bumper crops coming into head. Then, too, there was always Mr. Aberhart, who had a plan to bring them all out of the Depression.

Others also read the signs of a change in public mood.

At noon the same day of the parade, July 16, 1935, the United Farmers of Alberta at last got around to announcing the provincial election. For them it was a blessed release. The funk that had gripped them, that had paralysed them into allowing their full five-year term of office to expire the previous week, now seemed broken. There had already been ominous mutterings about their illegal status, their flouting of parliamentary precedent in using the feeble excuse of floods in the north to stay in office.

Now their moment had come. But they blew it again, for the premier, Reid, couldn't even bring himself to make the announcement. That he was more or less alive we all knew from his presence in the Mammoth Parade. So one of his ministers, George Hoadley, acted the role of premier in a government that no longer existed, technically speaking or in fact, and called the election for Thursday, August 22.

Those guys were really spooked. A couple of days earlier, Mr. Aberhart's view of the impending election was to reveal that he would be going on vacation! United Farmers' supporters like my father were enraged at their leadership, but as he said, rustling the newspaper angrily, his frustration was nothing compared to what Albert Roothe must be going through. Not only did Albert have all the gruesome ritual of his brother's inquest to endure, he had to wait it out until the Social Credit slate for the city was announced. My father's opinion was that Albert had read too much into what Mr. Bell had hinted at the day of Babe's death.

"Maybe not," my mother said. "They've obviously got something in mind for him."

Norm and I, of course, had blown our chances of ever getting to the exhibition, much less being taken to the gala grandstand show, "Fascinations of 1935." We were, however, given reluctant leave to attend the parade, the first such event held in eight years.

The short-lived heat wave had broken, bringing out the entire population to see an extravaganza that was two miles long, with forty floats, a thousand marchers, and thirteen bands, whose vast discordance pealed and echoed off the buildings. To us it was big-time stuff, a swell outing that only whetted our appetite to get to the exhibition and the Royal American Midway. We dreamt up all sorts of unfulfilled schemes for sneaking onto the scary ride called the Sky Rocket, which was forbidden, so the publicity warned, to kids. Only adults could play.

But the next day, in our thick Sunday suits, white shirts, and ties, like make-believe adults, our mothers dragged us over town to the inquest.

Ashamed to be seen with our mothers, we trotted ahead, north from Jasper Avenue towards the police station. The reality of being called as a witness confirmed in my mind what I had suspected:

that there was something not quite right about the assumption that Babe had taken his own life.

Now it seemed our whole neighbourhood had been evacuated by a disaster and was trailing along to Babe's inquest. Wednesday being a half holiday for the retail trade, there was no one out shopping, and those who worked in stores were free to come and catch the show. At the buff-coloured building we saw the Roothes unloading from a car driven by Jean Cullen who, as Albert had indicated to Mr. Bell, had probably borrowed it from her father.

Inside the door a policeman directed everyone upstairs to the second floor. Pausing on the main floor, we awaited our mothers. By the main entrance there was a glass wicket, as if they sold tickets. Two large men in hot black uniforms came out, hitching up their Sam Browne belts.

From the interior of this place came a clashing on metal and someone in cells shouting crazily. I wondered if it was one of the Cawners. So far neither Billy nor Neil had stirred himself to track us down. They were, no doubt, still in hiding at home, ready to jump for the bushes if the bulls felt their presence was needed to round off the blotters.

Upstairs there were various anterooms, including one marked "Press" where two men were having coffee. In a two-newspaper town they always seemed to surface in pairs. Through the open door of the courtroom we could see neighbours gathering quietly, as if in church. It was two in the afternoon, the magistrate's court having completed its petty tasks in the morning.

Farther along the hall two men stood talking outside an open door with "Chambers" lettered on its frosted pane. While awaiting the arrival of our slowpoke mothers — mine wheezing with blackened lungs and Norm's suffering from delicate feet — we hung around and listened to the two men. One of them was later identified to us as Dr. Candliss, the city coroner. The other man's role, as we found out during the day, was that of crown counsel appointed by the provincial attorney general. His name was Hedden, or Haddon — the latter, I think.

"I can understand the police interest in this thing, but why the AG?" the coroner was saying. He gestured with an unlit pipe.

Haddon (I'll call him) shrugged.

"You know how they've been since the scandals. The young fellow's brother is pretty well tied in with the Abie gang. They may have a vague hope something might come out. I don't know."

"You're saying you want to make sure I call him as a witness?"

"Whatever you say, Steve. That's all that's expected."

"Jesus, I hate this. My first inquest and it looks like a suicide, for Christ's sake."

When Dr. Candliss became aware of us loitering nearby, he let a slow beatific smile brighten his face. His thinning hair was reddish-blond, his lashes, behind spectacles as round as sealer rings, were almost as white as an albino's. There was a pinkness to his face, as though he had just stepped out of a steam bath. He was of a build that used to be called portly, bulky but not flabby, his bay window solidly packed into a suit properly cut to show off his weight as an affirmation of reliability. The smile fell short of kindly condescension. There was something else there, a trace of sympathy for us, for our age or possibly for his own younger days.

"You can go in now, boys."

His informality was further shown in the way he ran the inquest. Instead of using the magistrate's raised dais and witness box, he sat at the clerk's table down on the floor and asked the witnesses to sit beside him at the same table, facing the court. It was more like a consultation about aches and ailments held in his own office. Throughout the day I noticed he had heavy, thick hands and was surprised when my parents told me he was a prominent surgeon in the city.

The inquest began with a bit of ritual. An elderly constable in uniform opened the show in a high-pitched voice, as if he was practising drama lessons. He made us all rise for the coroner's entrance, introduced the coroner and the crown attorney, then yelled at the jury that they had been summoned to inquire into and determine for our Sovereign Lord the King the identity of the deceased, when, where, how, and by what means the deceased came to his death.

"Jeez, the King wants to know?" whispered Norm.

The old constable reported the jury present and correct. They were all men, obviously city people, with light red faces from the recent heat wave shown off against white shirts. Dr. Candliss then spoke to the courtroom.

"The jury has already been cross-examined for any conflict of interest or bias and the proper qualifications to be jurors," he explained. "They were sworn in on Monday when we assembled at the morgue to view the body of the deceased.

"Now, for those who are unfamiliar with this kind of thing, this inquest has been called under the Coroner's Act of 1927. In this city we don't have inquests very often. Only two have been held, one in 1906 and one in 1928. Shortly I'll be calling the witnesses. They will testify under oath. You should be aware that a witness is entitled to be advised by his counsel or agent as to his rights, but such counsel or agent may take no other part without leave. If there are any such counsels or agents present would you please identify yourselves and state whom you represent?"

There was a craning of heads, but no one stood up. A bunch of guys from school, who had slipped into the back row, waved at us. I was glad to see their ugly mugs.

After some more paper shuffling, the coroner repeated the purpose of the inquest, cautioned the jury to disregard anything heard or read prior to the inquest and to base their verdict solely on the evidence.

"The purpose of an inquest is threefold: first, a means by which the public can obtain the facts relating to deaths; second, to focus community attention on and possibly prevent such deaths; and third, to satisfy the public that the circumstances of the death of one of its members will not be overlooked, concealed, or ignored. Strict rules of evidence do not apply. No one is on trial.

"The first examination of the witnesses will be done by the crown attorney, Mr. Haddon. He's here as an expert interrogator and counsel to me, not as a prosecutor. Following his examination

I may then ask any questions I feel are necessary and then any juror may ask relevant questions. We'll proceed with each witness in this orderly manner.

"Members of the jury will retire at the conclusion of the evidence, after a summation that I'll give you. In this province your verdict has to be unanimous.

"Remember you must include in your verdict the name of the deceased person and also how, when, where, and by what means the deceased came to his death. However, you will not make any findings of legal responsibility or express any conclusion of law. You can make recommendations, though, that may help prevent deaths of a similar nature in the future. Your verdict will be submitted to the attorney general. If he feels it necessary he may then begin a criminal investigation. If it should happen that any evidence is of an incriminating nature, myself or the crown attorney will inform the witness of his rights to protection. You understand what I mean?"

As if shaking off flies, the jury members nodded their heads vigorously.

"I shall now summarize the sequence of events leading up to this inquest. This will, I hope, save time. I have studied the police reports and my summary is based on them. Witnesses will have full opportunity to correct any errors I may have made."

His pink face cherubic, a slight look of amazement intensified by his round spectacles, Dr. Candliss squeezed his stubby hands in front of him and spoke to us softly. We leaned forward in our seats to hear. He began very strangely.

"For Hamilton Roothe the bright heels of all those moments of youth ended at some point during the night of Sunday, July 7. After attending a political event at the Exhibition Grounds on Saturday, he came home around midnight. His mother was waiting up for him and remonstrated with him about the lateness of the hour. She told him he would have two choices: either to go to church with her and his brother, Mr. Albert Roothe, the next morning or to stay in the house all day as punishment. Mrs. Roothe records that he didn't seem unduly disturbed at this news and, in fact, seemed in an amiable mood. However, when questioned, he gave evasive answers as to where he had been for so long after the rally had ended. 'Just walking around,' Mrs. Roothe recalls him saying. He then went straight to bed.

"The next morning Hamilton's older brother awakened him about ten and told him to get ready for church. The boy declined. According to Albert Roothe there were some words. He will be called as a witness, but you should note Albert Roothe's statement that, while he accused his younger brother of neglecting his spiritual welfare, he did not consider it as anything more than the usual kind of spat they had had many times before. Around ten-thirty, Mrs. Roothe and her son Albert departed for church. Hamilton apparently turned over and went to sleep. His father, who is a carpenter, was busy in the basement, working on what he describes as a large screened bird cage for a neighbour who raises canaries for sale."

"That's old Mrs. Trotter," I whispered to Norm. "Her whole damned cellar is full of birds."

"Tweet, tweet," said Norm.

"Pipe down, for chrissake."

"What's that?" Dr. Candliss looked up with a smile for the foibles of the young. "Please remain silent, boys. . . . In any case, Mr. Roothe looked in at about one o'clock to awaken his son before the others returned from church. At this point the boy got up, dressed, and helped his father set the kitchen table. Then he went downstairs to watch his father at work and offered to help out in the building of the bird cage. They worked away for awhile and Mr. Roothe says he seemed a bit groggy and quiet, but otherwise pleasant enough. The other son and mother arrived home and at around one-thirty they all ate dinner together. Most of the talking, according to their statements, was by the older son, Albert, who had been involved in the political event of the previous day. Albert twitted his brother about his, and I quote, 'disappearance' on Saturday. By this he was referring to the fact that Hamilton had accompanied his parents and two other friends, who are present here today, to the rally at the Exhibition Grounds. Then, to put it colloquially, he had ditched them and hadn't been seen again until he arrived home at about midnight. At the dinner table Hamilton

evidently answered his brother in a rather cheeky manner—
something to the effect: 'Wouldn't you like to know?'—where-
upon Mr. Roothe told them both to stop it, that they were getting
on everybody's nerves. No further mention was made of the
incident. The only uncharacteristic thing Hamilton then did was to
offer to help his mother with the dishes. That was indeed unusual,
as I am sure you boys will appreciate."

There was some nervous laughter and Dr. Candliss beamed
pinkly.

"In her statement Mrs. Roothe says she had the impression
that Hamilton may have wanted to talk to her about something.
But he didn't. He went back downstairs to work with his father,
where he didn't offer any conversation except that related to the
work they were doing. About four o'clock Mr. Roothe completed
the work on the bird cage and Hamilton came upstairs, where he
fiddled with the radio for awhile, turned it off, and started looking
through a stack of books his mother had brought home from the
library. She states that he didn't seem to want to read any more of
the so-called pulp magazines, of which he had a substantial supply
in his bedroom, and finally took one of her books to his room.

"Hamilton was not ordinarily a great reader, but she recognized that he was probably bored at having to stay in. The only
unusual thing was his selection, a women's romance set in the
court of King Charles the Second—seventeenth-century stuff.
Once when she went into his room to do some dusting, she noticed
that the book was open on his bed and that Hamilton had pulled his
chair, a plain wooden chair, over to the window where he was just
staring out at the back yard. His room and the window, I might
add, are on the extreme south-west corner of the house, a single-
storey bungalow. All he could have seen from there would have
been his own back yard, mostly a vegetable garden, a corner of the
house, and some of the yard next door. These neighbours are
named Thorpe. He would have barely been able to see the edge of
the barn where he met his death. It is two lots away.

"Hamilton emerged again at six o'clock for supper, attended
only by his parents, his older brother having gone to a youth group
he conducts at his church.

"Mrs. Roothe states that by evening Hamilton was becoming highly restless. He paced through the house and hung around on the enclosed front verandah. At this point Mrs. Roothe asked her husband if perhaps they shouldn't lift the ban, but he said 'No,' they should stick with it. To keep him occupied, Mr. Roothe then devised some chores in the basement, sorting out and cleaning some of his carpenter's tools. Around nine Hamilton came upstairs, listened to the radio for awhile, then had a long bath. This also seemed a bit unusual to his parents in view of the fact that he had had a bath as recently as Saturday morning, before going to the political event. Then he got into his pyjamas and went to bed. That was the last they saw of him alive."

Now Dr. Candliss's voice cracked a little, intensifying the attentive silence in the room. His round face became sad, making him look more like the middle-aged man he really was.

"Because Monday was a working day in the household, Mrs. Roothe went to wake up Hamilton around eight. He wasn't there. His pyjamas were laid neatly on the bed and his window was open. At some point during the night he had lifted the sash to the top, unhooked the outer screen, and placed it inside the room. He had dressed himself in a clean shirt, pants, and running shoes.

"His disappearance, of course, caused great consternation in the household. Mrs. Roothe blamed herself for being so hard on the boy the previous day. Mr. Roothe, his taxi waiting, said Hamilton would be back sooner or later, and he left for work. Albert seemed deeply concerned, but advised against phoning the police until more time had elapsed. He went off to the Normal School where he was marking papers. Mrs. Roothe phoned around among the neighbours, but no one had seen her younger son.

"At approximately eleven A.M. the two boys, Fetterman and Sayers, ran into Mr. Headley's barn, which faces onto the lane two doors west. A subsequent interview indicates that they went into the barn to avoid a chum they felt was after them for something. In any case, they went up the ladder into the loft, where they found their friend Hamilton dead and swaying from the end of a rope. The police were called, the deceased was identified by his mother, and statements were taken. I am indebted to the city police for the thorough documentation they have provided to date on this matter.

"Now. . . ." Dr. Candliss took off his spectacles and rubbed his blunt hands against his eyes. "I have taken a lot of time in this summation, partly, I'm sure you will realize, to relieve the immediate family from spending an undue length of time on the witness stand. I think we have a difficult task ahead of us today. From all we know, the deceased had no history of mental disorder, criminal activity, or even acute emotional upset. He was no paragon of virtue — remember he wouldn't go to church with his brother — but he seems to have been a normal, high-spirited lad in every respect. He left no note, no message, no clue as to why he would wish to do away with himself — if indeed he did. Members of the jury have viewed the body of the deceased. I think we will start with medical evidence from Dr. Swansen, the medical examiner. Mr. Haddon?"

If others in the courtroom had the same reaction I did, they were stunned and angrily taken aback by the enormity of what had just been outlined. The nature of Babe's last moments seemed so commonplace they left us adrift, unable to comprehend. The details sifted through our minds, disbelief and bewilderment piling up like grey soil blown by the wind against the walls of a deserted farmhouse.

Under Mr. Haddon's interrogation the medical examiner said that in his opinion death was caused by asphyxia due to strangulation by hanging. He estimated the time of death as between midnight on Sunday and about two A.M. Monday, probably closer to the earlier hour.

"Was there any evidence of violence, or clues that someone else had been involved in any way?"

"No. There were no contusions or marks on the head, throat, or elsewhere on the body. There were no rope burns or marks on his wrists or ankles. His hands and feet were free. The police sealed off the barn, searched it for evidence, and found nothing that would indicate the presence of another person."

"And the rope itself?"

"A common type of half-inch hemp rope, not new. It's an exhibit there. In his statement Mr. Headley, owner of the barn, said there were lengths of that kind of rope at various places around the barn."

"When you examined the body of the deceased, did you find any indication of a fatal disease or disability? Was there any brain damage?"

"Well, of course, the asphyxiation resulted in layer-cell death in the cerebral cortex, caused by cutting off the blood flow to the brain."

"But no disease?"

"No, sir. Nothing. A perfectly healthy boy."

Someone in the audience let out a low groan. The coroner looked up, pained.

The next witness was Detective Sergeant Ewens, who had given us the third degree the previous Tuesday. He went on in detail about the barn, their search of the premises, their interrogation of the neighbours, including us.

"In Mr. Headley's barn," the crown attorney said, "did you find anything that would lead you to believe there had been illegal or illicit business done there? I mean, stolen goods, a still, or anything of that kind that the boy might have stumbled upon?"

I looked down the row to see how Mr. Headley was taking this slur on his integrity. Red-faced, he had bent his head over the big stetson on his lap.

"No, sir. We checked out Mr. Headley very thoroughly. He had no record, is well respected. We also searched his house and his wagons."

"One thing, Sergeant Ewens, how did the boy do it? Wouldn't it have been pitch dark in there?"

"It's hard to say, sir. There was no sign of a flashlight, candle, or lamp. I suppose a person's eyes adjust to the dark."

"Could there have been someone else with him, someone with a flashlight?"

"I suppose so, sir, but we could find no trace of any such presence."

"Could we have Mr. Headley next?" Dr. Candliss asked. Haddon nodded and had Headley sworn in.

"You know your own barn, Mr. Headley. Does any light get into it at night?" Haddon asked.

"Not much, sir. It'd be like ink in there."

"Do you keep lamps in the barn?"

"No, sir, 'fraid of fire. And I've never put electricity in."

"Where were you around midnight Sunday?"

"As in my statement to the police, sir, asleep. I start early in my work."

"You didn't see or hear anything unusual that would wake you up?"

"No, sir."

"Well, the animals were in the barn, weren't they? My notes say two horses and a dog."

"Yes, the dog sleeps out there."

"What kind of a watchdog is it?"

"Old Pal? He's all right, but you see someone like Babe — Hamilton — his smell'd be known to the horses and Pal. Y'know those kids've been around the barn ever since they were little. Pal'd just wag his tail, the horses might stomp a little, but that's not unusual."

"So if someone had accompanied the deceased, it would have to be a person equally familiar to the animals?"

"I'd say so. At least it'd have to be someone with a familiar smell."

"Are these exterior photos of your barn? Right. Are these large double doors with the crossbar closed up the same way they'd be shut at night?" Mr. Headley said they were. "If someone tried to open them at night, wouldn't they make a considerable racket: the bar being lifted, the doors creaking open?"

"Look at the other picture, the one taken from the side. See? There's an ordinary door there that anyone could get in and out of. It's always half open at night for Pal."

"One other question, Mr. Headley. When you went out to the barn at six-thirty A.M. to hitch up the team and the water wagon, and the deceased's body must have been up there in the loft, didn't your dog make a fuss, try to tell you something? Didn't you notice anything?"

"I can tell you that's been keeping me awake at nights. I wish I could give you an answer on that. All I can remember is that Pal did a lot of jumping up on me when I came in the barn. I noticed the door was wide open. And the horses were a bit gun-shy that morning, snorting and a bit skittish. But hell, that can happen if there's a weather change. That's all I can recollect."

Dr. Candliss put his head in his hands and muttered "Jesus" to himself. He asked Mr. Haddon if they could have Sergeant Ewens back for a moment. So far no one on the jury had asked a question; they stared at each witness, immobile and glassy-eyed. This time Dr. Candliss did the questioning.

"Sergeant Ewens, did you check out the ladder and the barn floors thoroughly for any evidence of a body being dragged?"

"Yes, sir. There were no fresh score marks on the floor of the loft. The lower floor is straw-covered, packed earth. We would've noticed anything like that. There are so many heel marks and the like on the ground floor there wouldn't be any point trying to take casts or anything."

"What I'm getting at is the possibility the deceased was done away with elsewhere and brought to the barn."

"That occurred to us too, sir. Especially after we'd found out that he was an apparently healthy boy with no mental problems. But to haul a dead weight up that ladder into the loft would require two people and there'd be marks or chips all over the place. No, we don't believe that's what happened."

"You're saying then that in pitch darkness, this normal, healthy kid took a butter-box, placed it exactly under the beam, found a rope, tied the rope securely and flung it over the beam, found the shovel, got onto the box, and knocked it away with the shovel?"

"That's the only conclusion we can come to on the evidence, ours and the medical report's."

"In all of this, the only unusual occurrences are those related to the two lads, Fetterman and Sayers: their reasons for going into the barn on Monday morning and the fact they stole money and fled the scene Monday afternoon?"

"Yes, sir, but as a police officer with some experience in dealing with juveniles, I can't see anything too meaningful in what they did. Boys are boys, you know."

"Let's get them up here," Dr. Candliss said.

Thus, ahead of more important witnesses, Norm and I took our turn on the stand, but not without the coroner first addressing the jury.

"When we have witnesses of tender years, as they call it, we are usually expected to call a recess and ask them some basic questions privately — such things as school grades, sports, and religious activities; their feelings about lying and stealing and punishments for same; the nature of an oath and the like." He smiled at Norm, sitting rigidly beside the clerk's desk. "But these two boys are partly grown up. They're fifteen. Despite their escapades they know something about responsibility. They come from good families; they go to school. I don't think we need to take time for a recess for me to establish their veracity. Is this agreeable to the jury?"

Another flurry of nods.

"Okay, then, Norman Fetterman will be sworn in...."

And, once again, he went through all of our movements from Saturday till Monday night.

The room seemed to have trapped some of the heat from the weekend scorcher; sweat gave lustre to the coroner's face, a sheen on pink dough. He appeared to be suffering visibly from mounting frustration. After he had finished inconclusively with Norm, he went over the same ground with me until he abruptly took another strange tack in his interrogation, a change of direction that caused the jury to exchange glances and raise eyebrows. He spoke to me softly in his rather slow, lazy tenor, in odd intonations that suggested he had spent a lot of time in some part of the States.

"What you're saying is you can't surmise a motive for your friend to...to do away with himself?"

"That's right, sir."

"Now consider this. Do you feel it's possible he might have

been in love with death itself?" I must have looked slack-jawed. "All right, take your time."

"No, sir. I don't really know what you mean, but I can't believe anyone'd have that kind of feeling. Unless he was nuts."

The doctor's face reddened.

"It has been known as a condition of the human soul. Someone so imbued with sin—even imaginary sin—and the need to atone for it, or the desire to protect someone else in the hereafter from the agonies of hell. I've seen it."

"No, sir. Babe wasn't like that. He wasn't insane."

"To have such a deep yearning is not necessarily a sign of insanity."

He paused to take off his glasses and wipe them, then he ran his pure white handkerchief, still neatly folded, over his forehead and neck. He seemed momentarily to be more concerned with his own memories than with the puzzle of Babe's death. After a pause to sip water, he smiled shyly and let me off the stand.

The afternoon slowed down into a baffled rhythm as witness after witness repeated the same details. By the time he had finished with the immediate family, the crown attorney was pale and droopy, his baggy clothes hanging on his spare frame as if he had just been on a crash diet. Dr. Candliss, who had begun to do more of the questioning himself, seemed exhausted. When the Roothes were called forward I couldn't bear to look at them and I rolled forward in my chair, head in hands, staring at mop shreds caught in the gaps of the floorboards. The voices receded until only their tones registered: gentle and brief with the parents; a rising sharpness with Albert (as they had agreed before the inquest); a sense of puzzled irritation creeping into Albert's resonant answers. I screened out what they were saying in a red haze and didn't remember a thing until much later.

Norm poked me. "You all right?"

It was not surprising that Dr. Candliss's summation for the jury was a shambles. As the inquest had gone on, he had become more agitated and upset, somehow emotionally involved, as though shadows from his own past were sitting in the clerk's chair beside the table. During his charge to the jury he stammered, shuffled papers, and repeated himself. I couldn't help but feel embarrassed for him as he struggled over the words, took his round glasses off, put them on again, mopped his gleaming face with a handkerchief that was now all crumpled and limp. At last the jury marched out, the elderly constable herding them off into another room, where he stood guard outside. The coroner and the crown attorney left. Just before going out the door, Dr. Candliss turned to the courtroom spectators, none of whom had moved.

"It's now four-thirty," he said to us, his kindly demeanour restored. "The jury may be out for quite a while. There are a few cafés around here, not the best in the world. Those of you who want something might go in shifts and someone could always come and get you. Remember you can't bring food into the court."

"I've got to have a smoke," Mother whispered.

"Can I have thirty cents?" I wheedled. "I'm starving and we'd like to go out with the gang."

Having successfully scrounged the money for Norm and me, we joined the bunch of kids from the neighbourhood and school to tear down the street looking for a café. We had to go all the way over to 97th Street, to the nearest Chinese café, for greasy hamburgers and Cokes. The patrons of the joint were a rough-looking lot who regarded our noisy entrance with contempt. It wasn't until five-thirty that Eddy Weir, doing his turn on watch back at the police station, came pelting down the street to haul us back. With much disruption we clattered into the courtroom, where Norm and I sat in the rear rows with the other kids. The coroner seemed to be waiting for everyone to file back in. I noticed that Mr. and Mrs. Roothe had left, that only Albert and Jean remained.

"Gentlemen, have you arrived at a verdict?"

The constable handed some long foolscap pages to the coroner, who read it all silently to himself. He frowned at the pages, then looked up.

"Gentlemen of the jury, harken to your verdict as recorded by you. The name of the deceased was Hamilton Roothe. The date and time of his death was July 7, 1935, at approximately midnight.

The place of death was the loft of a barn at the rear of the property known as (he gave the address). The cause of death was asphyxia due to hanging. The jury finds that the deceased, Hamilton Roothe, committed suicide by hanging from a rope attached to a beam in the loft of the barn previously described.

"We wish to make the following recommendations: first, that owners of barns, sheds, or similar buildings within the city should be required to keep them locked and secure at all times to prevent minors from entrance therein. Second, a comment rather than a recommendation. The jury found this to be a most difficult case because of the apparently normal mental state of the deceased. However, on examining all the evidence, we unanimously agreed that we could offer no other verdict than that of suicide."

Dr. Candliss gazed at them, his round glasses opaque.

"So say you all?"

The foreman answered: "Yes, sir." The others nodded for the last time.

The constable performed his final oration: "This inquest is now closed and the jury discharged. God save the King. All rise please."

Outside the courtroom Dr. Candliss and Mr. Haddon had their heads together, but the former beckoned to Norm and me and shook our hands. He viewed us again with that searching sympathetic look, as though he was trying to remember or recapture something.

"Thank you, boys. You did okay. Hope I wasn't too hard on you."

In the aura of his cherubic beam we smiled back. Then, forgetting us, Dr. Candliss turned to Haddon, who was a long mournful drink of water if I ever saw one.

"Sorry, sorry, I should've given them a better summation. I wonder if the AG will want a criminal investigation now?"

"Aw, don't worry about it, Steve. It's a bum verdict, but what else could they come up with? Still. . . ."

"Yeah, well, Lymburn is going to have a lot on his plate. He's into an election campaign now. And what about the legality — technically, they're no longer a government."

"Oh, they're still a government pro tem. You're still the coroner appointed by the province. You have to submit your report to the Office of the Attorney General, but I bet he ain't going to act on it now. He may not even be there by August."

"So it'll sit there in an empty office?"

"Yeah, even if there's nothing there but ghosts from the past."

That was a dig, all right, at the way the doctor had conducted the inquest. In a final blaze of pink, Dr. Candliss turned away.

The next day, without a word to anyone, the Roothes slipped away and buried Babe in Mount Pleasant cemetery, on the hillside facing south.

Somehow Albert had persuaded his friend, the Reverend Marant, to perform the ceremony. There was a small service in a funeral home with only the immediate family in attendance. Even with the exhibition on, there could have been a large crowd, including all the kids from school and the neighbourhood, but the Roothes were obviously so drained they couldn't face anything more.

Later, Mrs. Roothe, her eyes damp, apologized to me, saying they felt it was for the best. But, brooding, angry and curious at the verdict of the inquest, I had already decided to carry out my own investigation, to find out what had really happened to Babe. There were at least three witnesses, or those with some connection to the case, who should have been called: Neil and Billy Cawner, and Diane Thorpe. And, I noted to myself after a night of bad dreams — a dog with Babe's face running, its tongue hanging out — none of them had gone to the inquest, not one Cawner or a Thorpe.

There was a lot to do.

CHAPTER FOURTEEN

SOUTH OF THE CITY, AT THE SALISBURY SCHOOL, A SMALL
brick building with a peaked roof, Albert Roothe made the ninety-
degree turn to the east. He stopped cautiously at the CPR tracks,
then continued on the Calgary Trail, which ran along the east side
of the railway for several miles until it crossed over again to the
west side.

The Salisbury crossing was known as Death Corner, and I
wondered if maybe the infernal dust had something to do with the
high casualty rate. The 1929 Graham-Paige, a navy-blue brute,
seemed designed to create dust as a destroyer spews out a smoke-
screen. Along the edges of the road I could see the willows and
birches stuccoed with a clinging khaki grime.

Albert drove Jean's father's car gingerly, in the hope that
twenty-five miles an hour would somehow preserve the ageing
monster. Beside him Jean waved at herself with a Japanese fan
someone had picked up for her at the fair during the past week. If it
was a choice of heat or dust from the occasional passing car or
truck, Jean chose dust. Her window was open and she sat back,
apparently passive as usual, except for the odd irritable glance at
Albert for his slow driving. Even my unwelcome presence in the
back finally didn't restrain her.

"Albert, it isn't made of porcelain," Jean said.

I had been staring at a patch of her shoulder where she had
loosened her cotton dress and had pushed back its wide collar. She
had tossed her shoes into the back seat beside me so they wouldn't
get dusty on the floor. The shoes had slipped into a corner where
their slashed tongues, hanging over the laces, bobbed around with
each bump.

"Your dad told me all the trouble he had getting a timer chain. What'd we ever do for parts?" Albert said, a trifle sulky. "Haven't driven much lately."

Jean looked back, her dress slipping away from a deliciously smooth shoulder, and winked at me. My heart leaped. I craved a cigarette and fingered the five-cent pack of Turrets stuck to me through my damp shirt pocket.

While my father repeated that he had no use for Social Credit — "Fascists," he muttered once again — he grudgingly agreed to my accompanying Jean and Albert on the latter's weekend foray to speak for the Cause, the assignment Mr. Bell had mentioned to him the evening of the day Babe had been found. It seemed a bit indecent. This was only two days after Babe's private funeral, but I suspect that the Roothes may have encouraged Albert to go — to get him out of the house where he would only pace around and add fuel to their plundered emotions.

Much had flowed from our terrible discovery of Babe, not the least of which was my own crafty plot to go on this barn-storming expedition, where Albert was to regale the yokels at a Saturday night rally. We were heading a considerable distance for those days, to a small town on the fringes of the dry belt east of the Calgary Trail, about a hundred miles south-east of the city.

I had inveigled Albert into taking me for my own reasons: In hanging around the Roothes' kitchen on Friday I had heard Albert discussing interminably with his parents whether or not he should go. And when I heard the name of the town, I began to hatch my plot.

For the town, I knew, was the site of the Bible Institute where Diane Thorpe had been hastily exiled by her parents two days after Babe's death. Maybe they had scheduled her departure anyway, but there was just enough speed in her exit to make me wonder — especially now that I had found a clue, a memento turned up in my determination to fill in the gaps left by Dr. Candliss's highly emotional but sloppy conduct of Babe's inquest.

Diane had not been visible recently. When I saw Pete out on the sidewalk carrying his old man's duffle bag from the war, a long number and "L/Cpl Thorpe, W" stencilled on the canvas, I had asked him where she was. He told me and also revealed that he was being quickly banished to a summer Bible camp at Gull Lake. Someone was picking him up.

So both Thorpe kids were being sent off. After all, they had been deported every summer to those Bible camps, which were good fun and didn't cost the Thorpes hardly anything. All perfectly normal.

But Diane was not going to camp. She was being sent into residence at the summer school and would stay on in September to finish the rest of her schooling at the Institute. I noticed Pete seemed pale and morose, so withdrawn he could hardly appreciate his good fortune at my cordiality; but that too could have been an expected reaction at the thought of yet another summer of prayer meetings, outdoor activity among kids who never had a dirty thought and spoke as if they had learned their English from grammar books.

Another casualty at this time was Norm Fetterman. He had degenerated into a quaking jelly, a short distance at the best of times. Mrs. Fetterman, assuming it was "just nerves" from the sudden death of his pal, a malady she found hadn't responded to frequent doses of laxatives, packed him off on the train to visit an aunt in Calgary. Besides, Mrs. Fetterman had an opportunity to rent his cellar dungeon to a summer-school student.

Her assumption that Norm's state was the result of all the events that had followed Babe's apparent suicide was only partly correct. What really sent poor old Norm off the deep end was the local grapevine bringing us the message that Billy Cawner wanted "to have a gab" with us. Gabbing was the last thing we wanted to do with Billy Cawner. Ever since Neil had finally been picked up and arraigned with his brothers, Billy, as the only survivor and too young for all the trouble, felt secure enough to issue the word.

"They want to know who gave the tipoff," Sid Warren told us, relishing our discomfort. "And you guys are tops on the shit parade."

So, much to the amazement and suspicion of our mothers, we hung around home offering to do odd jobs. Most of the time I parked myself at the Roothes'. We didn't dare venture near our usual stomping ground down at the creek, but Sid Warren, who had obviously been spotted with the Thorpe expedition during the search for us, soon found out the score.

With some of our gang, he had gone down to spy on the barn, the one where Babe and I had once seen the man in coveralls about to stick it to the woman in the hay. Sid, Eddy Weir, and a couple of others had strayed through the ruined hacienda on their way down. While they were hanging around, they heard the crack as a twenty-two slug thunked into a concrete wall, its ricochet a warning buzz. They froze.

"Cripes," said Sid. "Twenty-twos they're using, not just BB-guns!"

They waited, listening to the brushing sound of cloth against branches, the scrape of a boot on rusty tin cans, until Billy Cawner appeared to stare at them from the top of a crumbled wall. He carried Neil's twenty-two and wore his brother's oversized cap, making him look like a top-heavy mushroom.

It was then that Billy had indicated that he wished to gab with us and took the occasion to wave the rifle under Sid's nose and ask him some questions. Sid, understandably frantic to account for his own lack of guilt, couldn't explain to Billy that we weren't likely to have tipped off the police.

"Yeah. Well, I want to see them."

Bandy-legged and dangerous, a smaller version of his older brother, Billy then faded back into the chokecherry bushes.

This incident was related to us Thursday noon, at which time Norm and I went into separate hiding. Norm fled home, where his mother found him in such a state she coughed up some cookie-jar reserves to send him packing off to the Calgary aunt.

Norm had left on the Saturday, the day I escaped with Albert and his girl, but that afternoon, on the Thursday, I had headed over to the Roothes' only to find the place silent and closed up. Of course, we hadn't known that they had slipped away to bury Babe. Perhaps my mother knew or suspected where they had gone, for I found her sitting alone on our front porch with no library book in sight; she just sat there smoking, her eyes shiny and damp, and she didn't seem to see me. When I saw her like that, looking older and so turned inward, I sensed it had to do with Babe and the Roothes.

The only sound was the clanking of the old mantel clock in the front room. I tiptoed through the house as if I was once again a thief. In my own room I fiddled jumpily with the junk on my dresser and at last found the flashlight in my hand. My thumb snapped it on and off, sending myself the message my conscience finally uncoded. I had known it all along, but now I realized I must do it.

I had to go back and look around Headley's barn. I had to find out for myself if the cops had overlooked something. But when I slipped through the side door and out into the empty lane, my excitement ebbed just as quickly. As the inquest jury had recommended, all the doors of the barn had been padlocked. Stirred up now, I let myself succumb to another inspiration.

Making sure that no one was watching, I sneaked into the Thorpes' garage next door. Without a car, they used the place as a cluttered storeroom, and it was so jammed with stuff I couldn't do anything more than stand in a small square inside the door and shine the flashlight around.

"Dumb, stupid," I kept telling myself, "Get out before someone comes along." I was about to take this self-advice when I found my clue.

The flashlight beam, watery and yellow with fading batteries, caught a splash of colour, something blue, like a rolled-up handkerchief. I knelt and saw that it was a small piece of cloth with an embroidered edge, scrunched up and stuck together by something akin to a starch solution that had dried. I picked it up with shaky fingers, let myself out of the garage, and high-tailed it for my room.

In the light of my window I could see the square of cloth had a jagged stain spread to the borders and outlined in light brown. That it was a woman's handkerchief I had no doubt, and my quick deduction, based on my exposure to the pulps, was that it could belong to Diane Thorpe. But she was gone, far away in that Bible Institute where she would be kept, maybe until the Christmas holidays. I put the handkerchief into an envelope and hid it in an old Tinker Toy cylinder at the back of my closet.

That envelope was now folded up in the side pocket of my pants as I lolled and dreamed imaginary, detective-like third degrees with Diane in the back seat of the old Graham-Paige.

The three of us would be away overnight, billeted with party supporters in town after the rally was over. We were to come back on Sunday and stop off en route for Albert to deliver another speech at an after-church luncheon. At the time I found the handkerchief, of course, I had no inkling I might be able actually to confront Diane with it. I had toyed with the idea of hitch-hiking all the way to the Institute, but I was too short of money and courage to do anything but day-dream about it.

On Friday morning my mother came back from the Roothes' with the news that they had quietly committed Babe to the earth the previous day.

"Look," she said, patting my arm, "why don't you go over and talk to Mrs. Roothe? I'm sure she'd appreciate it, poor dear."

My throat dry at the prospect, nerves jumpy at the discovery of the clue I couldn't reveal to anyone, I dragged myself over to the Roothes' where I found Babe's mother up and around, a wraith doing meaningless things in her kitchen. She seemed pleased to see me and held me in her arms for so long that I felt my own tears slipping off my cheeks onto the top of her head.

Soon she recovered sufficiently to make up some lemonade, at which point Mr. Roothe, apparently not at work that day, came up from the basement, a bottle of Bohemian Maid beer in his hand. Mrs. Roothe felt she had to explain, over and over again, why they had decided to have a private service for Babe. She asked me to stay for some eats, and while I was making my way through a great stack of thick peanut-butter-and-banana sandwiches, she suddenly darted from the table to return with an armful of photo albums.

Restless, Mr. Roothe made frequent trips to the basement to replace his beer and once apparently missed the bottom step, at least I assumed so from his muffled swearing and the clink of falling carpenter's tools. I tried to avoid dripping crumbs and peanut butter onto the photo album.

There was our first snap taken together: two moon-faced

little brats in winter garb, glowering fat faces in bulky coats and woollen hats that split those round heads as a globe divides temperate from tropical zones. A later snap of Babe and me showed us standing on the wooden sidewalk when we had graduated to cord breeches (pronounced "breeks"), with thick socks up the calves and the leather jackets we all thought aviators wore. This time we were grinning, but our eyes were enigmatic under peaked caps, worn low. So it went throughout the afternoon until I thought I would go nuts, the memories of Babe tearing us apart in that little kitchen.

I was glad I had stayed, though, when Albert came home early from Normal School to announce that he had been asked to take on two speaking assignments over the weekend. I couldn't help wondering if his fellow party-workers were really that unfeeling, or if indeed Albert had contacted them to hint that he would be available. While he stewed and fussed about going — all the time knowing full well he would — the name of one of the towns sifted through my cobwebs. By this time Jean had arrived with her father's car, which she said he was willing to lend to them if Albert would guarantee he'd get his twenty-five dollars on August 23, the day after the election.

"Your dad is a great kidder," Albert said.

"He wasn't kidding."

Albert continued to inflict his feigned indecision onto his weary parents. He seated himself beside his mother, clasped her small hand, and peered into her eyes.

"Do you really think I should go, Mom?"

At the end of his patience, Mr. Roothe retired to the cellar for good, the only sound being a bottle cap flipped off a fresh bottle of beer onto the cement floor. Jean wandered out to the porch and came back with the paper.

On seeing the newspaper, Albert leaped up, snatched it from Jean in rather unseemly haste, and rustled through it in an obsessive search.

"Still no word on the slate," Albert said, dropping the mussed-up paper. "He said it'd be this week." He seemed injured by the lack of news.

"Mr. Aberhart is going to win the election, isn't he?" I intervened slyly.

"God grant us His blessing, yes." Albert fixed his intense gaze on me, slumped at the table, the snapshot album open on the oil cloth. "You interested in the election?"

"I hear a lot about it from my dad. He doesn't like Mr. Aberhart very much."

"Ah, yes, your father. Look Doug, do you know what socialism is?" When I shook my head, he realized he had an audience. "It'd mean that the government would run everything: all stores, movie houses, businesses, the whole works. You want a government to tell you how to do everything?"

"I don't know."

"Well, holy mackerel, supposing that your entire life everything was run the way it was in school, with folks like teachers telling you what you could do and when you could do it. Would you like that?"

"I guess not."

"Okay, let's take it from another angle. You're aware we're in what we call a depression. Right? What's the main thing people are short of these days?"

"Money — and I guess, jobs."

"Right. But jobs are created when there's enough money. Now supposing someone came up with a plan to create money, or what we call purchasing power, without having to bring in a system of socialism?"

"Sounds okay. But where'd they get the money from?"

"Aha, you've hit the nub of the whole issue, this entire campaign, the struggle for hearts and minds."

"And souls," Mr. Roothe's voice echoed from the basement steps. "Don't forget the souls."

Albert allowed himself a tight smile. "That's what Social Credit means, Doug. It is a scientific method of providing the people with the purchasing power to be free again. I don't have the time now to go into all the details. But would you like to know more about it?"

"I sure would," I said, feeling a blush of shame at this

contrived earnestness. Bless her, Mrs. Roothe suddenly came alive, more like her old bright-eyed self, and brought up the suggestion that sealed Albert's fate.

"Why don't you take young Doug with you? He could see a meeting at first-hand and actually hear you speak."

Jean was making frantic "no" signals to Albert, but he was a sucker for a convert, no matter how young, especially if he was the son of an ideological enemy. It was plain they would prefer to be alone on this weekend journey, but Mrs. Roothe was not to be denied a favour for her new substitute son, if anything a partial improvement over her own departed one who had never taken any interest in the affairs of the world.

The almost pitiful transference of her love to me that Friday afternoon also spurred me on to complete the investigation of Babe's death. Here was an opportunity to slip away and confront Diane Thorpe with that stained handkerchief. Torn between Jean's beseeching signals and his mother's chirpy enthusiasm, Albert gave in to the latter and agreed I could go, provided I had my parents' permission.

"Oh, yeah, and Doug, ask your dad if he'll answer attendance for me tomorrow morning." Albert was referring to their Saturday-morning classes at the university. "I've got to work on my speech and we should make an early start."

At the time, of course, we didn't know that he was competing for the title of the slowest driver in the west.

South of Ponoka there was a stretch of narrow paved road, the only such mileage in the province, built during the short days of bright prosperity by the now collapsing UFA government. The dust magically disappeared and Old Heavy Foot cranked her up to about forty. The crunch of tires on gravel was replaced by the hum of asphalt. The air was clean and the foliage magically turned green. We revived and Albert began to warble a hymn. Jean passed around the Thermos of cold lemonade.

Like most places in the west the town where we were going had been built without any regard for scenery. The approach to it was a winding gravel road through a lovely valley, with enormous willows along a small river. We stopped on the bridge to rest for a moment before tackling the long hill up the other side.

Five grain elevators denoted the town's importance and the occupation of our host who, Albert told us, was an elevator agent for a line company, not the Pool, and therefore was one of the Movement's best organizers around. Gower, as he was called, had time for leisurely chats with the farmers about grain prices, taxes, purchasing power, basic dividends, cultural heritage, and all the rest of it.

On the other side of the railway siding, away from the town and where the open country began again, one could see three large gleaming frame buildings with a white picket fence along one side. I had already guessed, but innocently asked Albert about it.

"The Bible Institute," Albert said. "Wonderful place. Would do you good, Doug. Where young people are given a hypo against modernism and all the other false 'isms' that corrupt mankind today. They learn about the Bible as it really is. They study the Word of God and prepare for Christian service in an atmosphere of fellowship and purity. They all become soul-winners."

"Maybe that's where you should be teaching," Jean said somewhat bitterly. "If you're so sold on it."

"No, no, I'm not good enough, don't have the same dedication." He smiled at Jean. "I'm afraid I'm too worldly for that."

She flicked him on the ear with a fingernail.

I asked why they had built it so close to the tracks.

"There you are. You see, Doug, they're always concerned with the gathering of souls. It was built there back in the twenties so that even tramps would find a hot meal, a bed, and an awakening to God's mercy and love. Imagine what they're going through now with all those lost ones riding the rods."

The Gowers' house was a nicely painted bungalow in the middle of a large yard bordered by lilac bushes. Along one side there were two rows of Siberian crab-apple trees. The house was located right behind the main street, and as we turned off the main drag, I could see the town had once been an ambitious place, with its paved sidewalks, curbs, gravelled roads, and even metal lamp-standards. Now it seemed every other storefront was boarded up, the empty buildings fringed by weeds.

It was suppertime at the Gowers' and they were awaiting our arrival, a bit impatiently, I thought, with the table already set. There was a brief delay while we washed up and they set another place for me. Another guest didn't seem to bother them much once Mrs. Gower, a thin, sharp-featured woman, got over her fussing about where I would sleep.

We settled in around the table and I let my mind wander to the Bible Institute and Diane Thorpe. Somehow I'd have to figure out how to sneak away from this cozy place with the platters heaped high on the table.

As I shifted in my chair the envelope in my pocket crackled against my thigh.

The political meeting could be heard all over town. In the softening daylight, dogs barked.

The empty streets were lined with grimy cars and trucks, most of them old, square, and black, riding high off the ground. In a vacant lot some horses and wagons were tethered and there were even a few tractors in from the farms. At the two-storey brick hotel by the open door of the empty beer parlour, a waiter stood smoking, flicking ash onto his white apron, as though he could decipher the faint bursts of jeers and shouts down the street. I followed the noise and slipped into the Oddfellows' Hall to stand at the rear under some photos of men dressed in what appeared to be admirals' uniforms.

There wasn't a vacant chair or hardly standing room as hundreds of locals flooded the place with their soapy, Saturday-night patina, not unmixed with the sour mash of beer breaths, to yell and hoot in a din that was a thundering release of their frustrations.

Not at Albert, I noticed, who was standing silently at the podium, his fixed white smile directed in a chilling kindliness to someone in the audience who was on his feet. Near the front, the man waited out the catcalls, his hands on his overalled hips. A man next to me leaned across to speak to someone on my other side.

"Who's he trying to kid in that getup?"

"Overalls? Hasn't bulled lumber in years. Tells others what to do. Bastard."

They resumed their yelling at the man in the audience, still upright and waiting for the uproar to subside. That he was in the lumber trade was apparent when there were more shouts of "Woodenhead" and someone suggested he take the splinters out of his arse and sit down.

Albert, sensing that the tumult had gone on long enough, raised both hands, pressing down with his palms as though trying to put the heckler, or whatever he was, back into his box. Albert's voice finally penetrated.

"All right, all right, friends. This is a democratic meeting. But the people have a right to the facts so that they can vote for the results they want. If you want to persuade these people, go get your own hall." Cheers.

"Quiet, please, friends. Now we don't have any objection if you want to come up here and state in an out-and-out way the principles you stand for and what your party, whichever one it is, will do to relieve the misery we're all suffering. It seems to me, though, that all of you old-line parties have had your chance — and yes, I include the Communists and the Socialists, too, for nothing could be older than the slavery they preach."

Roars of support.

"But, my friend, let me tell you this. Don't come here to insult us. Don't come here to ask stupid questions. If you want to learn, you're welcome to sit down and find out something. We'll give you lots of reading material to smarten you up. But don't think you can get by with any cheap tricks around here. All these good people know a two-by-four politician when they see one."

In the deafening laughter that followed, I realized how smart Albert was. Someone had probably told him the heckler was in the lumber business and Albert had turned it around — very neatly, too. That boy'll go far, I said to myself. Unlike one Doug Sayers, who obviously had no talent as a Nick Carter. After all the deductive reasoning that had led me to this crummy burg in the company of Albert Roothe, I had struck out.

My expedition had been a failure.

Doubly now, I resented Albert's obvious triumph as he went on, uninterrupted, into what was evidently an anatomy lesson. Today I realize he was merely repeating the Master's famous analogy (but without charts) of money as the life-blood of the economic system. Such stupefyingly boring stuff, yet they sat silently and craned their necks to hear every word. Even the heckler, completely surrounded, sat on his hands, probably leery of what might happen to him if he made any kind of move.

"Just as the blood flows to every part of the body, feeding, clothing, and sheltering every cell, so must credit flow to every individual and his own productive enterprise, including farms, for the same purpose. Nothing must be allowed to interfere with this flow of credit. But when the financial institutions call in their loans and cut back on credit, they commit their crimes against humanity and inflict upon us all the foul disease of anaemia. So, my friends. . . ."

As he hurtled towards his wind-up Albert's voice changed more perceptibly into an imitation of Mr. Aberhart's, until I felt I could have shut my eyes and pictured myself back at the Exhibition Grounds only two Saturdays ago. Whether consciously or not, all their speakers tended to take up Bible Bill's soaring tones, as if there was a secret school of oratory somewhere that trundled them off a conveyor belt.

After Albert sat down to cheers and the dry smacks of calloused hands, the chairman introduced three red-faced men who had been seated on the stage. These, he reminded everyone, were the three fine "gennulmen" who were duly put forward as nominees to the Central Committee by the local Social Credit association. One of these worthies would soon be announced as the official candidate and everybody would get behind him.

From the look of those three stubble-jumpers I could understand why Albert had been imported as a speaker. I saw Jean, flushed, aroused, and adoring, get up from the front row and say something to Albert, looking up from his feet on the stage and into his eyes. Albert blew her a kiss off the top of his fingers. A woman brought the piano to life with a rendition of that same hymn that had resounded across the race track at the Exhibition Grounds, sung once more with that emotion they put into it, and bringing a lump to my throat as I thought of that day and our last moments with Babe. Following the hymn there was a rush for the homemade baking and coffee in the hall basement.

To try and shake off deep waves of foreboding, I drank too much coffee and gobbled a stack of sandwiches. I made my way through the crowd to Albert and Jean and told them discreetly, trying not to leer knowingly, that I would find my own way back to the Gowers' place, thus leaving them with the car which they could take somewhere for some sparking or whatever they did, if Jean could ever get Albert back to earth and away from the public adulation enveloping him. I realized then that politics is a horny game.

Down in the Gowers' basement, on a jangly cot near the root cellar, I thrashed around and couldn't get to sleep. A twinge of propriety kept me from masturbating and possibly leaving telltale signs for my hostess, Mrs. Gower, who slept upstairs with Jean while Albert had to bunk with the old man on a double bed.

The Gowers had a daughter about my age who had made up a soft cocoon of flannelette sheets on the front-room sofa. Earlier, over our supper, the Gowers had said they would never send their daughter to the Bible Institute. Albert had been shocked and, with all charity (as he put it), probed to find out why.

"Oh, Matty's too outgoing for that bunch," Mr. Gower said with a significant look at me, a warning not to take advantage of his slip. He must have been over six feet with wrists as thick as my shins, not someone to cross. Yet I became intrigued with his remark, seemingly an odd point of view in a household that had dark religious pictures on the walls.

The object of the remark, Matty (her name was really Martha), was silent as a tomb, but she had flickering blue eyes and her boobs, in a green sweater with a wavy yellow design, gave the impression of two watermelons about to be served on the table. At any other time I would've asked her to show me around town, and while her parents seemed relieved when I announced I was going out to wander around on my own, Matty gave me a flash of those blue eyes to signal her disappointment. After all, I was tall, not bad-looking, and a worldly sophisticate from the city. Another time, kiddo, I said to myself.

"You should see the poor dears," Mrs. Gower amplified. "They come here wearing nice dresses and lipstick, but after they've been over there for a while, you can pick them out a mile away. They look drab and wear those shapeless sacks. They can't have any kind of jewellery, not even a birthstone ring or anything."

"Aren't there both boys and girls at the school?" Jean asked.

"Oh, yes, but they must do everything apart. Skating parties are held at different times, boys or girls only. Even after supper, about this time, they promenade in separate groups around the grounds."

My ears pricked up at that. Albert was quite shocked at these revelations.

"In this day and age it's probably good for young people."

"Up to a point, sure," said Mr. Gower. "The ban on smoking and drinking, okay. But no dancing, no listening to the radio?"

"I don't see how else one can train them, instill the fibre necessary for their mission of worldwide evangelism," Albert argued.

"Oh, I grant you, they do good works. Do we have time for me to show you the elevator before the meeting?"

This was my cue to excuse myself. Avoiding Matty's puzzled ire, I headed quickly towards the railway tracks, which I crossed by the station, a good-sized one with a sweeping pagoda roof. Slipping between some boxcars on the siding, I soon came to the main gate in the picket fence.

A neat sign invited all wayfarers in need of refreshment to present themselves at the main office housed in the middle of the three buildings. I reviewed the possibilities of presenting myself as a hobo, or pretending I was interested in enrolment, or just going to the main office to ask for Diane. From the Gowers' table-talk, though, it wasn't likely the school would welcome a male caller.

My feet were taking me inexorably towards the three frame buildings, dazzling advertisements of white purity, along a path, a straight line of fine gravel that cut through a field of potatoes, each hill carefully and freshly hoed that day. There was the smell of cooking in the sultry heat. Somewhere, by an open window, an inmate was practising badly on a trumpet, part of the students' training, no doubt, for those little combos that floaters like the Thorpes must have found in every fundamentalist church.

As I came closer I realized the three frame buildings were of a good size, each one three storeys high, with wings built on that weren't visible from the tracks. They were placed in an open-ended quadrangle, and between them I could see movement, stiff shapes passing across the gaps. Without a plan and a bit scared, I headed towards this shooting gallery. I found myself amid the evening promenade, the gospel according to separate sexes.

There they were, all right, out on the prowl in two wavering circles, slowly revolving flywheels on well-tramped pathways between the buildings. Varied ages and heights, some carrying their Bibles pressed to their hearts. There was an overwhelming sense of drabness. No horsing around among the boys, no playful tripping or jabbing in the ribs, no shadow-boxing, no hoarse yells of cracking voices, no dirty jokes or lewd guffaws or fumbling attempts to get fresh with the bimbos. And among the girls, no irritating giggles, shrieks, or sharp nudges and knowing glances.

"What a place!" I groaned to myself.

They had sent the beautiful Diane here to lose her identity among these sublime pudding faces in shapeless, sacklike dresses. Where was she? As no one had yet paid any attention to this lanky outsider gawking at their little ritual, I slid along the rear of a building towards the female group. A kitchen helper in a stained white smock, his mouth chewing on something, stared at me from an open window, but did nothing.

Closer now, I scanned this harem of soul-winners, as Albert had described them, for a glint of platinum, Diane's bright corona of hair.

At last I saw her.

She was on the outer ring in a row of three girls, and I had to blink twice to make sure it was our Diane, the unattainable, who just might have made herself available to Babe. Well, poor old Babe wouldn't have given her a second glance now. Her long, flowing, silvery hair had been chopped off in spikes, stiff and uncontrolled as though seldom washed. Her budding figure was enveloped in an oversized garment of bleached grey with a white-trimmed collar and short sleeves. Even in this heat she wore grey stockings and her feet seemed swollen in some kind of square-toed work shoes. That unblemished, creamy complexion was now brown as a berry, weathered and dark, as were her arms.

More devastating than all of this was her expression. Some of the others seemed happy enough, had a glow, perhaps of the inner faith the Institute was supposed to inject into them. As they chattered away, quietly mind you, but not unlike the familiar, high-pitched whisper of dames in a school corridor, Diane seemed apart and lost in her thoughts, maybe in the dumps from the awesome burden of conversion and faith that she now had to master, or possibly she was reliving a faded memory of Babe's trembling, sweaty hand on her pure skin. Nunlike, her head was down, her face not especially serene but rather withdrawn; there was an outer blankness while the doubts and convictions tumbled around inside, the way washing got itself all tangled up inside my mother's old copper-tank Beatty.

So there she was, already revolving in her new world, well along in the process of being transformed — into what?

"Hi, Diane. It's me, Doug."

She stopped.

"Got to talk to you, Diane."

There was a hissing now in the moving circle, and its form became less certain, wobbly and fragmented as some of the girls stopped, gasped, or giggled at this heresy of a male from the outside appearing out of nowhere to break up their secure routine.

Diane came awake, her green eyes snapped open, wide in disbelief. She may have wondered if I was a visitation from the nether regions, a throwback from the leering, corrupt world she now had to forgo. I think she was almost ready to reach out and touch me, just to make sure. But all around her a rising mutter of female voices held her back.

"Di, Di, who is he? The rules, tell him to go. Hey, you, you're not allowed here. Scram. Beat it."

Amid this growing clamour I moved closer to Diane, near enough to catch a whiff of earthy sweat and strong soap. I held out the envelope to her.

"Here, take this, it's yours. Babe wanted you to have it."

Cruelty was the only way to break through, to shock by violation the tenets of love, devotion, and self-sacrifice that glued the place together. I knew I was an unsettling presence, possibly in their eyes almost satanic with my gawky, aggressive height, the slicked hairline with the point dead centre in the forehead, and my hand outstretched to press something obviously obscene on one of them.

Diane took the envelope and pulled out the crumpled blue handkerchief.

"Come on, Diane. You know, don't you? I found it in your garage."

Her voice, at last forced out of her in the uncontrolled tones of someone who has just been cured of deafness, was harsh and flat.

"It's not yours," she said. "Not yours."

I was just about to follow up with the clincher question — It's yours, isn't it? — when she dropped the envelope, clutched the stained, crackling handkerchief in her hand, and ran from me, her square shoes thudding on the dry turf. Ignoring the rising pitch of female voices behind me, I whirled around to follow her and ran into a tall, bespectacled man in a white shirt who had suddenly appeared.

"You don't belong here, son," he said. "Please go."

Almost his height, I tried to stare him down. Out of the corner of my eye, I could see that the male promenaders had broken their wheel and had formed a jagged arrowhead aiming in my direction. My courage was plummeting fast, but I tried one last effort.

"I must see her. An urgent message."

"Are you from her family?"

"Ah, no. I guess not, but it's important —— "

"An old boyfriend, eh?" He glanced back into the darkness of the hallway. "No, she doesn't want to see you. You'd better go. I know she will pray for you."

I'll just bet she will, I thought. There was no point in trying to do anything more. The troops were closing in from all directions. I grinned cheekily, deliberately took the time to light a Turrets, and slouched off between the buildings, back along the path between the potatoes. At the picket gate I looked back and saw that the man in the white shirt had followed me part of the way.

At the railway station I sat on the platform, dangling my legs over the edge. I smoked and thought for quite awhile.

What did it mean? Were my suspicions confirmed, or had I brushed too closely against inexorable, universal laws by causing pain to the survivors who, no matter what was found out, could not bring Babe back anyway? It was possibly a warning, in a way, to accept one's fate, a hint to await whatever revelations might be doled out or made known when our own souls were cleansed enough to receive them in grace.

Being around so much fundamental religion and its emergence as a political movement was having its effect. One thing I knew from that expedition: I was not equipped to cope with manifestations of the Divine Will. Oddly enough, my parents' careless disregard for such matters, their failure to arm me with any spiritual muscle, now aroused a sort of resentment towards them I never thought I would feel.

There was no prospect of my conversion, but I did begin to worry about my inability to understand the forces that drove so many others to those teachings in the white clapboard buildings, a simple type of education that might create another species beyond my limited perceptions of what people believed and how they acted — as foreign to me as the political euphoria that now engulfed Albert and his friends.

On the way back to the city I half dozed in the back seat of the car. My sleepless, caffeine-twitchy night near the root cellar had finally caught up with me. A guilt settled on me and would adhere in a gummy layer the way dust stuck to the trees along the roadside. It had been a dumb thing to do, to shatter what might have been a terrifying struggle and spiritual rebirth that Diane had to master—especially difficult for her if she now knew that someone else had made the connection between her stained handkerchief and Babe's death.

Or maybe there was no connection. She might have kept it as a souvenir of her first arousals, there in her garage or in Headley's barn. On the other hand, maybe they had been discovered, maybe there had been exposure and confessions. Or threats? Enough to make a fourteen-year-old going on fifteen sneak out of his house in the middle of the night and go into a pitch-black barn and hang himself?

I awakened as Albert, belting along at thirty, swerved to avoid an oncoming truck.

"You're driving faster today, Albert," Jean said lazily, curled up and leaning into his shoulder.

"I'm still all wound up, Jean. Yes, yes, what a marvellous meeting. Golly, what a time!"

CHAPTER FIFTEEN

ALBERT WAS WOUND UP, ALL RIGHT, BUT BY TUESDAY HE HAD wound down again.

The Social Credit Advisory Committee had been in session in Calgary, making the final selection of candidates from the names put up by the constituency associatons. The long-awaited list was finally released by Mr. Aberhart on July 23. Albert snatched the newspaper, scanned it, then let it drop onto the kitchen table where I was seated with Mrs. Roothe. He almost knocked over my lemonade, and Mrs. Roothe glanced up at her surviving son, wondering, no doubt, if he might bring on his own early demise from sheer frustration. She had read the newspaper and knew that his name wasn't on the slate.

"I guess it just wasn't meant to be," Albert said. A deep vertical crease appeared above his nose as he contemplated his fate and the injustice of it all.

Another heat wave in the nineties made it too hot to be outside. With Norm away I was still hanging around, partly to avoid any threatening gab with Billy Cawner, partly from a need to atone silently for my brutal handling of Diane Thorpe at the Bible Institute, and, maybe just once, to hear the Roothes ask "Why?"

Over and over again, Mrs. Roothe darted out with the snapshot albums, or Mr. Roothe would come upstairs from his work in the basement to lean against the door and study me with a crooked grin, or just the two of them would stare expectantly as I gobbled sandwiches. But not once did one of the Roothes ask "Why?" or "What do you think happened?" or "What ever possessed him?" Least of all Albert, who prattled on about his politics.

Watching Albert savaging the newspaper, I finally grasped how he had misinterpreted Mr. Bell's friendly encouragement the night of his visit. Albert, I am sure, had become convinced he was going to fill the vacancy on the Edmonton slate for the deceased Mr. Cameron. But although he had been among the eighteen names considered for the six spots in Edmonton, he had not been chosen. Instead, he tried to save face by babbling on about the virtues of the choices made by the Advisory Committee.

"All fine men," he went on, chopping at the newspaper. "Not surprised about Dr. Hall, after all he's chairman of City Central. A dentist, you've met him, Mom: glasses, wavy hair. Your dad must know Dr. Willis, Doug; was a high-school teacher at Vic, now vocational head over at the Board. Good man. Gil King is one of our best organizers, but in all charity, I'd say I've done as much. Mr. Mullen I don't know that well, a cattle dealer or something. I wonder about Barnes and Mark Robertson, though, both of them active in other parties before. Barnes was chairman of the School Board, but I always thought him a bit left, used to be in the Labour Party. And Mark, well, he's a railway-union guy and ran as a Conservative. Now why would they pick those two?"

"Balanced slate," offered Mr. Roothe, arising from the basement where he had just discarded his white coveralls on his return from a job. He had the usual bottle of beer in his hand.

"We don't have to resort to the old political trickery."

"Oh, Albert, don't feel too badly. They must have some plans for you."

"I wonder, Mom." Albert tried unsuccessfully not to be too bitter. "More speeches?" He peered at the paper again. "Mr. Aberhart says he's trying to free the Movement from the old-line politicians, but then he goes on to say many of the candidates named ran for other parties in previous elections. I don't know why he did that when there are so many of us, so many others, who aren't connected with the old-line parties in any way."

"Come on, Albert, if he's anything, he's a smart politician."

"That's not so, Dad. He is different. We're not like the others. We're forced into political action because the old liners won't listen. Mr. Aberhart isn't even running for a seat. If the people want him after the election, a place will be found for him."

"See what I mean? The world's oldest boondoggle."

Disgusted, Albert got up.

"I'm going to phone Jean. See if she can get the car tonight. We'll go to the rally over at the Franciscan Hall and see how our new and wonderful slate handles itself."

He spat it out. Albert was quite capable of surges of anger; the fixed smile stiffened and, to ensure self-control, the words were nipped off at their roots.

Once, before all this had happened, I had seen his fury unloaded onto some smaller kids who were burning caterpillars over an oil drum in the alley. While the kids giggled and poked each other, the caterpillars, the colours of a Scona school sweater, curled up on a white-hot screen and smouldered in vivid furry balls. The immolations had incensed Albert, who had been doing some chores in the garden. He roared in on the kids and kicked over the drum, causing a running fire in the dry weeds. Then he had to rush for a garden hose before the fire reached the Fykes' garage behind us, unaided by his brother who leaned on the fence and grinned impudently.

In a way, I suppose Babe was getting even for Albert's constantly badgering him to join his youth group at the church. Usually reticent about his family—not from shame or a sense of privacy, but rather, I suspect, from a sense that anything about them would not come under his mandate to amuse us—Babe did go through the motions of asking for our advice.

"Albert's after me again about his church group," Babe told us a week before he died. "He says if I join, I can go to a summer camp at Seba Beach."

"Any dames?"

"I told you, the time I went to case the joint, all dogs."

"What the hell, you'd be at the lake. Why not?"

His eyes shifted as he gazed at something beyond us.

"I've got other things to do."

There we were once more, up against Babe's opaque reserve, the sudden clang of a shutter that blocked us out, that same cool rejection that had baffled Albert. One could picture the two brothers staring each other down: Albert's eyes pinpoints and eager over the fixed smile; Babe, amiable and blank.

At the inquest, Dr. Candliss had been equally puzzled by the relationship between the two brothers and had watched intently while Mr. Haddon, doing his duty for the boss, the attorney general, went after Albert. The two sleepy reporters over at a side table came to life and started to take more notes.

Oddly enough, though, it was the coroner who at this point took over the questioning from Mr. Haddon. Why he did so, I'm not sure, but again he seemed to be probing for some clue to Babe's death that he could relate to an experience from his own past. Dr. Candliss was a strange coot. Wearily, his moon face pink and shiny, he spoke to Albert in a voice that was slowing down the way a gramophone record dies away on an old hand-cranked Victrola.

"Now, Mr. Roothe, I've been trying here to search out motive, why your brother would do this. I just want to understand it, if I can. Now you're a religious and a political man, I believe?"

"Religious: yes. Political: no."

"Oh, I understood you are very active and well known in a certain political movement. Well, I'll say it: in Mr. Aberhart's movement."

"That's not political."

"I'm not trying to be funny, but what is it then?"

"It's more a form of education: to show people how they can realize their heritage and get the results they want."

"You're a teacher, too?"

"Yes, sir."

"Did your brother not belong to your church?"

"No. I tried to get him interested in our youth groups. He came a couple of times, then quit."

"So he was not a religious boy? Would you say he was a sinner?"

"No more so than other boys his age."

"On the political side ——"

"I don't know what you mean. It's not political."

"All right. Did you try to get your brother involved in your activities for Mr. Aberhart's movement? Did you put any pressure on him to take part?"

"Once school was out I asked him to come to some meetings with me. We've started up a youth movement that has Mr. Aberhart's full blessing."

"Go on."

"Well, he wasn't interested."

"Did you invoke any visions of damnation or eternal fire when he wouldn't play?"

"No, no." Albert looked across the room at his parents, a pulse fluttering in his jaw. "I wouldn't go that far."

"Not even for the Cause?"

"Of course not." He turned angrily. "I—I loved my brother."

The implication that he might have misused beliefs that had such deep meaning for him, that he might have driven his own brother to suicide, was too much for Albert. Furious, he returned to his seat in front of me and muttered something to Jean that sounded like "old fool."

With his deep commitment to the Movement, it was easy to see why Albert felt spurned and unappreciated when the slate of candidates came out, loaded as it was with apostates. Perhaps he wondered if his outburst at the inquest, duly recorded in the newspapers, had had anything to do with his rejection. If his background was pure, his ideology correct, in Albert's eyes those others, who had been mysteriously chosen by the leader and the powerful Advisory Committee, were a lot less pure—publicity from the inquest or not.

Having been put forward by the South Side organization among the eighteen hopefuls, he had been subjected to rigorous interrogation and obviously had made an impression on the leadership strong enough to stir the memory of Mr. Aberhart himself, whose remark—or promise—on the night of the rally of the Exhibition Grounds continued to stick in Albert's mind.

I had no idea what he had been through until many years later when I went to bed with Jean Cullen. This was during the Second World War. By that time I had the maturity and insight to realize what it was Albert had endured in accepting and confirming his faith, a process that possibly would never have been clear to me if I hadn't run into Jean while I was on leave in London.

By January 1944 I had my two pips (one year at Normal School before joining up gave one a nudge towards "officer material" rating) and, like most Canadians, except for those who were toiling uphill in Italy, was languishing in the south of Britain awaiting the invasion of the Continent.

Those of us who were old enough in 1939 or 1940 tended to go into the army. Later, the air force and the navy — oddly attractive to Prairie boys — were the fashionable services. As the war went on, the army also absorbed womanpower, and Jean Cullen had arrived overseas for a desk job at CMHQ in London.

I should describe how Jean and I met again. Such encounters were surprisingly common: there you'd be in a strange place far away, say Antwerp, and you would run into someone from home.

Did I say Antwerp?

That came afterwards, in the same year but seeming like a century later. Let's just say that a very pretty lady near Guildford had dropped me for an Eighth Air Force colonel, my own age too, with twice the money and the chocolate tunic and beige slacks that were a kind of aphrodisiac to the English women — not that they needed any.

So I had skulked off to London, passed up all the raucous companionship of my own bunch, and paid a large bribe for a solitary room in a small hotel on Half Moon Street. I had brought with me a bottle of gin, obtained with another exorbitant outlay to our mess sergeant, and had gone out prowling in the vague romantic hope of finding someone to share it all with, yet sufficiently innocent so that I wouldn't end up at the blue light with a dose.

At that time Jean worked for a branch of Transport Control in a building on Sackville. Every noon hour she and a group from her office would walk half a block to Piccadilly, then cross over to the alleyway beside the battered St. James's Church to a pub off Jermyn Street where they would have Scotch ale and a cold lunch.

All Jean said when she saw me in the pub was: "Doug? Is that you? Oh, Dougie."

She didn't even take the time to introduce me to her friends, but came over to my end of the bar, put a hand on my arm and squeezed. Under the long peak of her service kepi her eyes were feverish, her sallow skin ruddy from the English cold and damp. Although I noticed a few crow's feet and a slight puffiness that may have been the result of a starchy diet and too much ale, the rather large pores that had formerly given her face a slightly coarse, oily look had gone.

"Oh, I want to talk to you," she said, her fingers digging into my arm. "Oh, it's good to see you."

Outside the pub, I kissed her and we almost ran along the gleaming wet streets to my room, where we gulped some gin and made love quickly, almost to get it over with so we could share our memories of home.

We didn't leave that room for a long time.

As the double daylight-time dawn brought a slow, grey light to the hotel-room window, I got out of bed, opened a tin of meat and a package of crackers from home (one always carried tins of stuff around, either for personal use or for bribery), poured out more gin, added some shillings to the gas meter, made sure we had a fresh pack of cigarettes from my kit, and crawled, shivering, back into bed with her.

We chatted on about people we knew and, of course, Albert's name came up.

"So you two never married?"

"No. You know, even as a snot-nosed kid you always looked down on him."

"I don't know, maybe I thought he was a phony."

"He wasn't, you know. He believed in it all, still does, I think. You have no idea what he went through to test and reaffirm his faith."

While I brushed cracker crumbs off her bare shoulder, Jean told me something of Albert's ordeals when he had been on the prospective candidate list for the city. It was, she said, as if someone had been subjected to a lodge initiation, fraternity hazing, and priestly ordination all at the same time. She seemed determined to prove her point, and went on.

Even before they got in for an interview all eighteen prospects were checked out with the city delegates for their religious affiliation, former politics, platform abilities, anything that could be used against them by opponents or to disqualify them. The zone captains and others who had put forward a name were asked if they thought the aspirant was in the Movement for personal gain. After all this, the nominee was then eligible for his third degree on Social Credit principles.

Because of the importance of the six spots in the city, Mr. Aberhart himself, along with the secretary of the Advisory Committee, E.C. Manning, and a carefully selected panel, ploughed through all eighteen interviews. That was why it was all the more remarkable that Mr. Aberhart had remembered Albert the night of the rally. Certainly Albert had emerged from his interview fired up and so convinced he had done well he couldn't resist telling it all to Jean.

"I was privileged," Jean said.

She reached for a Sweet Cap cigarette (a precious commodity from home) and took another swig of gin, a few drops spilling crystalline jewels onto her bare breast.

"It was as though a Mason came out of his initiation and spilled the beans."

Thorough as always, Albert had immediately sat down to make notes of his interrogation.

"Useful points for speeches," he had told Jean, as she sat beside him in the Roothes' front room. He began to read out each question he could remember and, with some pride, repeat his answers.

This took place in June, about a month before Babe's death. Albert wouldn't tell Jean where the interviews took place — "Somewhere over town," she guessed — but he did say it had been a cordial atmosphere, the questioning friendly and sympathetic. The members of the Advisory Committee sat at a long table with the nominee facing them on a straight-backed chair. No smoking was allowed. Albert seemed a bit puzzled that Mr. Aberhart, while there, said hardly anything until he asked the two final questions.

On reflection, Albert mused, this made sense, because the committee was vitally concerned with a nominee's grasp of the subtle differences between the doctrine espoused by its inventor, Major C.H. Douglas from England, and Mr. Aberhart's adaptation of it to the realities of Alberta. Albert's interview took place before the publication of Aberhart's famous Blue Book, the Social Credit manual, although there had been tracts of many hues issued before that.

"Did they wear hoods?" I asked. "Masks?"

Jean gave me a love slap on the shoulder.

"Oh, Doug, you sound like your mother."

Albert Roothe, in his only navy-blue suit, is tautly upright on the straight chair in the airless church basement.

He is trying to will the sweat back into his pores. The sharp edge of the dazzling white collar bites. He tries not to fiddle with his seldom-worn pearl-grey fedora, which rests on his lap as though to cover his private parts. He who will mark exam papers later that summer is now on the receiving end.

Has he done his homework?

The test begins. He relaxes a bit as they start off with the basics: rock bottom doctrine, the A Plus B Theorem, the famous Douglas formula of purchasing power that is being debated up and down the hustings by politicians, farmers, and merchants who want to believe.

Albert feels his mind clearing as the sun dissolves the ground fog from an early frost.

"Now, Mr. Roothe, during the legislative hearings and since then, some so-called learned professors have been pooh-poohing the theorem. Are you aware of these attacks?"

"Oh, yes. It makes me wonder why they can't see anything so obvious, or who's been getting them to pick on us."

"What do you say when they claim that the Social Credit plan would result in inflation?"

"People who attack us on those grounds confuse the amount

of purchasing power needed with the amount of money or credit. What they can't — or won't — see is that the amount of purchasing power depends on the amount of real credit available and the rate of flow of credit."

"Do you think that some of the confusion comes from the difficulty of understanding Social Credit? Is it too hard to get across to the working man?"

"Not at all. Ours is a very simple idea. If there is any public misunderstanding about Social Credit, I believe it's because some find it difficult to make the distinction between credit and currency."

"That's interesting. How do you explain the difference?"

"What I do is, I use Mr. Aberhart's examples in the fourth white leaflet where he correctly points out that the total value of trade or economic activities of some 6 billion dollars in this country is done with only 350 million dollars of currency in circulation, or that one dollar has seventeen times its own purchasing power. Then I go on to point out that currency is a matter of Dominion control. But the province has sovereign authority over its own credit. It can issue this credit to those whom it considers worthy to receive it."

"On what authority do you base that opinion?"

"Property and civil rights belong to the province. The Bank Act, Section 138, gives three exceptions to federal control of currency and credit, which would give us the right to issue non-negotiable certificates through the Alberta Credit House."

"So you don't agree with what certain splinter groups, who claim they are pure Douglasites, are saying?"

"You mean that Social Credit can only be implemented on a Dominion-wide basis? No, I don't agree at all. I feel sure we can do it here. We must!"

"Then how do you feel about their attacks on Mr. Aberhart's modifications to the Douglas system?"

"Obviously the Douglas plan for Scotland is not suitable for us. One almost infers he had imbibed too much of Scotland's best-known product."

"I can see why you're in demand as a speaker!"

"Oh, is he?"

"Indeed, he is. We've been using Mr. Roothe at quite a few places. Once school's out we expect to see more of you."

"Don't forget I'll be marking papers."

"That's important to you — I know. What subjects?"

"Math, mostly, sir. Then, too, I've got summer school. But I'll give every moment I can."

"Good for you! We take it you approve of Mr. Aberhart's adaptation of Social Credit to Alberta?"

"Very much so. Your — his — teachings on the need for an immediate basic dividend of say twenty-five dollars a month; his insight into the flow of credit — the bloodstream illustration is brilliant! — the automatic price-control system and the Just Price and, what we've just been talking about, implementation at the provincial level. Yes, I fully support Mr. Aberhart's improvements on the basic theory. And I'm not just saying that because you're here, sir."

"No, we understand. We're not trying to embarrass you. To change our tack a bit, how do you look upon the larger picture — I mean, the non-monetary aspects of our movement? You had said it means a new way of life."

"I've given much prayerful thought to that question. Not now: I mean I've prayed and asked for guidance ever since I heard of Social Credit. I have absolutely no doubt in my mind that it is the key to a better social order. I really believe that."

"Suppose we are successful in putting it in here. What then?"

"I'll be frank with you: Sometimes I despair at the forces lined up against us, but when Mr. Aberhart speaks, my faith is refreshed again."

"Well, what are these forces that cause you such despair? I'm asking because some of us have been through the same thing."

"You have? That's good to know. I didn't mean it that way. I meant to know that you — the leaders — have been through it too. As I see it, it goes much deeper than the misguided, tinhorn politicians who oppose Social Credit. Or even the Fifty Bigshots.

There are more sinister powers arrayed against us, or, rather, against the people, denying them their individual freedom, their access to the heritage that flows from our modern production system."

"Go on."

"The nature of these forces makes it difficult to put faces or names to them. That they exist goes without saying. They are mostly alien, conspiring with like forces to suppress freedom. We do know they control the banking system, international finance, the press, political parties, legislatures, and parliaments."

"How do you see them doing that?"

"By a network of overlapping influences. Well, gosh, you take the aliens who control Wall Street, they're of the same racial stock — Turko-Mongolian mostly — who run the Communist movement and the Free Masons. And they're all tied in with the Zionists. Their affinity seems to be almost primeval, based on dark racial urges that bring these unlikely elements together against everything that is white, Anglo-Saxon — especially the British Empire. They're also non-Christian, atheistic, or adherents of more primitive religions before the revelation of the Cross. I'm sure their names will eventually be revealed, and the public will be shocked beyond belief."

"Against such forces, what can we do here?"

"We can be steadfast. We can continue to educate the people. We can build a solid base through Social Credit. Above all, we must win the next election so that we will have the foundation, a rock against which those alien forces will destroy themselves."

The vehemence of Albert's reply brings about a respectful silence in the room.

Mr. Aberhart, who has seemed to be half asleep, doodling on a pad, sits up, suddenly a large imposing figure, transformed from the slumped, fatigued fat man who hasn't said anything much until now. Mr. Aberhart adjusts his glasses and stops Albert with his clear blue eyes.

"Have you ever said to anyone that if not chosen you would run as a candidate anyway?"

"No, sir. I would never do that."

"If not chosen, will you definitely work for the candidates chosen in this city?"

"Not only here, sir. Anywhere in the province you want to send me. I'd consider it a privilege. I've already done some speaking and hope to do more wherever you need me."

"Thank you very much, Mr. Roothe."

Albert brings his eyes up from the fedora codpiece on his lap and basks in the smiles and nods. He is sure he has made a fine impression.

Albert thought he had a right to the candidacy: He had studied hard, passed the tests, and pitched in on the sweaty work of organizing and speaking. At that moment in his career, when he read out the list of city candidates, he must have felt almost suicidal, convinced that his political life was at an end.

Just what had Mr. Aberhart meant, then, when he had said on the night of the rally at the Exhibition Grounds: "Maybe next time, Albert?" His gloom deepened after the Liberal victory in Prince Edward Island was announced on July 24. In another legislative milestone they had swept all thirty seats in a provincial election, leaving no opposition at all.

"Maybe the Liberals are stronger than we think," Albert growled. "As Mr. Aberhart has said, they'll do anything to get elected, will take anything anyone suggests, even pretend to adopt Social Credit if they have to. Then this Economic Safety League, rich businessmen trying to turn the people against us. Yet, you look at the crowds we're drawing: two thousand at Chipman, fourteen hundred at Willingdon, fifteen hundred at Rimbey—and remember the papers are calling the crowds as small as they can. That must mean something."

Jean snuggled down into the bed, her satin dampness arousing me again in yet another bout of that outpouring of sexuality brought about by the heady release of wartime. All of us young people whipped into top physical shape, then released far from home into blessed anarchy! No wonder old vets live on their memories.

"He grumped around," Jean said after awhile, her cool arms loosely around my neck. "More disappointments came. He was in a terrible state. I — I just felt I couldn't handle it, so I decided then and there I'd never marry him."

She released her arms and gave me a meditative look. "What did you eventually find out about Babe's death?"

CHAPTER SIXTEEN

IT WAS AS THOUGH OUR CLAMMY BED HAD BEEN DRIFTING IN a soft summer haze along a river, and now Jean's question was the ugly hawser that blocked the way and swirled us around into a past I didn't want to visit again. I wondered why she was so determined about it.

"Not much."

Which was true at the time.

"Come on, you snooped around."

"How'd you know that?"

She dug a sharp fingernail between my ribs.

"I wasn't blind. That day we went on the speaking tour, what happened when you went to see Diane Thorpe at the Bible Institute?"

"You figured that out? I didn't get a chance to talk to her."

"You think it had anything to do with girls — sex?"

"We were kids, for God's sake."

"No you weren't. I saw you watching me. The way your eyes'd cross when you'd see Albert and me together. And sneaking up on us when we were smooching on the porch."

"Babe wasn't even fifteen."

"So what? He was a handsome hunk, fully developed. I saw him once in a bathing suit at the South Side pool."

"How'd we measure up?"

"He was the best looking of the bunch of you, even at that age. Had more pizzazz than Albert."

"Anybody would."

"Albert was repressed. Self-discipline he called it. Both of them were dreamboats."

"What bothered me, and it still does, is there was nothing wrong with Babe."

"Well, if he hung himself, there must've been."

"Sure, if he did. If anyone was nuts in that family it was Albert, not Babe."

"Albert may've had a one-track mind, but he was no booby."

"Yeah, well he sure acted strange after Babe's death. He wouldn't talk about it or mention his name."

"Oh, there was a reason for that."

"Such as?"

Coy again. "You own up first on what you found out."

"I don't know, Jean. Honest I don't."

She subsided for a while and drank her neat gin, gagging primly. The truth was I had difficulty focusing on Babe. He was fading like an old print, unformed and locked forever in an adolescent path. More immediate losses were sharper. At that point in the war they were mostly in the air force, those who had slipped over the shimmering line we all knew was there waiting for us, but we didn't know when or where. Letters written (When're you getting some leave? Canst meet in London?) were returned, ugly "missing" stamps smeared on them. The memory of Babe kept receding.

Odd, too, that Jean seemed to realize that I had been prowling around on my own, indulging in fantasies of the private eye — like the Hardy boys — trying to unravel the enigma of an apparently normal, healthy pal who had hanged himself in a barn. Was I that obvious? In her indolent way Jean must have been taking in more than anyone had realized. Her laxity was a cover for an acute intellect and enough common sense never to have married Albert Roothe.

As it turned out, though, my gumshoeing led nowhere, and I was overwhelmed by other forces. Oh, I kept going, all right.

Once I rode shotgun on the water wagon with Mr. Headley, a slow journey over heaving, rutted tracks to the edges of the city, a long day mostly of silence, for he was not used to company. He clucked at the horses, spoke to his dog who sat between us for a while, and waited for me to broach the subject of Babe. He knew why I had volunteered, but he seemed to welcome my presence and the help. After I had bulled three cream cans of fresh water into a shack for a frail woman who coughed in a dry rhythm like a one-cylinder pump, Mr. Headley allowed a few words as a sort of payment for my services.

"Still eating you, ain't it?"

"I can't figure it, Mr. Headley. Can't figure it at all."

"Sure didn't like the way that fellow at the inquest went after me."

"Nobody's blaming you for anything."

"Hope not, Dougie."

That was the end of my snooping with Mr. Headley. He withdrew under the brim of the big stetson and said no more. Somehow I had thought he might know something, but he didn't, or wouldn't let on.

Next day I confronted Diane's tubby girlfriend, Mabel, who went to a daily Bible camp in the city. I caught her coming off the streetcar around five o'clock, made a big play of walking home with her, and finally broached the question of Diane and Babe. All she did was to giggle and run off home ahead of me, her ankles turning over as she sprinted along on the edges of her thick brogues in a remarkable display of speed for someone of that bulk.

Then the storms came. The elements, as they say, had gone wild. As cattle stomp around in a barn during a weather change — perhaps their tiny brains have visions of their ultimate fate, dismembered and sizzling hunks in the stoves of those people who fed them — so, I found, are humans caught up in blind forces. The shift in barometric pressure set off a brainstorm or two, squalls that swept in on me like the sheets of hail that billowed across our garden on Saturday afternoon.

With these storms came the end of hope for the farmers and everyone else. What mighty hand felt the need for further punishment? Up to that point in central Alberta there had been almost ideal growing weather: enough rain mixed with sporadic heat waves to achieve that delicate balance that ripens the heads until they fill out into tall, bending stalks.

Only the weekend before, on my drive with Albert and Jean, I had been given some understanding of what the land was capable of releasing to us. From the car window I watched a light wind sweeping up crests of golden light on the rises, the soft burnishes of green in the hollows where the ripening was slower, all of it sighing and bowing on top-heavy stems.

"By gee, sixty bushels to the acre. At least," Albert had said. "The Lord is bountiful."

Or so it seemed.

On the North American markets, especially in Chicago, July wheat futures had shot up past ninety cents, then closed around eighty-five. The stem-rust disease that had infected over four million acres had not yet devastated the crops in central Alberta, and it looked as though our part of the country anyway would once more have a taste of prosperity. Wheat up to a dollar by fall?

But the end came for this last holdout on the ocean of misery that was the prairies. It came during the weekend of July 27, when the first in a train of hailstorms swept in over the foothills.

It being cool and showery that Saturday afternoon, my mother, not inclined to stir from the comfort of the house and her library book, sent me to the local grocery store to buy a pint of ice cream as a special treat for supper, to celebrate the completion of the exam-marking at the Normal School. Father was not yet home from his morning summer-school classes at the university.

The atmospheric changes must have affected my own better judgement for, instead of treading the slippery boards of the front sidewalk, I took the back lane. On the street I had a clear view in both directions: Our boulevards were wide and the trees too spindly to conceal an ambusher. The laneway, though, with its garages and fences blocking off the view at the end of each thirty-three-foot lot, was a series of traps.

No sooner had I passed Headley's barn than I stepped right into Billy Cawner, no twenty-two across his arms, but his stare glinting and angry under the floppy tweed hat he now wore far over to one side. If it hadn't been for their local renown, Billy Cawner would have been a comic figure instead of a menace. He wore one of his brother's windbreakers, the long sleeves giving him the appearance of a penguin, hilarious with the flapping gestures — as long as you kept your distance. But keeping out of reach was something I was in no position to do. A grimy hand like that of an old man held onto my heavy rubber slicker. A light cool rain mingled with the sweat on my forehead.

"Okay," said Billy. Possibly because of malnutrition his voice was uncertain. "Okay, we have the word you bozos weren't around. So you couldn't have squealed. So who did?"

"Search me, Bill. It wasn't us."

"That's not what I'm getting at. You hung around with Babe. What'd Babe tell you and who'd you pass it on to?"

"Babe didn't tell us nothing."

If I have cultivated one attribute over the years, it's the ability to size up people quickly, to do the artist's trick of taking an image from flesh and tone and creating signs of strength or frailty. Even at fifteen, I was beginning to develop the talent and sensed, in the hand grasping my rain slicker, a slight tremor. My logic told me the whole scrubby Cawner clan was in the jug, either over town or, in the case of the two older brothers, already inside Fort Saskatchewan with its sculptured gardens. They'd literally been sent down the river. So what was there to fear from a scrawny Billy Cawner without his twenty-two and only his poor mom, the only parent in the area who knew how to howl to the moon, to deal with now?

"Look, Bill, we're pals, okay? Well, let me pass on a tip. The bulls are poking around about Babe. They don't buy it that he hung himself. See?"

The grimy hand dropped. "Naw, I don't see."

"Don't you figure they're grilling your brothers about it? The cops ain't that dumb. Suppose they put two and two together? Who d'you think'd take the rap?"

"Jeez, Doug, they won't tie the can on us for that one?" He peered at me without any menace. "Didn't Babe string himself up?"

"Ever wonder why?"

"Aw, come on. That's nuts. We didn't do nothing." He restored his hand to my rain slicker and shook it again. "See here,

Sid and Eddy and others say it was old man Thorpe who turned us in. That right?"

"How the hell would I know? Norm and I weren't around."

"What about your old man? Or Albert?"

"Come on, Bill, my dad wouldn't do anything like that. He's no squealer. And Albert was too broken up to do it."

"You sure, huh?" He retracted the hand into the flapping sleeves of the windbreaker. "Okay, so Babe didn't tell you nothing?"

"Who, old Babe? Not old Babe."

Billy Cawner squinted at me while his wheels slowly meshed. The light drizzle thickened up into fat drops. He slid along the side of the barn as if scratching his back. When he was a safe distance away, I called after him.

"Yeah, well, you sure, Bill? You guys sure about Babe? Better ask your brothers."

Drenched, I returned home with the carton of ice cream, for once unmelted by my loitering or gossip along the way. When I arrived in our kitchen I found my father and three of his teacher friends from the Normal School sitting around the table. They had pooled their money for a mickey of rye and were making it last by filling their glasses with slivers of ice chipped off the block in the upper compartment of our old brown icebox. They were celebrating the finish of their summer job marking exam papers. The following week the results would be sent out to some seventeen thousand kids, including me, in grades nine and twelve. Around our table the chatter was about the recent selection of new teachers by the City School Board and the fact that only two new high-school teachers had been hired for the entire city system.

"Goddamn lottery," one of them was saying. He was younger than my father and wore thick glasses. "Over twenty applicants for each job. And those goddamn trustees sit around and vote by ballot on the names. What the hell kind of system is that?"

"It isn't a system," one of the others said. "It's a form of torture."

They looked up as something like a handful of gravel was

thrown against the kitchen window. There was a pause, a clap of thunder, and a roar of falling ice drumming on the roof. My grandpa came in from the living-room, his stubbled face ashen and stricken.

"My God, you see that? That's the end of the garden."

"And every poor bastard of a farmer," said one of the others. "Come on, grandpa, take the weight off your feet and have a drink."

On our small back porch — with its raised box for laundry baskets and a clothes-line wheel attached to a post, it was nothing more than a covered platform for hanging out the washing — I watched the white curtain of hail.

The faint haze of rain had been swept aside by a solid wall, pounding in slanting waves of rolled ice that bounced and clattered off the ground and steps. The garden disappeared under jiggling piles of hail, a plague of bluish-white frozen termites seething in a mass. The short stakes with bits of cloth on them to scare off the birds were knocked over; the wire rods with jam-tin lids, also to deter the birds, rang briefly against the deep roar of the hail, then collapsed.

I picked up some marble-sized stones that bounced at my feet. They were still so frozen they wouldn't melt into a larger ball in my hands. The air turned chilly, not the dry cold of winter, but a gasping dampness that soaked into the bones.

Then I saw the apparition. At first I thought it was only a shadow, a kind of mirage (my God, Babe's ghost?) thrown up by the wavering sheets of blue and white. It began as a faint impression of a human form out by the garage, not a looming outline, but one that became more distinct as it moved closer. My throat dry, I stood numbed, the ball of hail, forgotten, now beginning to melt in my hand. Before my fantasies took hold in complete panic, I could make out the figure of a small man sprinting towards our house. My momentary relief at having to confront only an earthly creature was short-lived.

It was Mr. Thorpe. He saw me on the back stoop and came sliding and slipping up the steps.

Thorpe's fedora, always far too big for his small fleshless skull, was pressed down to his eyebrows, its wide brim crowned with a band of unmelted stones. The shoulders of his shirt were wet and plastered down under suspenders, and his dark trousers were spattered with spots. He came straight at me, his hypnotic green eyes reflecting the jumpy lights of the falling hail. In his hand he had an envelope which looked battered, either by his damp hand or the attacking hailstones.

"You!" he began, his anger barely making room for his voice. "You molested my daughter! You had the nerve to—to——"

I was sure he was going to whip me, and backed up with a thump against the door.

He came on, shaking the envelope in my face, a letter, I began to realize, that he had probably received that morning from Diane. What had she told him? I couldn't think of anything to say, but my father, who had heard the noise on the back porch, came out from the kitchen, a glass of the cheap rye in his hand. He had been having a nice time with his pals and wasn't in any mood for small irate apparitions waving pieces of paper at his son.

"Now, now, Mr. Thorpe," Father said in his best classroom tones. "What's all this about? What're you doing here with Doug?"

"Your son went all the way to the Institute to assault my daughter," Thorpe went on, his eyes bulging. "Of all the un-Christian, evil——"

"Wait a minute. This true, Doug?"

Shivering, I told him that I had dropped in to see Diane while on the speaking tour with Albert and Jean the previous Saturday. My voice faded in a massive clap of thunder that seemed to rock the small porch.

"While we were in that town, I just thought I'd go and see how she was," I said as innocently as I could.

Father didn't quite buy it, but he wasn't going to give in to Thorpe either.

"Mr. Thorpe, what does your daughter actually say in her letter? Come, now, what's her complaint?"

His face mottled in blue shadows under the brim of the large fedora, Thorpe hesitated, then took the crumpled piece of paper out of the envelope and passed it to my father. I sidled over to read it.

The opening part of her letter seemed to have little to do with the problem. Diane related an experience she'd had during one of their classes.

We had a revelation the other day. Tom, who comes from Stettler, leaped to his feet to tell us he had been visited that morning. The Lord had instructed him to rise and confess his sins aloud. We all got caught up in it and began to shout out our own confessions, our failures to fully accept all His mercies.

I could picture them all: pudding faces and shapeless clothing, suddenly frenzied, tear-stained and pouring it all out.

We went on for several hours as the Spirit of God entered us all until we reached a plane of glory that none of us had ever witnessed before.

I wondered what she had confessed, and wished I had been a fly on the wall, assuming they allowed any flies in that place. It came as something of an anti-climax to read that her reference to me was only a P.S., a footnote to what for poor, gorgeous Diane was another step in her withdrawal from the lustful world outside.

Her postscript merely said: *Meant to tell you, I had a visit last Saturday from one of the neighbours. It was Doug Sayers who told me he wanted to see me about something. I didn't want to see him so they sent him away. Hope he never comes back.*

Father, closing ranks, handed the letter back to Mr. Thorpe.

"All right, the boy shouldn't have done that. I guess he didn't know the rules. He won't do it again, that I promise you."

"It was sinful and stupid," Thorpe went on. "I want to know what it was he wanted."

"That's for me to find out. As far as I can see, no harm was done. At worst, it was a dumb prank. I'll talk to the boy and I'll thank you not to bother him about it again. We're sorry. That's that."

"All you have to say? Here he goes into a place of Christian study with his cheeky manners to disturb a poor girl who is trying to find her way to the Truth, and you——"

"Enough, Mr. Thorpe. That's it."

Father, possibly for effect, grabbed me by the scruff of the neck and pushed me back into the kitchen ahead of him. He slammed the door on Thorpe and turned to me, his friends at the table now looking up, puzzled but amused.

"I think I know why you went to see her." His saturnine face was grim. "We'll talk about it later. You stay out of his way. Now beat it."

As things turned out, I was far from done with Mr. Thorpe. On Monday morning, when he stepped out of his house to leave for the Civic Block, he found his front steps had been decorated with a pile of evil-smelling garbage, gooey and dripping down the sides. Someone had scrawled an arrow in white paint on the damp wood of the sidewalk; the point of the arrow aimed at his door and led back in a wobbly streak to the latters "R-A-T" daubed across several boards on the street.

Billy Cawner had started.

Our supper hour that day was interrupted by another visit from Thorpe, and this time my father took him outside into the yard where they stood out of earshot on the sodden grass.

"You weren't mixed up in that, were you?" my mother asked.

"No, no, not me. I'm pretty sure who it was."

"I can guess," she said with a shrug.

After the next night's calling card, a pile of manure topped by a dead cat, Mr. Thorpe called the police. Despite my parents' assurances, it was obvious I was first on the suspect list and, once again, I had to sit and fidget while a cop, this time in uniform, grilled me. Fortunately, my mother was on hand to swear that I had been in the house all the previous evening. The cops went elsewhere.

At midnight we were awakened by the sound of breaking glass, and we rushed out onto the verandah too late to view the brick being heaved through the Thorpes' glass window in their front door. I thought I saw a small crooked shadow slipping away, but this time the crafty bulls were waiting, and Billy Cawner ran headlong into a cop who had been squatting, no doubt cold and shivering in his wet slicker, behind a hedge across the street.

So was an immense burden removed. For if the Cawners had thought I was the one who had set the police onto them, my life would have been so cheap I might as well have gone down and joined Diane in that Bible Institute. When little Billy was nabbed that night, Thorpe came rushing out of his house triumphantly and had to be restrained by the cop making the pinch. The whole neighbourhood was awakened by the shouting, but I breathed deeply with relief. I heard my father out on the sidewalk chatting with Albert Roothe, who had burst out of his house, crowbar in hand, to subdue any mayhem.

"What a racket!" I heard Albert say to my father. "I thought someone was being murdered out there."

Also greatly relieved that the culprit had been caught, my father now relapsed into his usual cynicism.

"Aw, it was just Brother Thorpe having a prayer meeting."

Not long afterwards none of us was surprised to learn that the Thorpes planned to move over town to another district on the north side, far from our quiet, friendly neighbourhood. I had visions of them now setting off on an endless quest for the perfect house in the same way they floated from church to church. Whether they did or not I can't say, for they never came back to look us up.

When I had snuggled down in that London bed and tried to divert Jean from her questions about Babe, she came back again to Diane.

"You're lovely," I said. "Do you know that?"

"A frump compared to Diane. She was the most gorgeous creature I've ever seen. No wonder they kept her penned up like a nun."

"She faded fast. When I saw her at the Institute, she'd lost all her looks. I've often wondered what happened to her."

"Oh, her friend Mabel — you know, the fat one? — she's here in the CWAC's. Slimmed down a lot, smokes like a chimney and cusses a blue streak. Mabel told me. Diane married one of the teachers while she was still at the Institute, an older man, and they went off to Africa on missionary work. They're in the Belgian Congo now, Mabel says. She still hears from her."

"Poor Diane."

"Why do you say that? Listen, even Albert noticed her."

"Albert did? I thought he only had eyes for you — aside from himself and Abie, that is."

"That's not fair."

"He let you get away, or are you here to get away from him?"

"That's mean, Doug. We've just grown apart. That can happen."

"Yeah, and he never joined up——"

"He thinks he's doing essential work where he is. You know what he's like. You've seen it. That summer of Babe's death, he was right on the edge. You have no idea of the frustration he was going through."

"You could have remedied that."

"Not what I mean," she said.

What she had meant was Albert's burning urge to play a major part in the advent of a new millennium. As prominent as he was in the Movement, he still hadn't reached the inner circles. This was again brought home to him when the candidate situation in Edmonton became unstuck again.

By July 30, Jean told me, Albert had got all excited with rumours that Dr. Willis was about to withdraw as a candidate. That evening, as Jean once more drove up in the old Graham-Paige, she saw that Albert had taken special pains with his appearance; his suit was freshly pressed, his shoes gleaming. They were on their way to a Social Credit rally at the Alberta Avenue Community Hall, where Dr. Willis was billed as one of three speakers.

"They just might call on me to speak," Albert said.

But they didn't, and his time still hadn't come. By Thursday the official announcement was made. The campaign manager for the city, a man named Gould, confirmed the withdrawal of Dr. Willis and his replacement by one Orvis Kennedy.

"Know him well," Albert told Jean. "A grand fellow, very active in the Movement. Like myself, interested in young people."

"How'd they decide on him?" Jean asked.

"It'd be done by the selection board in Calgary."

"Isn't Mr. Aberhart away on vacation?"

"Yes, yes, a well-deserved time of meditation to ready himself for the responsibilities of office. I'm sure they must have consulted him."

"Albert, he isn't even a candidate. Why wouldn't he take the vacancy himself?"

"Not a good idea for a leader to risk all in a six-member riding with proportional representation."

"Why not? Two of the party leaders, Mr. Howson, the Liberal, and Mr. Duggan, the Conservative, are running here."

"They're just two-bit politicians. Why, if they went out to a country seat they'd be tarred and feathered. No, someone will make room for Mr. Aberhart when the time comes."

He made the best of it, but he was, as Jean suggested, bleeding inside. I had visions of Albert's inner cavities filling up with tomato soup, the way the soft-water cistern in the basement rose to the overflow pipe during a rainstorm. Jean was also of the opinion that Babe's death had affected him more deeply than he would admit, that it had drained away some of his resilience. But, as we both agreed, Albert always seemed to bounce back.

Wrapped around each other in the warmth of that bed, Jean and I paused in our, or rather her, reminiscences. Far above we could hear the morning drone of the American B-17's with their overpaid crews heading out for their daytime bombing, an unwelcome reminder of why we were here together in the first place. The intrusion of wartime sounds set Jean off on another train of thought.

"Hey," she said, wriggling out of my arms and sitting up. "You remember the Nazi rally? You were there, weren't you?"

Yes, I was. I told her I thought it was probably Albert's finest hour. Jean said she agreed: It was those speaking assignments that kept Albert more or less under control, from thinking too much about why Babe had died, while at the same time building up a stack of unclaimed markers from the Movement. His willingness to take on this particular event must have earned him a blue chip, all right, for it appeared the Movement had agonized, then decided not to be represented at it. There were enough enemies going around the province hinting that there was a touch of fascism in Social Credit to give them pause about appearing on such a platform. Apparently Albert convinced the local mucky-mucks that he could handle it, and as he wasn't a candidate anyway, someone — perhaps an unfriendly soul — had finally agreed that he should be there to extend greetings.

"Let's see the poor sap handle that one," my father said gleefully, after Albert, unable to contain himself, broke the news to him. "Why don't you hop on your bike and head over there to see how he does?"

So, with nothing else to do, I persuaded Sid and Eddy to come with me. Off we went to 104th Street, where we turned south and pedalled along the pavement to the South Side Athletic Grounds on the Calgary Trail.

This was on Sunday, August 4, during the long civic holiday weekend, an overcast day with spits of rain. My pals started to grumble, but I kept them going by promising (based on my father's prediction) that there'd be trouble. How he knew this, I didn't know, unless perhaps some of his socialist friends had told him they had something in mind.

To be fair, the event was not billed as a Nazi rally. Its official moniker was the Eighth Annual Picnic of the German-Canadian Reunion Association, featuring such harmless pastimes as a potato race, the hundred-yard dash (seventy-five for women), the high jump, and a tug-of-war, city *versus* country. We had heard there was to be a parade from Market Square across the High Level Bridge, with a line of floats loaded with dignitaries, including Mayor Clarke himself ensconced in the second car. By the time we got to the grounds, the parade was already over and, with much milling around, the big shots were taking their places on the platform, including, I noted, Albert Roothe in his one and only dark suit.

It was nutty, all right. The place was wall-to-wall sauerkrauts jabbering away in German and some English, all types and sizes in varying degrees of non-prosperity. And in the crowd of some four thousand, one could sense a suppressed excitement, an expectancy that formed a mystic bond among them, thick as a hoar-frost haze at forty below and deliberately excluding those of us who weren't on the same wavelength.

Someone was taking a photo of two slim ladies in slouched hats who were trying to lounge elegantly on the fenders of a car that had swastika flags stuck on the hood ornament. Little blond kids ran around at our feet.

The programme began with the singing of "O Canada" as the Union Jack was run up a pole in front of the platform. Then, with a sigh that let out pent-up anticipation, in a louder burst of deep voices, they sang "*Deutschland über alles*," and on either side of the Union Jack they ran up the still official flag of Germany, black, red, and gold with horizontal stripes.

There was a curious stillness as all eyes turned to the third flagstaff, where the swastika, within a white circle against a scarlet background, shook itself loose. There was a collective sigh, an outburst of chattering voices, and the pointing of fingers. A flurry of smaller swastika flags waved in the air.

Because I was interested (and instructed) to see how Albert performed, I followed the speeches more closely than I normally would have. The visiting bigwig was one Herr Doctor Seelheim, the German consul-general for western Canada, who had made the trip all the way from Winnipeg. Unfortunately he spoke entirely in German, but I picked up snatches of a translation being muttered beside me by a large man in a dark suit who was evidently conveying it to his English-speaking wife.

"He's saying that Hitler is carrying on the work of rebuilding Germany which Hindenburg had started when he died in 1934," the big man muttered in a loud stage whisper. He paused. "He says that nations cannot progress while the spirit of the French Revolution still prevails—its anarchy. In Germany a sincere attempt is being made to develop a new system, that of National Socialism. We fight bitterly against the excesses of capitalism. Business in Germany is being made to serve the people. Only the best of capitalism is being retained. Good point, *ja*?"

Then the other speakers had their turn.

Mayor Clarke, a crusty-looking old duck with horn-rimmed glasses, led off. He was followed by Lymburn, the attorney general in the UFA government, the one referred to by Haddon and Dr. Candliss during Babe's inquest. Trying not to look too strained, he dwelt on the fine qualities of the German people and how, perhaps more than those of any other race, they were needed during these difficult times to help in the work of building the province.

"Give us jobs and we'll try," a man next to us growled in English.

I craned to see the other two party leaders who had so often been described by Albert as "tinhorn" or "two-bit." I had expected to see sneaky-looking little creatures, shifty and malevolent in starched collars and top hats, and was somewhat surprised at the two rather presentable-looking geezers who took their turns at regaling the throng.

Duggan, the Conservative leader, had a ruddy face, and was big and stocky but immaculate in a neat suit and a flower in his lapel. His voice was soft and persuasive. But he pulled his punches and didn't incite revolution, no doubt because his political mates were still in power in Ottawa and a federal election was in the offing.

"I appeal to all German-Canadians to join with us to preserve, during the present times of unrest, that which has been built by the pioneers," he intoned. A conservative message, for sure.

There was a polite spatter of applause.

Next came the Liberal leader, Howson. He was formidable looking, with a prominent jaw, steely eyes, and an aggressive speaking style hampered by a scratchy voice that kept cracking on him.

"We should honour the older people who came to this land to give their children greater opportunity." A big fat mistake on their part, I thought. "I urge you younger ones to remember the toil of your parents in carving out new homes in this new land and to carry on in the same pioneering spirit." At the height of his oratory, his voice cracked and there were giggles around us.

Now came Albert's turn to swim upstream against all the

clichés. He came to the microphone, poised, tall, and slim, to convey the springiness of someone fresh who, like those in the Fatherland, represented something new.

This is what Albert Roothe said on that day:

"I bring you greetings from our leader, Mr. Aberhart, who, as you know, is of German ancestry himself. I know he would have wanted to be here. Doctor Seelheim" — Albert must have had a translator nearby, but then I remember that one of the officials had been whispering in his ear during the speech — "has very graphically described the new winds of change that are sweeping Germany today. A similar urge for change now grips the people of Alberta, faced as they are with the modern dilemma of poverty in the midst of plenty. Germany, in the light of her own history and culture, has chosen a distinct course. From a different background, the people of Alberta will soon be making their choice. We, too, stand at the crossroads, where we must decide to continue as we have been doing these past few years or to seek a new way, a new order. In this sense, we are all pioneers again. Thank you."

That was all, but it was enough. The applause was louder and all kinds of bullet-like heads nodded.

The others on the platform were furious. Both Duggan and Howson glanced at each other and turned to glare at Albert. He had broken the unwritten code of such non-partisan gatherings without a trace of remorse, and as he took his seat among the bigwigs, he returned their scowls with an impudent smile of confidence, as if to reinforce his message that the old ways were gone and done with forever.

After a wind-up oration by the chairman of the rally, there was an outburst of cheering and a loud, discordant crash as the German United Band struck up a march.

"Holy cow, look at that!" Eddy murmured.

Up went the arms in the Nazi salute, a sea of pointers to the sky and to the future. We were puzzled, ignorant of its meaning. It seemed more like a primary classroom running riot: May we all go to the bathroom, huh, teacher? We poked each other and snorted. It was funny.

As a light drizzle of rain began to dissolve the crowd, we saw the trouble begin. There seemed to be a flurry of men running and a waving of arms off to one side of the stands. Now a clump of men gathered around a policeman who seemed to be holding them back. One large fellow with a swastika armband was shredding some pamphlets and stomping on them like ants at a picnic, his face purple with fury. As we approached this bubbling, agitated bunch of heads, we could see their wrath was directed at a lone individual, a small, baldish man who was trying to hug the remnants of his pamphlets. The cop had turned to bawl out the little guy who was scared white, but equally determined not to move.

"Look, okay, it's a free country. But these people've rented these grounds. It's theirs for the day. So I'm going to take you to the gate and you high-tail it out of here and stay out. Get me?"

The little guy kept shaking his head in a kind of stubborn palsy, until the policeman, one arm holding back the looming bulks who wanted to shred the small fellow along with his pamphlets, grabbed hold of his collar and marched him through the menacing crowd towards the white fence at the edge of the field.

We trailed along for the excitement, expecting any moment that the huge German-Canadians would take the little man away and pound him into the wet turf. They seemed satisfied, however, to stride along as outriders and spit threats in that language which seems designed for the purpose.

At the entrance to the grounds stood the harness bull, arms folded to make sure the agitator did go on his way and didn't come back to spoil the good clean fun. As the little man was straggling away, shaking his head and muttering to himself, I caught up to him and asked for one of his pamphlets.

"Good for you, sonny. You know what those ginks stand for?" He had a thick accent that also sounded German.

"Nope, not me." I put the leaflet in my pocket. "It's for my dad."

He seemed disappointed, realized there wasn't much point in expending energy to explain it all to a grinning teen-aged lout, and headed off in the direction of the McKernan Lake streetcar line. On our way back into the grounds, looking to see if we could snitch some food somewhere (their great sausages), I thought I should have picked up one of those pamphlets for Albert who, I had noticed, had started to raise his arm during the Nazi salute, then thought better of it and placed his fedora over his heart. But when I looked back, the little man had disappeared from sight and the beefy men in their armbands were wandering back, jabbering among themselves and shaking their heads.

CHAPTER SEVENTEEN

ONE EVENING MY FATHER CAME HOME FROM A MEETING IN THE Flats, arranged not by the UFA but the rising CCF, the socialist party formed in 1933 that was to inherit the cause of the people if Social Credit didn't get there first. Perhaps he had known what to expect and deliberately passed up this opportunity to give his son some exposure to something other than Albert's ramblings about Social Credit.

The meeting had been a bust. Only a dozen stalwarts had shown up, and some local bully boys had let the air out of the tires of those who had cars and had daubed white SC's on the car hoods.

All bottled up. You could almost see his inner turmoil, as if it were two colours of paint mixed together, folding and swirling in different threads until they finally merge into something different. For my father, the bright stains were his beliefs in a kind of agnostic humanism, not in rational man but in a more sensitive one, and his darker swirls were despair that any form of humanism would ever work as long as there was humanity. In such moments of inner agony he would briefly become much older: The seams on each side of his mouth became scars; his usually alert, aquiline expression drooped. Chin down, he had a bulge over his collar, showing that he was not as lean as he seemed, or that imperceptibly time was eroding the flesh.

He couldn't have arrived in our kitchen at a more inopportune time for me. I had one of the little swastika flags lifted at the rally in my hand and was doing what was to become a cliché, a Hitler imitation with a black comb under my nose. Mother was doubled up in a wheezing fit and even grouchy old Grandpa allowed a yellow smirk to crack his stubbled jaw.

"Holy smoke, do you know what you're doing?" My father's voice was a notch lower and scary.

"Oh, John, he was just kidding around."

"Well, stop it. Look at this." He rustled through the evening paper. "Near Kurpark, Frienwalde, a notice was posted reading, 'The smell of the Jew is deadly in the pure forest air.' In Coburg all municipal officials have been ordered to cease all business and social intercourse with Jews. And not just them. See here. In Breslau they've ordered the confessional synod of Silesia dissolved and they've set up a Reichsbishop to take over all the Protestant churches. That little man is no Charlie Chaplin. And Albert and his bunch aren't that much different. All their talk of Zionist plots. You know over in England they parade around in green shirts?"

"Not Albert, surely."

"You hear what Dougie told us about the rally, how he toadied up to them. They're dangerous!" Then he told me what they had done to the cars.

I put my comb back into a pocket. Father slumped at the table.

"Where's it all going to end? It's a nightmare."

Collective visions of gleaming towers and new orders had reached even to our small bungalows on dusty streets. Not surprising that we would be so affected — my father not immune in his own mirages of equality — but I wonder, too, about the subtle influences of weather: those roller-coaster rises and plunges in atmospheric pressure: heat, rain, and the frozen killer, hail.

A nightmare, he had said. And premonitions, I could have added. Or, years later, I might have told him of the dreams that had dogged Albert, and may have explained something of his peculiar reaction to his brother's death and his own immersion in a cause. In my own nightmares, Babe kept coming back, trying to tell me. . . .

The roof of the barn has disappeared and he walks up a ladder into a yellow dawn, pausing only to wave back at me with a sardonic grin. When he tries to speak, worms drop out.

The dreams go on, even after Headley decides to demolish his barn.

One morning we were awakened by squeals and creaks and the voices of men shouting. As my father had no summer-school classes until the afternoon, we had all slept in, even my grandfather, who had sourly given up on his hail-flattened garden. We straggled out into the back yard as if there had been a fire in the house, and stood around to watch the gang of men tearing and ripping at the roof of Headley's barn three doors away from us. Going into the lane along with other neighbours, we came across Mr. Headley, his big stetson pushed to the back of his head while he watched the men demolish his barn. His two old nags were tethered in the vacant lot across the lane and Pal was running in circles around his fast-disappearing home.

"After what happened," Mr. Headley told us slowly, his eyes crinkled and squinting up at the workmen, "figured it ought to come down."

An era had come to an end, for Headley's barn was our visible link to the surrounding countryside, the lumbering wagons and horses a reminder that we were only a fake city with false fronts plunked down in the midst of a vast farm. So it appeared that the violent atmospheric pressures had brought on yet another human brainstorm, this time in the mind of the stolid, slow-speaking Headley, an unlit roll-your-own stuck to his bottom lip as he wiped out a memory — or evidence.

The question of evidence had already been put to me by my father following Thorpe's outburst the day he confronted me with Diane's letter. When I finally told my father about the discovery of the handkerchief, he looked worried — for me, I think, and my curiosity. At such moments he could not resist delivering a lecture.

"Any policeman or court would consider that as circumstantial evidence," he went on. "You know what that means? Unless there was some kind of corroborating statement, it'd be useless, only a vague suspicion. It wouldn't prove anything about Babe's death. Anyway, you don't have it now. She's probably destroyed it."

"Or she's kept it."

"Oh, come on, Doug. Why'd she keep it? Her letter indicates

she's adjusting to the school, is putting her past behind her."

An image came to me of Diane hoeing spuds, her dress like a potato sack itself, her arms and face tanned a deep brown and tears streaming down her face to drip into the green leaves. That was too romantic. For one thing, there probably weren't any potatoes left.

The hailstorms had swept in over and over again, creeping barrages of white shrapnel, destroying the gardens, so vital in those days for extra food, as well as the crops; cows and horses were driven mad in the slashing torrents, chickens pulverized until only bloody clumps of feathers. East of Calgary the hail had lain over a foot thick on the ground, and after it had melted, they found partridge and pheasants beaten to death, their wings stretched over their dead young. Nearer to us, hailstones the size of eggs, in large swathes six miles wide by forty miles long, had wrecked the almost-perfect crops. All of this was mixed up with cyclones and lightning that burnt the Lutheran Church at Ellerslie to the ground, that smashed in windows, tore shingles off houses, thundered a destruction that was now thought to be almost total. Again and again that first week of August, the massive thunderheads piled up in grinning skulls of deep bluish-grey, picked the targets they had missed, then struck.

The disaster was almost complete; the survivors scanned the horizon to see if they would be next. While in the city we had been hit mostly by heavy rains and a two-hour power failure on Sunday, Mr. Headley's barn now looked as though hail had torn off its roof and ripped holes in the old siding that came crashing down in long strips.

Yet, as I confided to Jean in that London hotel room nine years later, we were glad to see the barn go. Its presence had become a malign reminder of Babe.

"I wonder if Albert ever felt that way," I mused to Jean.

"Surely you weren't that smart, that perceptive as a kid. You're just fooling around with old memories, eh? I didn't have the impression anyone noticed at the time."

"Noticed what? Was there something, then? I guess you saw because you were closest to him."

"Not as close as we are now."

"You mean, you two never —— "

"No, there wasn't any place to go. He was always so busy and I was scared of getting knocked up. But there was something there. I mean before Babe's death."

I sat up. "Before?"

"Yes, before. You do realize that Albert was going through an intense mystical or religious dedication to the Movement? At times he pushed himself to the edge. Somewhere, at some point, he had taken on himself the responsibility of being a messenger, of bringing to all those beaten, shabby mobs the good news that here, at last, was an awakening, a kind of millennium within their grasp. Unlike anything else that had gone before, morality and religion would be actually bound together within a government, under a leader who had received an obviously inspired revelation from Above, a handing down of the tablets that would bring economic recovery: food, clothing, jobs, money, and Grace to go along with it all."

"Who was Grace?"

"Oh, stop it. And all of this was to be done simply through a mechanism of economics that had escaped all previous great thinkers. So there had to be divine inspiration. Otherwise, how come no one else had received the answer, the solution, with such clarity? That's pretty heady stuff. You probably weren't aware of how many people actually shared these convictions. The old-line parties, the newspapers, and the Economic Safety League sneered at the dumb clucks who were led along by the promise of twenty-five smackaroos a month. But it was much more than that. Much more. The burning light that shone on people like Albert is tough to see now. Maybe the whole world was getting like that and we had to have this war to purge ourselves of fevers of the mind so intense something had to give. And because we were so distant and alone away out there on the prairie, the pressures were all the more intense. You see?"

"Maybe. I didn't think you —— "

"Had the brains to figure it out? Jesus, Doug. Something had to give—like this war. And it did in Albert too. Being so close to him, so wrapped up in him because I was unemployed and had nowhere else to put my energies. Try as I did, though, I couldn't share his commitment. Night after night I left him and went to bed all wet and writhing with sex. I ached all over and slept with a wrinkled, damp pillow in my arms.

"About this time, I began to notice some curious lapses in Albert. When alone with me, or if he didn't think I was watching, an odd expression would appear in his eyes and he would stare off somewhere. It happened often enough for me to ask him if he wasn't feeling well. Eventually, I forget just when, but it was after Babe's death, he told me. He had been having visions or dreams. They had become so frequent he was almost afraid to go to sleep. He finally told me about them. He saw himself alone on the Avenue, walking in a glowing, bright aura that seemed to shed heat, like a hot Wednesday afternoon, say, when all the stores are closed and no one is around. Then, he told me, he would become aware of something unseen, a substance that was transparent, yet tangible, that began to follow him, flowing from doorway to doorway beside him — a sneering, vicious presence reaching out to him with some kind of horrible message he couldn't understand. Whatever it was, this substance slithered and crept along with him in the hot blinding sunshine until he woke up covered in a sweaty slime. So there we were, both of us far apart in our separate bedrooms, awakening in the middle of the night, all sweaty and upset for different reasons."

"Surely he must have had the odd moment when he, too, mashed up a pillow in your image."

"If he did, he didn't tell me. We were close, you know, not intimate. It was only after Babe's death that he could bring himself to tell me about the dreams. He thought they were visions, premonitions."

"What do you think?"

Jean got quite agitated and sat up straight in bed.

"After Babe's death, the dreams stopped. So what are we to think? But he kept going, you know, always hoping, always trying."

"Wasn't he even a bit curious about why Babe may have hung himself? He never asked me anything about it."

"I'm not surprised. Sure he wondered, was as mystified as the rest of us. But it's my opinion that the dreams so frightened him, he was afraid to involve anyone else. Besides, he was too busy."

She was right. Albert Roothe's long struggle for recognition came to an end the weekend of August 10, only twelve days before the election. In a way, I suppose it's more accurate to say he cleared the first major hurdle. He had secured a foothold.

On Saturday morning Albert was called out of his summer-school class at the university with an urgent message to call Mr. Gould, the campaign manager for the northern part of the province. On the phone Albert was invited to go to Calgary for an interview early Sunday morning at the Prophetic Bible Institute. He wasn't told why, and Mr. Gould would not answer his questions. So Albert rushed home, borrowed the fare from his father, and managed to catch the slow afternoon train at the CPR's Strathcona station.

He stayed overnight in Calgary at the YMCA, and in bright warm sunshine the next morning he walked all the way along Eighth Avenue. He didn't want to spend his money on a streetcar ride, so he strolled along the empty street, absorbing the peculiar oily smells of the city. An empty orange-and-brown tram clattered past him, adding to the strangeness of such a different place. The only signs of life, he told us later, were the rustling and stirring of hobos emerging from their newspaper cocoons among the garbage cans in the alleyways.

One can imagine his inner tumult as, for the first time, he paused under the large electric sign that hung out over the street. The sign was shaped like a giant dog bone and had the words "Alberta Prophetic" across the top part, "Bible" in vertical lettering down the shank, and "Institute" across the bottom. It marked a two-storey building of dark brick, with steps leading up to double doors under a square portico.

By the energy and will of one man, this was where it had all begun.

Following a legendary fund-raising campaign among the ordinary folk ("five dollars a brick"), the Institute had opened its doors in 1927. William Aberhart's original idea had been to have a place where young people could "secure a good training in Bible Knowledge without having their faith undermined by atheistic, sceptic, and modernistic teaching." This was where he had perfected his dramatic teaching methods and taken up the Lord's instrument — radio — to broadcast the Word. Here, shattered and full of compassion for the sufferings of the people, he had first begun to preach the economic salvation the Lord had seen fit to reveal to him. Here young people could learn not only the true gospel, but worthwhile skills in shorthand, typing, music, millinery, domestic science, and motor mechanics.

The Institute, the well-spring of the Movement, had now become its nerve centre, the setting where Mr. Aberhart always felt most at home and brought forth his best oratory. And now Albert was being asked to go there, by an urgent summons that was all the more mystifying when it was known that Mr. Aberhart, having returned from his vacation, would actually be arriving in Edmonton the next day, Monday, for a week of meetings in the city.

What was it all about?

Albert found a polite young man who led him past the open door of the auditorium, where a huddle of youngsters seemed to be taking a Bible class, to an office where he was ushered in to Mr. Aberhart himself and several other men sitting around in chairs. So taken aback was Albert that he didn't catch the names of the other men in the room, although he thought two of them looked familiar. Mr. Aberhart's protégé, Ernest Manning, didn't seem to be around.

Dizzily, Albert sat on a chair in front of the desk and tried not to sweat too much. The leader appeared fresh and rested, slightly reddish and sunburned in the face from his vacation on the coast or from being outdoors during the campaign.

"I was very sorry about your brother. I hope you got my note. My prayers go with you," Mr. Aberhart said. His voice was soft and rich, not the way it sometimes was when he bellowed from a platform.

Albert nodded his appreciation.

The leader clasped his big hands in front of him, as if about to pray.

"You know, three years ago this summer one of my most

talented students at Crescent Heights committed suicide. He was tops in Grade Twelve and a swell kid. His family had been wiped out by the Depression and it was too much for him." He made a half turn and spoke to the others, who nodded. "I'll never forget that summer. I think that was the year we were marking papers at King Edward School, before the Normal School reopened. Oh, I was feeling low that summer. That's when I first started to do some reading on economics." He turned his blue eyes on Albert again. "Did the inquest help to reveal the reasons why he would do such a thing? There was quite a bit in the papers."

"No, sir. Not really. We don't understand it at all."

"Perhaps in good time it will be revealed to you. Let us hope that the Almighty in His wisdom will set your family's mind at peace." He sighed. "On a more cheerful note, Albert, we've been receiving fine reports on your work. I'm told you wowed them last Monday at that German rally. That you just said a few words, but knocked the spots off the leaders from the old-line parties."

"I'll admit I was kind of uncomfortable about it all. I don't know your own feelings, sir, but that crooked cross of theirs gives me the willies."

"Yes, it's a primitive symbol, you know. There's something about it I don't much care for. We can only pray that better elements will prevail over that man Hitler."

"From what one reads in the papers about the persecutions of Jews and Christians alike——"

"No, it doesn't look promising, does it? Well, I have a confession to make to you, Albert. It won't have escaped your attention that none of our Edmonton candidates was there. There was much prayerful discussion by our Edmonton group, I gather, before they decided not to send any of our candidates. But they agreed you would do a fine job—which you did. So we are grateful."

"Thank you."

It's difficult to guess what Albert must have thought about the revelation that he had been a patsy. As Albert related his interview, over and over again around the kitchen table, Mr. Roothe kidded him about having been a fall guy, but Albert hotly refused to accept the idea that his buddies in the Movement would throw him in to see if he could swim. In any case, what followed next must have driven any lingering resentment from his mind.

"Albert, you've no doubt been wondering why we asked you to take all the trouble to come down here when we could have met in Edmonton tomorrow. You are aware that nominations close at two o'clock tomorrow, Monday?"

"Yes, sir."

"Are you knowledgeable at all about the constituency of Strathcona-White Mud?"

"Yes, I've given three speeches there. It's just south of the city limits, a narrow band between the city and Leduc riding. I know quite a few people there. The candidate, Fred Tarrow, is a fine man. He shouldn't have any trouble getting elected."

"Then you haven't heard what happened to him?"

"No."

"Late Friday night, driving home from a meeting, Fred hit some loose gravel, sheared off a telephone pole, and was badly smashed up. He has a concussion and several broken bones."

"I'm sorry to hear that. Fred's a hard worker."

"Yes. He's in the University Hospital and will be out for the rest of the campaign. As you may be aware, he has a good campaign organization and the chances are he could get elected even from his hospital bed. At least, if we're reading the trends right."

"I'm sure you're right. Everywhere we go there's nothing but admiration and support for you."

"Except for one minor but important fact about Fred's accident. He was obviously driving much too fast for his fatigued state. Worse than that, the police report says he had been drinking. There's a possibility of a charge, something like 'wanton and furious driving,' or worse, a charge related to his drinking. I don't believe they'll proceed until he's out of the hospital, but even so."

The import of the message was beginning to reach Albert. Up to that point he had thought maybe they had wanted to slot him in somewhere as a campaign manager, which hardly warranted a special trip to Calgary when he could have been assigned the job by the regional organizers themselves. Now he tried to suppress a mounting exhilaration over what he realized must be coming, the reason for a Sunday meeting with the leader himself. You could picture Albert holding onto himself, every twitch under control, voice carefully modulated; yet his excitement must have shown in the lights of his pale eyes.

"Frankly, Albert, we can't afford to have any of our members elected under a cloud of that nature. We have gone to the voters saying that we are honest, clean, Christian, a new wave of dedicated politicians who won't be corrupted or side-tracked from our duty to the public. Mr. Gould has been to see Mr. Tarrow and has obtained his resignation. Of course, the public explanation will be easy to get across — his disability due to the accident. Fred is a good man and knows his onions about Social Credit, and we're sorry to have to do this to him. In a sense, I suppose, we could say he did it to himself by not getting enough rest, not being temperate. But we must have an upstanding candidate in that riding who will make a good member. Hence — and I won't beat around the bush any longer — your name has come up."

"Well, I don't live in the riding, and there must be others who could be put forward by the local association."

Mr. Aberhart glanced at one of the others, who now spoke.

"Mr. Roothe, we'll continue to speak frankly. While Fred was an excellent candidate, the others fall considerably short of the qualities we seek. In any case, two of them have already indicated they are no longer available."

"What we want, Albert," Mr. Aberhart resumed, "is for you to accept the nomination. Yesterday a very extensive phone canvass was made of the local executive. Knowing you as they do, they are agreeable. The fact that your name has been in the papers hasn't done any harm. There wasn't one dissenting voice. If you find it within your heart to accept, we will make the appointment official."

"But the names for my nomination papers?"

"If you accept, Mr. Gould will see that's looked after today and that our papers are filed by two o'clock tomorrow."

"I don't know what to say."

"We appreciate your feelings. Regretfully, though, we must

have an answer almost immediately. If you wish to take a while to pray and meditate in the chapel —— "

"No, no, it's all right. I'd be honoured to accept."

"Fine, fine. Very good."

"Now I think I would like to retire to your chapel, if I may." They laughed and nodded.

"My, my. Well, thank you, all of you. I hope you'll pray for me."

"We shall," smiled Mr. Aberhart. "We shall indeed, Albert."

By Wednesday night, when he sat on the platform at Strathcona High School to hear himself introduced then lavishly praised by his leader, a dazed Albert looked around as though someone else was being mentioned.

"Ordinarily," Mr. Aberhart said, "someone running outside the city wouldn't be on this platform tonight. But an accident that struck down our fine candidate in Strathcona-White Mud has brought forward a replacement who is not only well qualified, but is known to many of you as a teacher, a church worker with young people, and a graduate of this very high school: Mr. Albert Roothe."

When Albert stood up, there was a satisfying cheer from the some thousand people who packed the gym on the top floor of the old high school. While the six city candidates tried not to look too miffed, their egos were rescued by each being allowed to speak, a privilege denied Albert, possibly because the local powers didn't want him to show up the others.

"Ha. He'll be gloating, silently lording it over them," my father said to us before we left for the meeting. Although my mother was accompanying Mrs. Roothe, my pinko dad was having no part of any Social Credit rally. "He's got a cinch. A one-member rural riding with the single transferable vote. Just a straight one-two-three count until someone gets fifty per cent. He's all set. And the others know it. He's got the last laugh."

I didn't realize what he meant, and how important it was to have a rural riding until I sat scrunched up on a wooden chair in the packed, sweaty Scona auditorium with the gym mats stacked against the walls.

Instead of a high-flying oration about bloodstreams and credit and the Fifty Bigshots, Mr. Aberhart gave a lecture on election-day tactics. I didn't have a clue what he was talking about until we got home and my father sharpened up his classroom skills with another practise lecture.

In essence it was this: There were no wards or constituencies in the two major cities, Edmonton and Calgary. In our city there were six members of the legislature elected at large in a complex method of proportional representation. There were twenty-seven names on the ballot and you voted one to twenty-seven for the whole works, or you could plump for, say, a slate of six representing one party.

How could you develop an election-day strategy with that mess?

Mr. Aberhart told them.

"Outside each poll, cards will be distributed with the numbers already printed opposite the names of the Social Credit candidates. I urge you to follow the voting order indicated on these cards. We've got it all organized so that each candidate gets a proper share of first choices and so on in different zones of the city. If you follow this plan when you come to vote, and look for our cards, we'll make a clean sweep."

His six candidates tried to look confident that this would actually happen.

During this interminable detail, which kept his audience more rapt and silent than the Scona kids would ever be, I allowed my mind to wander. I gazed around the room and tried not to yawn openly. It seemed that the entire neighbourhood was there, many of them to view Albert on the platform. The main reason I had gone along was to have a first inside look at the place where I'd be starting my Grade Ten in the fall.

It was no bargain. It was a much older school than King Edward, with dark wood, blackened oily floors, and the fetid smells of long occupation. It seemed dingy and cramped, an ageing firetrap where I would have to spend the next three years or more because my parents believed in education (their only deity) and there wasn't any point leaving to become yet another unemployment statistic or a hobo. I began to get drowsy. Although it was cool outside, the mass of people in the gym had built up a sticky, thick heat.

A mention of beer woke me up and, I noted, brought Mr. Roothe upright from a low, bubbling snore.

Aberhart was referring to some letter that had been sent to all hotel owners warning them that Social Credit would put beer parlours out of business. Was this what my father meant by fascism?

"The opposition parties have permitted their candidates to stoop to anything, to fight fairly or foully against our movement. If they permit such things before the election, what can the people of Alberta expect if they get into office? I'm not spoofing you. If you vote for men who lie and misrepresent themselves before the election, don't squeal if they take all you've got after they get into power."

On he went, his skill and sincerity working up the audience into a quickening sense of excitement. After the mention of beer got him going, Aberhart was back into the style I had remembered at the Exhibition Grounds all those weeks ago.

Along our row of wooden, folding seats, where the neighbours had more or less clumped together, I saw warm smiles break out on faces I had always assumed were forever frozen. I saw them start to bob their heads with an animation never seen before. I caught the shine in their eyes, sparks shooting out from those I had thought incapable of fervour. I watched amazed as they jiggled, craned their necks, and waggled their heads. For the first time I had seen the long-suffering, quiet sleepwalkers having fun!

And, as I turned once again to Albert, seated at the end of the row of the six local candidates, I caught him carefully sizing up friends and neighbours. A broad grin lit up his face; he nodded to someone in the audience and pointed a finger at his leader.

"Atta boy, Albert," someone shouted behind me.

CHAPTER EIGHTEEN

THE WINDOW. SHADOWED AS IT WAS IN THE NARROW passageway between houses, my bedroom window showed the first scratches of the frost. That morning, Friday, August 16, there was a design of tiny jagged stars, white against the outside greyness, as though a distant shotgun blast had spattered its pellets during the night. I padded in bare feet on the cold boards to squint at the random beauty that had slipped through the screen. I stared at the pane of glass. Something was trying to edge into my consciousness, but it kept slipping away out of reach.

A nursery rhyme I thought I had long forgotten began to unravel, one I once had known by heart; it was from the six-volume *My Bookhouse*, the 1925 edition acquired by my parents during their first enthusiasm over having a son who had made it to the age of five.

> For, creeping softly underneath
> The door when all the lights are out,
> Jack Frost takes every breath you breathe
> And knows the things you think about.

Someone went downstairs and lit the gas furnace, and soon the hot-air registers creaked and snapped. In windbreaker, hands deep inside the pockets, I went out into the back yard where my grandfather was glaring at this last, low blow from the elements. White-coated blades of grass crackled and snapped off underfoot. The rows of potatoes, beans, and peas, their leaves already tattered from the hail, some of them partially buried where they had been pounded into the soil by the heavy rains, even the dahlias, were edged in white; and there were the black stains, the beginning of rot. Creeping softly underneath, as the nursery rhyme puts it, the frost not only finished off the gardens; it had destroyed the remaining crops in the countryside. There was nothing left for them now.

"And knows the things you think about. . . ."

An ominous note, as though J. Frost was a lurking deity checking up on the impure thoughts of the nursery set, hinting that they'd better not play doctor any more behind locked bathroom doors or a cold finger would freeze off their dinks. Had my own thoughts been stolen by the silent visitor? Or had he implanted something chilled in my own brain that was waiting to be thawed out?

After my attempts at deductive reasoning, my mind had slipped back into its usual state of low gear, the unaccustomed exercise having caused a few sprains upstairs. I had pretty well concluded there wasn't anything more I could do about Babe; my leads had all dried up; my assumptions had curled up like the leaves in the garden; and with Norm away, there was no one I could talk to about it. Yet, those stars on the window were trying to tell me something about someone who was no longer with us. But who?

They had gone. The last of the Cawners, Billy, was in a youth detention home. Once, when I had slunk down the alley, I had seen Mrs. Cawner; her bloodstained fur coat — possibly overlooked when the police repossessed their loot — worn over a ragged house-dress, she was feeding the chickens in the back yard, her soft cursing loud enough to deter me from stopping to ask about the health of her departed brood.

So, too, had the Thorpes gone, a yellow MacCosham van appearing one morning while Mrs. Thorpe stood alone on the sidewalk, watching. No one from the neighbourhood knew they had found a place over town or had turned up to help clean the house, as if it ever needed it. Even my mother's infallible intelligence system had failed on this one, and she had ventured out to say a few words of farewell, at least to find out where they were going; but she came back, her eyes downcast from Mrs. Thorpe's guttural, offhand rejection. Mr. Thorpe hadn't bothered to take the day off for the move. The Thorpes would soon be replaced by some bewildered family who would always be referred to as the "new people," and for years they would feel they had entered that neighbourhood as though arriving in the middle of a movie they didn't understand.

Then, too, I had been unable to resist an impulse to kick around in the strewn lumber from the demolished barn, until I looked up and saw Mr. Headley watching intently, his tanned neck reddening. For he knew, and he was right, that my poking around was a further attack on his integrity, that I was really asking: Was the tearing down of the barn what he had implied it was, a gesture to still the muttering tribe ("Come on, I'll show you Headley's barn where that kid hung himself"), to take away a grim local monument and erase its memories — or was it something else?

Usually amiable and tolerant of the ignorant young, Headley's voice that day, when he saw me poking around in the debris, was empty and flat.

"Still looking?"

I stopped.

I didn't know what more I could do about Babe, but there was something trying to get out, a hint on the window I couldn't read.

More and more, too, we found ourselves drawn into the election excitement and tension. Like the frost, it crept in under doors and, in fact, this advance touch of winter seemed to intensify the headlong search for an answer to blind forces, natural and economic. The day before the frost, the advance polls had been swamped and the police were called in to keep order.

"I can guess what that means," my father said gloomily. "Albert's going to make it, the whole damned lot of them."

Even my mother was beginning to get a little touchy. She lit a cigarette while another one was already burning in her ashtray.

"Is it really so bad, John?" she said.

Father's reaction was one of surprise. Startled by her fervour, or rather the hint of possible disloyalty, he dipped his knife into the golden tin of Empress Jam with its white ocean-liner forever sailing to parts unknown, and piled more of the gooey, red mess onto the concrete biscuits my mother, in a fit of energy unusual for her, had made that afternoon. It was a sign that the pressures she so carefully hid behind her library books and tobacco smoke were beginning to wear through her placid shell. There seemed to be a few more grey strands in her rich auburn hair.

As far as I could make out, their only flash-point of daily conflict was the mail. Mother refused to open any mail, even letters addressed to her—not, I think, out of sloth, but from a fear or distrust of the tales of woe from aunts or cousins who seemed to have joined in a contest to see if they could shake her up.

"Charlie cut off his left index finger today fixing the binder. Came running into the house and knocked over the cream separator, bruising my foot, so I'm all laid up. The kids have the measles and our dog was run over by a truck. Uncle Alf, the one with all the back trouble, has come to live with us since Trudy threw him out. Could you take him for awhile? Half the wheat is hailed out." And the like.

Possibly she simply didn't want to give up valuable fantasy time with her library books. Certainly she never opened an envelope that might contain a bill. When he got home, my father would take a kitchen knife, angrily slash open the mail, scan the contents, and dump the letters and bills onto the table, where my mother sanctified them with billowing cigarette smoke. I suspect it puzzled him: that she, who somehow quietly gathered in every crumb of gossip in the neighbourhood, could sardonically refuse to learn any news of their own kin.

Father stared at his biscuit, its crown of strawberry jam shaky on a thick layer of yellow butter. Blueberries were stuck hither and thither in the white baking-powder dough. He flicked one of the blueberries onto his plate as if it had been a dead fly, accidentally baked in.

"Oh, Albert's all right, I suppose," he said. It was a peace gesture, almost an apology for the derision he had heaped on his neighbour. "I guess they mean well. It's just—well, they're so sanctimonious, so sure of their economic rubbish and all the other stuff. You know they won't be able to put it in, and I suspect they know it too. That's what's wrong."

Grandpa got angry. "How do you know they won't? How do you know, eh? Least we can do is give them a chance. So why don't you just shut up and watch and see what they can do."

Arguments of this kind were causing indigestion, family rifts, and storming in and out of kitchens all over the province. Obscure jargon such as "monetization of credit" or "Just Price" filled kitchens with an exotic aroma. Those who couldn't talk with knowledge or supportively of these new ideas, or at least nod their heads in agreement, were outcasts. Anyone who dared to question the new gospel was declared an enemy, none with more contempt than the businessmen who ran the Economic Safety League, or the poor deluded twerps in the local Chamber of Commerce who went to the trouble of delivering to every household in the city a pamphlet entitled "The Dangers of Aberhart's Social Credit Proposals." The public yawned.

The target of these counter-thrusts, the great man himself, was fending them off during a heavy schedule of meetings across the city in crowded halls that reeked of Lifebuoy soap.

On Monday night he took care of his critics at Oliver school, then rushed on to the Edelweiss Club where he attacked the Economic Safety League by labelling its president with the ultimate insult: "a super-hetrodyne Liberal."

Tuesday night he was up in the north end in the Alberta Avenue Community Hall to follow with more scientific allusions.

"You don't have to know all about Social Credit theory before you vote for it. You don't have to understand electricity to make use of it, for you know that experts have put the system in and all you have to do is push the button and you get light. So all you have to do about Social Credit is to cast your ballot for it, and we'll get the experts to put the system in."

Then there was the rally we had attended at Scona on Wednesday night. The next evening, when he was in the west end at the Westmount Community Hall, Aberhart said something that brought back memories of Babe: "If we are so foolish and fanatical as they say we are, why don't they let us hang ourselves?"

An inadvertent ploy maybe, when so many of his audience had stood out on Portage Avenue to await the arrival of Will Rogers and Wiley Post, who were supposed to have been on their way to Edmonton. They never made it, but when a call went out to that crowd in Westmount Community Hall for a standing vote of Social Credit supporters, there was a clatter of chairs and everyone got to his feet.

Aberhart's last rally in the city was held Friday night at the Memorial Hall, known locally as the Legion Hall, where the vets consumed vast quantities of suds and argued about angels in the sky over Mons. On McDougall Drive, next to the main branch of the library, the Hall was only spitting distance from the Edmonton Club, the last post of the Economic Safety League and the Chamber of Commerce, where members could sit in deep armchairs and look through huge windows at the valley below and wonder if the remnants of their world were going to hell in a basket.

"Look me straight in the face," Mr. Aberhart told them. "Do I look as if I'm trying to put something over on you? I'm not running as a candidate. I don't want honours or a parliamentary post. If I can be of service when the members are elected, yes, but not otherwise. I don't need it."

To a mob of over a thousand, inside and outside the hall, perhaps taken away by the waves of teary hope that washed over him, he at last fell to temptation and held out even more expectation, possibly leaving them with their yearning to be near him, to touch him, to believe. For on that night he threw out a strong hint that the basic dividend to be paid to every bona fide citizen could well be seventy-five dollars a month instead of twenty-five. There was a hush in the hall when he said that, and a low gasp of anticipation whistled from the craning heads.

From one of the anterooms along the side of the auditorium, someone shouted out the final epithet of the campaign.

"You're crazy!"

Perhaps he was one of the besotted vets, or someone who just couldn't take the scientific talk of a new millennium any more. As irate supporters closed in on him, he fled and got through the overflow crowd gathered outside. Later he may have sat on the wooden railing along the Drive, as we used to do after the next war, and tossed beer bottles down the hill.

Except for his appearance on the Scona platform, Albert Roothe no longer had time to follow his leader around. In the last few days of the campaign he had apparently arranged to stay with some folks in his constituency, just south of the city. He had, so Jean told me later, also arranged a virginal bed for her in a nearby parsonage, more, she judged, to have her father's car handy for his frantic dash around the riding to transform his name into a household word.

The weather began to warm up again, but occasional thunderstorms turned the clay sideroads into soupy gumbo. Jean said she got muscles in her forearms wrestling the old Graham-Paige as it slithered, sometimes sideways, up or down a slope. Albert gave up his city shoes for thick socks and rubber boots into which he tucked the wide trousers we all wore in those days.

Once I overheard Mr. Headley tell my father that he had seen the two of them out in one of the shanty towns beyond the city limits where the watermains ended. When Headley came along in his cart to fill up the cream cans outside the front doors, he saw Albert rushing from door to door while Jean lurched along beside him in the mud-spattered car.

"Nothing like rubber boots to give ya the clodhopper look," Mr. Headley grinned. "He was loping along as if he'd been busting sod all his life."

On his one and only visit home one afternoon, a quick drop-in to pick up some more clothes, I couldn't help but notice how Albert's style had changed. As usual I was in the Roothe kitchen stuffing myself to compensate for the lousy meals we had at home. Albert left his rubber boots on the stoop and slid across the linoleum in his stocking feet, heavy grey socks with white caps on the toes. He hugged his mother, glared at me, then tilted back alarmingly on a kitchen chair while Mrs. Roothe piled up a lunch of breaded pork tenderloin on a plate. Already he seemed leaner, more tanned, with white sprays around his eyes from smiling at voters. Jean wasn't with him, having probably slipped off home to get some laundry done or something. Albert's mother darted around with some of her former sparrow-like energy while he recounted his deeds. This was the first thing I noticed about him, how his voice had slowed down from its normal machine-gun delivery to a kind of drawl, a slurring of words and the dropping of g's.

"Yes, ma'am," he was saying, "I figure we're gettin' a mighty fine reception from the folks. In an ordinary campaign it'd be nuts to go in at the last minute the way I've done, but all you hafta do is say you're the Social Credit man representin' Mr. Aberhart and the doors open up, the smiles come out as if they'd been kept in the root cellar. We're goin' to make it all right." He smirked. "Not sure how our boys are doin' in the city, but we're doin' fine."

As I soon found out, the new Albert had also absorbed a rural shrewdness in sizing up people. What I mean is he saw through me, perhaps had realized why I had gone along on his speaking foray, not out of any interest in the Movement or him, but to see Diane Thorpe for my own nefarious purposes. I would have thought he might have been appreciative of someone so concerned with the unexplained and sudden death of his younger brother, but he wasn't about to give anything away. When I asked him — with a feigned shyness — if I could come along on his rounds, he smiled with the sagacity of a farmer about to shoot down a sharp deal from a travelling salesman.

"'Fraid we don't have room for ya, Dougie." I could almost see a straw jiggling in his mouth. "But the city boys sure could do with some help. How'd it be I phone the South Side committee rooms or Mark Robertson, eh? They could probably use you on election day. You could round up a gang of your chums."

The look that came at me across the table was one of careful appraisal, and it said: Don't try to pull anything off on me kid, your interest is just a lot of hooey and I know it; I'm going to call your bluff.

Which he did. A lady from the committee rooms phoned, asked if I could come and bring any of the bunch who had bikes, and named an address on Whyte Avenue. With nothing else to do, I managed to corral five of the guys who thought there might be some dough in it. Their larcenous instincts were right: They paid us a dollar each in advance to stand outside the polling booths on election day and hand out the voting cards Mr. Aberhart had talked about at the Scona meeting. The lady in the committee rooms — she wore a white slouched hat with a black band and there were stains in the armpits of her blouse — told us the law required that we stand no closer than one hundred feet from a polling station.

"So if you're not a very good judge of distance and someone comes along and says you're standing too close to the poll, don't argue, move away — until they've gone. You'll have to be there before nine and stay around until the polls close at seven. I suggest you get your mothers to make lunches for you. It's going to be a long day, but it'll be a great one."

Then she gave us each a dollar bill and wrapped up bundles of the cards, which I hid under my bed that night so my father wouldn't confiscate them to burn in the oil drum out by the garage. Although he had assumed a passive role in the campaign (he didn't say so, but I can guess he had given up on the UFA and was awaiting greater things, a more decisive cause with the CCF) I felt it wasn't safe to leave enemy election stuff around the place. I stayed awake half the night trying to calculate what I could do with the dollar and, just before sleep, got the inspiration to spend half on flowers for Babe's grave.

That way, I figured craftily, I might not have to return the whole damned thing to repay my mother for the dollar I had stolen.

Witnesses to revolution, that's what we were.

On that bright warm morning in August the mobs, as if they had been stacked up, waiting in small cages, came pouring out of the rows of tiny frame houses. They came downstairs from attics, upper floors with hotplates on linoleum-covered sidetables, back rooms over grocery stores; they came upstairs from basements in the old two-storey buildings and homes put up during the pre-war land boom. The wooden sidewalks thundered with a clatter of heels pounding out a revolt as surely as if they had been carrying their shotguns and twenty-twos instead of the voting cards with the candidates named and numbered in bold type.

They marched in family or neighbourly clumps, in extended lines, in wedges or pairs, not to gather in the Market Square or the Legislature or the Civic Block to clamour for the heads of those who had betrayed them. Instead, they rushed to the big let-down of doing number work on long sheets of paper. Truckloads of men from the relief camps as far away as Jasper rumbled through the streets, brought to the city to be sworn in and vote.

There had never been anything like it. Before nine in the morning there were line-ups of dozens, scores, even hundreds, crammed around school doors, houses, or community halls, all itching and ready to burst in and work their way through twenty-seven names on the ballot paper, enough to give pause to any revolutionary.

Before noon the polls were overwhelmed and the panic-stricken electoral officers sent out calls for more pencils, for carpenters to slap together more booths, for police to keep order.

And they kept coming, jamming up in lines to wait for an hour or more while the bemused voters inside the booths struggled over their complex decisions, some of them openly marking their numbers on ballots held against a wall or on their knees, some of them naively asking the poll clerks how to vote, some snitching the markers so that the deputy returning officers had to send out for pencils, cleaning out every stationery store in town.

By one in the afternoon the tide was still rolling in, even though over half of those on the lists had already voted.

"Are elections always like this?" I asked the old geezer who had been paired with me to hand out cards at King Edward school.

He was shrivelled, with bandy legs, and he sweated in suit and vest, heedless of the warmth. His crinkly eyes were hopped up with nothing more than the flush of being in the vanguard of the revolution, as people snatched the cards from his hands and he told them how to mark their ballots for Social Credit. But I never learned his name. Although he was friendly enough, and actually a lot of fun, he obviously regarded me as a kid, and you didn't give your name to kids.

As the day went on, we sneaked closer and closer to the school, moving right into the groups of voters lined up at the big double doors to make sure they had the correct order of numbers for the Social Credit candidates.

"Nah," said the old geezer. "It's the biggest ever, and it's all going to be for us."

We were at Poll Number 30, the old guy told me, of 40 voting locations in the city containing a total of 171 polls. The school, he explained, contained 9 "split" polls for the bulk of those in our area of the South Side. At least fifty people had lined up before nine o'clock, just when we were ripping the wraps off our parcels of cards. A lot of the early starters were women, including my mother and grandparents. Father had said he'd drop in on his way home from the university, as if, he said gloomily, that would make any difference to the outcome.

Someone came out of the door, pushing his way through the crowd.

"Was in there for half an hour," he told a neighbour. "Took the fellow in front of me twenty-five minutes to mark his ballot. What a mess!"

One of the city candidates (I remembered him on the Scona platform) cruised up and down the line, shaking hands and exhorting his supporters to talk to their neighbours before they went in. As he left for his car a small cheer and spatter of applause came from the crowd.

"Is he allowed to do that?" I asked my aged partner.

"Who's to stop him?"

At that point, Eddy Weir, one of my pals who'd been dishing out cards at another entrance, came running around the building with a policeman loping after him. He sought shelter with the wise old party man who seemed to know everything.

"This lad was inside the poll," the cop said. "And you guys move out to your hundred feet. Watch it!"

"You'll be sorry when we get in," my partner told him.

The cop grinned. "Not the way I voted, I won't."

"Must be one of ours," said the old geezer. He told Eddy to go on back with the others and to stay his distance as long as the cop was around.

On they came until I had to ride my bike over to the

committee room for more cards. The workers in the committee room were jumping around as though they could sense what was happening outside at the polls. Someone was arguing that they had too many cars and drivers hanging around, that the fine weather had inspired people to walk to the polls instead of calling in for free lifts. At noon, back at the poll, we asked one of the other kids to hand out cards while the old man and I sat down in the shade of a poplar tree on the front lawn, an area that had been forbidden to us kids all the years we had been at the school.

After lunch I slipped over to a nearby lane to take a leak behind a garage, and came back to see yet another mob arriving and lining up on the cement steps. The two of us moved up and down the grinning ranks, passing out more cards.

"If it takes one man twenty-five minutes to vote," I asked the old guy, "how long'll it take them to count the ballots?"

"You really want to know?" He pushed a card at a man who refused to take it. "Come on now, sir, this is your ticket to a better future, a finer way of life for us all."

The man took the card, scowled at it, and tore it up.

"What's his name?" the geezer growled. "Somebody tell me his name. He ain't going to get his twenty-five bucks." There were snickers in the waiting line. "Damnedest system you ever saw, kid. Guess I don't have to give you a card, Mrs. Ames, you'll mark it the right way. After the polls close at seven they sort out the ballots by first choices into twenty-seven separate piles, the number of candidates, see? Then they go over town and they start with the first choices and go through the second choices and so on down the line till six of them have reached their quota. May take them a couple of days before we get the final count."

"Sure sounds complicated."

"That's why we got these cards, kid. If we can pile up heavy surpluses for the Social Credit candidates, we'll get them all in. And that's what we're going to do."

As old men often are, he was wrong.

Late into the night, when the radio was spouting out the results of the Social Credit sweep across the province, the City of Edmonton stood out as a maverick, a collection of sceptics or a sufficient number of burghers with property to fear the onset of Social Credit. By eleven the radio announced that the Liberal leader, Howson, the one with the failing voice, had been elected on the first count. He had gotten his quota of first choices, so he was home free. The radio announcer said that Howson's second choices would now be distributed for the next count.

But elsewhere in the province it was a sweep, with Social Credit elected in twenty-one ridings, leading in thirty-eight.

"Looks like a split vote in the city," my father said with a faint smile.

"There'll be at least two Liberals," I said smugly.

"How do you know that?"

"With Howson's surplus, there's got to be."

"By God, Dougie, at least I taught you something."

I didn't tell him that it hadn't been him, but a geezer with wispy white hair and crinkled eyes who ran like a fiend up and down the lines of waiting voters, pressing upon them his Social Credit cards.

By nine the trends were in on the radio making it clear that Abie had his majority, an enormous surge of faith, hope, and a good gamble on charity, namely, twenty-five dollars a month. Along Whyte Avenue there were cars tooting their horns and there were bunches of people gathered around the Social Credit committee rooms, laughing and whacking each other on the back.

This was exciting enough, but I wanted to rush home and find out what had happened to Albert. My father had taken the unprecedented step of spending a nickel for the *Journal* extra, but there was nothing in it about Strathcona-White Mud.

"Must be a close one then," he said with some self-satisfaction.

It wasn't. The only reason for the delay was the scattered nature of the constituency, the difficulty of gathering the bits and pieces together. Shortly after eleven P.M. the radio had it.

"Albert Roothe, an Edmonton high-school teacher, has been declared elected for Social Credit in Strathcona-White Mud. Here are the results provided by phone by the returning officer: Boland, UFA, 201 first choices; Bower, Liberal, 452; Moffatt, Conservative,

103; and Roothe, Social Credit, 1,539. Roothe declared elected on the first count."

The phone rang.

It was Albert's father asking everyone to come over and have beer. He hadn't gone out to his son's committee room because he had been busy all day, running up taxi fares as he rushed around to hammer together more voting booths. In the Roothes' front room I was offered a Coke and stood in the doorway to watch the adults, their conversation stilled as they clustered around the radio, listening to the excited voices describing the incoming tidal wave.

Tears glistened in the creases on Mrs. Roothe's shrunken face, and she came over to clutch my hand as though she had lost two sons and was afraid her adopted son would also go from her forever.

When the votes were finally counted, there were fifty-six Social Credit members elected, none of them with any previous legislative experience. The Liberals got five and the Conservatives two. The United Farmers of Alberta didn't elect a single member. In the city Albert Roothe had the last laugh. Only two of the Social Credit candidates filtered through the twenty-seven names on the ballots to win seats. They were Barnes and Mullen. Three of the other city seats went Liberal and one Conservative, with their leader Duggan elected.

When Albert finally showed up at home the next day, my dad and I went over to shake his hand. Already there seemed to be a change in him. Thin as he was from gadding around to the shacks, the farm houses, the grain elevators, and the general stores, he seemed to have gained a weightiness, a kind of ponderous awe at what had happened to him. It left me with a sense that he would be thin and jumpy no more, but would gradually expand into a heavier person, more thoughtful and careful, brow furrowed as the beginnings of a pot began to push against the vest of his new navy-blue suit. I noticed, too, that his gaze, once so intent and piercing, boring into you with the death ray of his beliefs, had become looser, more fluid. He could hold onto your eyes for only a moment or two, then his stare became unfixed, passed over you and looked beyond, either to greet another constituent or someone of more influence, or to contemplate what they had done and what they now had to do to bring the people the results they had voted for. That night our prairie tract leaped to world attention.

People sat up and took notice of this first glimmer of a new era of monetary reform, a way of reviving the dead capitalist system, a means of giving the people control over their own destiny by driving the money-lenders from the tabernacles, a grass-roots expression of popular will that would make parliaments no longer necessary.

It held out an answer to the dull heresy of communism and the brutality of ascendant fascism.

It was the way out.

The Dean of Canterbury wired William Aberhart: "The Douglas scheme is the fulfilment of Christ's teachings: 'Here are the hungry, let us feed them.'"

In the City of London there was a parade of men in green shirts to celebrate the victory. They gathered on Threadneedle Street and marched seven times around the Bank of England.

In California a doctor named Francis Townsend read the omens and came up with a plan to give everyone over the age of sixty two hundred dollars a month. Three and a half million people became adherents of the Townsend Plan.

The next week Albert Roothe went off to Calgary for the first Social Credit caucus meeting. He was among those who gave Mr. Aberhart unanimous authority to select his own cabinet. They offered him any seat he wished to select.

The caucus meeting took only fifteen minutes.

On being asked when the basic dividends would be paid, Mr. Aberhart told the press: "No person can say just how soon we will be ready to pay the basic dividends, because we don't know what difficulties may arise in the pathway of building the foundations of a new social order."

As the first frost had done, the clue sneaked up on me in the night. Sometime around midnight, maybe about the hour Babe had left his bedroom forever, I awakened from another nightmare into a bright moonlight. The window again. I padded over and stared out at the brilliant stillness and felt the slight breeze, clammy on my sweaty pyjamas. How long I stood there, I don't know, but I do remember pushing up the sill of the inner glass window. Then I unhooked the screen and tried to jiggle it around and take it off from the inside. There was a groove that held it in place and the four outer tabs made it impossible to push out. It rattled and refused to move.

Lights came on. I heard my father muttering sleepily and making his way around from room to room until he arrived outside my door. He opened it carefully. By this time I had returned to my bed, but did go through the motions of sitting up when the hall light hit my face.

"Sorry, Dougie. You hear anything outside? Thought there might be prowlers."

I managed to rub my eyes and shake my head. He left and went back to bed, and from the dining-room I heard my parents' sleepy voices wondering.

As I stared open-eyed at the ceiling, I realized I had at last found out something about that night when Babe had gone. Someone else must have been outside to push the retaining tabs on the screen into a vertical position so it could be lifted off. Babe must have unhooked the screen from the inside, dressed in his whoopee pants and running shoes, set himself carefully onto the grass, and made his way to the barn.

Someone had called on him. There had been a message. From whom, and what was it?

I didn't find the answer that summer.

CHAPTER NINETEEN

ABOUT A YEAR AFTER I HAD SEEN JEAN IN LONDON I WAS twenty-four and a captain, but with the mental age of sixty-five.

A lot of us were like that. We had gone through the process of survival, which meant getting wounded early enough to miss the shattering counter-attacks after the landings and to come back later when the enemy was beginning to unravel that superb fighting machine. You start getting surrenders after a casual fire-fight, and you get so many prisoners you can't take them off in small clumps to look for those with the underarm tattoos so they can be taken aside and shot.

From those early wounds I still get the occasional wandering splinter of metal poking through the skin on a finger or toe. When that happens I slit the skin and use my wife's eyebrow tweezers to pull it out, then I wash it under the tap, a gleaming antiseptic memory of a long time ago. My daughter Anne says I should try floating in the middle of our circular pool without moving and I'd probably end up pointing north, a handy compass for any low-flying aircraft.

The ageing, the constant fatigue, some said could have been avoided had I, like them, stayed a private and turned down the commission. There has always been that ambition inside me. Look at the business I've built up today, which the government is now plundering in the same way we would go through an occupied town. But there is also the sybarite who likes nice clothes, sheets on the bunk when back in barracks, the better food officers get no matter what they protest to the others, and someone to shine shoes and buttons in the days when a batman wasn't just a comic-strip character.

It was when I was a captain, ancient and crafty at twenty-four, that the first rocket brought the answers and the second destroyed both the only evidence and my own certainty that I had really found the solution.

By that time I had been through enough of their ancient cities not to gawk any more at the solid masonry buildings, which made even our brick ones back home seem flimsy, or at the cobble-stoned pavements; and not to believe that the war would really change anything. Even where the explosives had torn out the innards, leaving the stone walls, the buildings exuded the trapped gases and smells of centuries, leaking a protective musk, a minor haemorrhage of bottled culture and slyness that told us: You will pass through and we will go on unchanged as we always have. There are no comparable smells in the new world.

The weekend before Christmas 1944 I had gone in to Antwerp on some Civil Affairs' business and maybe to do a bit of shopping. I was having a respite, detached from my unit for awhile because of yet another splinter in the calf of my left leg. This was more of an accident than anything, the result of overconfidence when, in November, we reached the Mastgat, north of the East Scheldt. Contempt of mortars, that's what did me in that time, a tendency to wander around too close to them when they were plunking down in soggy ground.

But that's neither here nor there. The point is I was scratched up enough for light duty and sent off to Civil Affairs in a town just inside the Belgian frontier, where a problem had developed concerning spies and collaborators in the local civic administration. I had taken a jeep into Antwerp to pick up two women who had been in the underground; they would, it was said, sort out the situation in the town in a hurry and would have the necessary papers to identify any unreliable types. They also had the authority to have the collaborators shot or hanged if that's what they felt had to be done.

After lunch at the officers' hotel near the station, I decided Antwerp was too hot for any hanging around or shopping. The buzzbombs and the V-2's were pouring in that day, destroying the old port city. From the rim of our new world came the rattletrap buzzbombs and the more deadly silent missiles, unheard and unseen, from somewhere above the bulging grey overcast. Without any more fooling around, I made the rendezvous with the two women, and the four of us, including my driver, set out to return to the town near the frontier.

The two Belgian women sat together in the back seat, their identical hair pulled back from pinched faces, as if the good rations they were now getting hadn't yet been soaked up into their tissues. Nor, it seemed, could they put aside their dangerous years in the underground, for they both wore American field jackets, issue pistols in web holsters, and each had a grenade hooked carelessly on her top pocket.

Both women spoke English, but they stared at me with such glittering, bitter amusement I couldn't get any small talk out of them, even with the bottle of excellent red wine I passed around. Perhaps because of it, their wrong assumption that I had liberated it from some house: Who knows? We pulled away from the central railway station near the empty zoo and headed along the main drag where Christmas shoppers tried to put on an act of normalcy, refusing to glance up into the sky.

In this strained silence we were on our way when the V-2 rocket hit the Rex Theatre full of a matinée crowd, mainly troops on leave. There were twelve hundred or so people killed instantly by that one warhead tumbling out of space.

And, as I found out much later, one of the dead was Jean Cullen, who had just been sent to the Continent with a CWAC detachment. I almost joined her under one of those little white crosses.

That same rocket tried to slit my throat. To this day I have a wavy white line that extends from the hairline in front of my right ear, down the face, and under the jawbone. It looks like some kind of pale tropical worm trapped and frozen under the skin, coming alive when I talk, trying to break out. My teen-age daughter Anne is always after me to grow a beard, but my wife quietly tells me afterwards that she doesn't want the fine skin of her inner thighs prickled by bristles. Thank God for electric razors.

The eruption of sound, hellish gases, and volcanic rubble launched our jeep off the cobblestones, the hands of my driver, Corporal Thomas, who was already dead, still on the wheel. As we crashed back down again, I was flung head first through a plate-glass window, noting clearly in the concussed silence of my skull that it had diamond patterned tapes to prevent flying glass. But it had shattered anyway with enough jagged edges to nearly slit my throat.

The odd thing was that I got up almost immediately and walked past the tilted cash register in the store as if I had just been haggling over some ration coupons. A flap of skin hanging down over my collar and the warmth soaking through into my chest, I opened the door of the shop and stepped out into the silent duststorm of the street. The street, of course, wasn't silent: It was just my concussion.

Outside the shop, my eyes stinging with the dust and smoke, I stopped long enough to remove the small field dressing we carried in the right front pocket of our battle-dress, tore off the tab, and held it against my ripped jaw. The jeep had landed sideways on one of the two women, squashing her across the chest so that her grenade had been imbedded in her lungs.

She was dead. Red soda-pop foam gave colour to her lips.

In the haze I couldn't see the other one and I couldn't bring myself to go any closer to the body of Thomas, who lay nearby, his feet towards me and his jacket smouldering. When I saw the square hulk of the first ambulance approaching through the smoke, I had enough sense to press myself up against the overturned jeep, one arm looped through the bent roll bar so they could see me, so I wouldn't be run over or left for dead in the confusion. Hanging by one arm I propped myself against the vehicle, did a quick but useless wrap-around of the field dressing over my head to try and stop the blood flow, made sure I could see more ambulances coming up and figures running through the eerie and soundless chaos.

As the dust began to settle I could see that only one wall was left of the Rex Theatre. The rocket had brought down the ceiling and killed them all in a torrent of falling rubble.

I wish I could remember what the movie was that day. I try to think of Jean sitting there, maybe with someone else she had met, nibbling on a chocolate bar sent in the latest parcel from home, away from the war and packed in with all the others exuding the oily disinfectant of worn battle-dress, savouring the ninety minutes' reminder of our own culture in the flickering images, perhaps believing that this was the way we really lived in the new world: that the film was reality and not the silent missile tumbling at random out of the grey overcast. It must have been instant, as they say, but I wonder if there are last pinpoints of consciousness, a final microscopic flash of memory or a second's montage of those of us who made up her past. Did she see Albert then? Or, I have always hoped, perhaps she had a last glimpse of me leaning over her in our clammy bed in the hotel on Half Moon Street.

There was a blurred Christmas in a civilian hospital in Antwerp until they got the paperwork sorted out, or needed the beds, and I was doped up for a chilly ride in one of our ambulances to one of our own hospitals in Holland. By that time I had been refilled with plasma, stitched up like the proverbial monster, and probed and X-rayed. They said I was really getting somewhere when I stopped shouting in order to hear my own voice, although they warned me against getting into any arguments that might pull the stitches along the jawline.

The final tangible proof of recovery was the issuance of out-patient blues, the shapeless blue-denim jacket and slacks with white shirt and orange tie that people pay over a hundred bucks for these days as pre-wrinkled leisure outfits. Contrary to what you might think, most of us were so grateful to be restored, to recover, that we didn't think it through — although we joked about it — that the patched corpus was once again on its way to becoming certifiable cannon fodder.

The blues meant one could walk out, at first only a turn around the building, weak and shivering in a greatcoat in the watery winter sun. Then the body thermostat begins to adjust and you start taking longer walks, rushing back famished to delectable mounds of sticky rice, grey mutton, and soggy balls of brussels sprouts.

The hospital was in an old convent—there were so many convents and seminaries around, one wondered if they had been built just so they could be used for something else in wartime—some distance from a town between the Maas and the Waal, not too far from Nijmegen. All we could do was explore the frozen muddy grounds or hang around the officers' canteen, where you had to have a special chit to get a beer, otherwise you were stuck with tea, coffee, or Perrier water which had apparently been liberated by the caseload. The convent was shaped like an E with one wing for officers and the other two wings, each three storeys, for what the army used to call "other ranks."

One sleety day I crossed the invisible boundary, pacing the deck indoors, and found myself in the farthest wing for other ranks, where I decided to prowl around to see if there was anyone from my unit. I was careful to skitter past the intensive-care wards and, eyes averted, the surgeries and the sickening traffic of mobile stretchers lined up in the halls.

On the second floor I had peered into a long room I quickly identified as one for loonies, and was about to go on my way when I found myself looking into a pair of familiar, motionless grey eyes. He was sitting on the edge of his bed in a blue dressing-gown, hands clasped between his thighs, and from his place just inside the door, he sat unmoving, still as death. The skull flesh was stretched and yellow, the hair lank and sparse, reminding me of his father, but there was no mistaking who it was.

"Pete," I said. "Pete Thorpe?"

CHAPTER TWENTY

THERE WAS NO ANSWER. THE EYES WERE FIXED ON SOMETHING beyond the wall as though he was peering into the ether for someone new to copy.

I motioned to a passing sister.

"I know him," I told her. "We grew up together. What happened?"

"You do?" She must have been in her late twenties, but she had whitish hair. The nurse went over and checked the charts and documentation at the foot of Pete's bed while I stared at his blank face and wondered why he hadn't been evacuated farther back, where the specialists could work on him. "You sure you know him?"

"Yes, Pete Thorpe. An old buddy. What's wrong with him?"

"Well, for one thing he's a non-ID. They've sent off his fingerprints, but you know how long that takes. When he was picked up he didn't have dog tags, paybook, or anything personal on him, not even a snapshot or wallet. He was wearing coveralls and he had no unit flashes of any kind. No one in the area seemed to know who he was and Casualty Clearing even wondered if he was one of ours at all. Hasn't said a word, but obviously understands English. So you're sure, eh? Look, if you feel up to it, I'd like to have you talk to Dr. Knowles and the chaplain. Okay?"

Before we left, I spoke quietly to him.

"Pete, it's me. Doug Sayers."

There was no response.

"Doug Sayers, Pete. I'll call for you on the way to school tomorrow."

"Watch that," said the nurse. "I don't know if that's the right way. We'd better talk to Dr. Knowles first."

She stopped off to have a word with the head nurse on her floor, then led me down the wide stairs to the ground floor and into a kind of cell that was furnished with beautifully carved antiques. Dr. Knowles was in, an exhausted pale man with glasses and a greying border of hair around his ears. His white smock was dirty and he was sighing over a stack of forms. The nurse told him her story. I introduced myself, then she ran off to find the chaplain. Dr. Knowles waved me to a fragile drum-shaped chair which had inlaid pearl in the arms. The chaplain, a worried-looking type with army-issue steel-rimmed glasses, joined us while the doctor fished out Pete's file.

"So you're sure you know him, eh?" Dr. Knowles leafed through the file. "He's only been here a week. Was picked up away over at Kapelsche Veer on the Maas Channel, you know, where those paratroop kids were giving us such a hard time. He was found in an SAR tank that'd been hit by a Panzerschreck. Recovery crew found him huddled in a corner. Well, you know what those things do."

I said indeed I did.

"Now, no one could've survived in there, and so they say he must have crawled in after it happened, but no one knew him or could identify him. Field Ambulance took him to Casualty Clearing who sent him along the line. He was shunted around a bit and ended up here for transfer to Number One Neurological, except I've got a whole ward of S-5's up there and we can't fly them out — the weather or lack of transport or the Neurological is all filled up, I don't know. I'm getting the runaround and I'm going to need the space next week."

This was the end of January 1945 and we knew there was a build-up going on.

"You know," the doctor went on. "It's no secret. The big U-turn to clear the Rhine and the Maas — all that bush, we'll be full up. You tell me, you've been all through it: How come we get the dirty ones, Caen, the Scheldt, and now this? We're taking over every school, convent, or anything we can find. You heard who we're up against? The First Parachute Army, for chrissake."

Knowles had the puffy jowls of someone who overeats to kill the stomach pains.

"Is there anything I can do?"

"You can help me trace him now," the chaplain said. "We can get a letter off to the family — it'll be a blessed relief for them."

"What I meant was, should I try to talk to him or anything?"

Dr. Knowles glanced at the nurse and bit at his thumbnail.

"I'm not a psychiatrist. Oh, if I had the time, some drugs, maybe a bit of shock therapy and he'd come out of it. But who's got the time? He should be back under proper care. They all should be. Look, I don't see any harm. Use your head, your common sense. Be careful and see me if there's any sign of violence or further deterioration. What the hell's there to lose? What d'you say, Padre?"

"Captain Sayers seems like a responsible person. It could help, I suppose."

"Okay, then, we'll draw some blues and you can sign him out under your care whenever you want, as long as you let the sisters know exactly where you are and what you're doing. Try getting him outside and walking him around. How long are you likely to be here? May be back sooner than you think. Well, take him outside, dredge up some common memories, and see what happens." He moved his head around as if the entire psychiatrists' association, or whatever they have, was behind him listening in.

"Try it. Try anything. Who cares?"

He threw the file back onto the desk.

Now don't expect me to give any kind of rational analysis of the forces that plunged me into messing around with a human's mind and later his emotions. We were all messed up: The stresses of war hit us in different ways. Even Norm Fetterman, who was always walking into things, one day kept ploughing ahead when everyone else wasn't moving, until he got far enough to win the Military Medal. Yet he too had his moments, which he told me about after the war, when we hung around briefly at the Legion to see who was going to show up.

Belching and a bit glassy-eyed after his eighth beer, Norm told me how it had hit him.

"Right out of my head," he admitted when I told him — not all of it, of course — about finding Pete Thorpe in the loony wing.

Norm had been with the First Brigade in Italy, and after Ortona and all the mouseholing house-to-house, he had gone temporarily crackers. He pinched all the loot from his pals and wandered around trying to give it back to the Eyties. With little success, as it turned out. They were understandably suspicious or, when he pressed jewellery or some artifact on them, they in turn offered him mama or the nearest sister or a bottle of vino. Norm couldn't make them take anything back, and he came to his senses after some of his comrades, incensed at the theft of their loot, dumped him into a shit pit. Shock treatment. I wondered what would have worked for Pete, but I recall how determined I was to do something for him.

So there are probably several explanations, some of them deep. Maybe it was partly that old sense of community that surfaces when you're far away from home, the compulsion to help a neighbour who was never really a pal; but that was also combined with a need for a diversion from the boredom. A sense of pity was mixed with the callousness that warfare breeds in the young; and I needed, too, to indulge my curiosity as a contrast to the careful detachment of day-to-day comradeship back at the unit, where you don't get too close to others when they may die, become horribly injured, or just go away. And also the old ego.

For I knew something the doctor didn't. I knew that Pete Thorpe was the greatest mimic I'd ever met, and that it was just possible he had slipped away and crawled into that tank to play a role. I knew about those years when his puniness and cowardice — a fear of personal contact or even a casual touch — would send him skittering away from any sports or to the edges of the crowd when horseplay loomed, slipping out of the melee with a stream of wisecracks from radio, somehow perfected in a household where no radio was allowed.

Because we were rarely in that household we never knew

how he did it, but I suppose that somewhere in his tiny room was a crystal set, the copper wire painstakingly wrapped around the cardboard tube from inside a roll of toilet paper, the crystal and needle itself nailed down on a small board, and the earphones and wire for the aerial all rolled up in some secret niche in that small house where there wouldn't be much space that wasn't bulging with something. I had decided perversely to probe the recesses of his mime, and went at it crudely and with that aforesaid callousness because my time, too, was short.

The first day I deliberately clasped tightly onto his arm and led him like a blind man down the stairs and out into the grounds, past where they were unloading piles of metal cots for the imminent wave of fresh victims, and along the path that led to the gardening sheds out of sight of the main building. I kept up a running patter about shared childhood memories, when he suddenly shook off my grip and stopped. I clutched his arm again and was brushed away. I tried to imitate the nasal tones of a famous comedian, then walked on a few steps ahead.

When I checked on him, he was following along. I figured that was enough for one day—my own head was starting to ring again—and I turned him around. He followed me to the edge of the gardening sheds and stopped, until I again took his arm and led him back to the hospital.

"Either you're coming out of it, or you're a fake, Thorpe," I said.

The next day I felt much better, so decided to give it a real try. Instead of invoking our joint past—those dusty gravel streets with the small wooden bungalows pressed side by side—I tried another tack. Over and over again I told him how lucky he was that the war was over for him, but not for me: I had to go back (possibly not true) and would never see him again. I asked him to take the word back home because he'd soon be there; he was one lucky stiff.

Pete's immobile features gave nothing away, but then his eyes did blink. We're getting there, I told myself, but how long? Is there time?

During the crib game in the ward that night everybody

remarked on the rumble of hardware going up the road outside the convent, on the way to the Reichswald no doubt. After lights out I thought up yet another stratagem for the next day.

Right after breakfast I picked up Pete and, instead of heading towards the sheds at the back, led him through the growing boxes of medical supplies piled up at the front door, in the direction of the steady thunder of the stuff going up the road. And that's where I made my breakthrough, even — as it turned out — if that equipment wasn't enough for the other big breakthrough, its fate to become rusty, bogged hulks in the flooded lowlands.

The armoured fighting vehicles we used in that distant war were ferocious in appearance, but so fragile they had to be transported to the arena in much the same way, say, as you might ship a lion in a cage through traffic so it won't injure itself. On huge multi-wheeled platforms these siege engines — some of them, indeed, had zooish names: Buffalo, Weasel, Kangaroo — were delicately lifted to their arena. It was their endless rumble we had been hearing back in the wards.

Pete Thorpe had allowed me to lead him to the growing tidal noise at the iron gates of the convent where, as luck for the pseudo-therapist would have it, one of the transports had broken down and its cargo, blurred in a camouflage shroud, was clanking its way backward down the ramp on the verge of the roadway where it had pulled over. I noted the tank had red fluorescent panels on its hull and turret, a sure guarantee it'd be strafed by our own planes.

Military policemen flailed their arms, trying to keep the oncoming stream moving: more tanks, personnel carriers, bridging equipment, and every kind of field gun in the book. This was going to be a big one, all right, and I was glad I wouldn't be there. I studied the Sherman that now rested on the ground in front of us. Part of its veil had been pushed back, like a mourning widow who lights up a cigarette, so the driver could keep his head outside, a trophy mounted on the forward deck.

At first Pete Thorpe did nothing more than stop, listening to the screeches and whines of metal and engine with his head cocked to one side. So, as I suspected, he could hear. At this point I became unforgivably cruel.

"There it is, Pete. They brought it back just for you. Go take a look. See how they've cleaned it up. Go look inside."

The regret did not come until later, after much reflection amid the heaving snuffles of a sleeping ward, that most terrible of night sounds: the crunch of grinding teeth by a sleeping neighbour — you'd think he'd be down to mashed and splintered stumps by morning.

Then, and only then, was there one of those sudden drops into nocturnal insight, when it came to me that there was a strain of placid arrogance in the Sayers, its daily appearance in my mother's soft-voiced dissection of our neighbours, mumbled from behind a library book and flowing as one of her thin gravies over the mashed potatoes at the supper hour.

Now I had taken my supper-table conditioning to another level, a much more dangerous one.

Not that Pete Thorpe reacted in any of the ways I had envisaged. There was no way I could have foreseen what it was he perceived in front of him; or that somewhere beyond those blank eyes he had made a decision to risk retaining his pose (mustn't get sent back) while, I realized later, making use of our short time together to unburden himself of the complicity he had kept locked up all those years. For he did shuffle over to the tank where it now sat tilted on the gravel shoulder, and he did seem to be seeing it for the first time. He didn't seem to notice the others standing around waiting for the village idiot in rumpled blue to do something they could laugh at.

Pete acted as though the tank was not there at all. He lifted a corner of the draped green-and-brown camouflage netting, snuggled in under it, and sat with his back against the bogey wheels, cross-legged and humming to himself within the porous tent. He extended one hand as if holding out a candle. The crew, in their black coveralls, possibly at last realizing this could happen to them, began to call at him to come on out and finally turned to me to do something about it.

As I moved forward to lift away the netting, it came back to me.

When we had been much younger, around twelve or so, the

Roothes had let Babe, Norm, me, and some others put up a hut in their back yard, a flimsy thing framed by badly nailed two-by-fours that we then covered with pungent gunny-sacking redolent of dusty potatoes. When we were seen trying to entice a couple of girls to come in with us for some feels, Mr. Roothe told us to take it down. We stalled as long as we could, of course, and it was Pete who saved us the trouble. He had brought some candles he had no doubt pinched during one of the mystic rites held by one of those strange sects his father was always joining. Not knowing of Mr. Roothe's ultimatum, he offered them to us for any nocturnal trysts we might have there in the hut — if he could have the privilege of watching.

Except his father came storming out of the house next door in that crazy, jerky way of his, and roared at Pete to bring back the candles and stay away from that den of sin. Pete was so startled that he dropped a candle he had just lit to demonstrate how he could make a monster nose with melted wax. Whoosh. Up went the gunny sack in a whomph of blue smoke that sent us running for the garden hose.

And this was where Pete Thorpe was sitting now, cross-legged in that hut, holding the candle in front of him and mashing imaginary wax onto his nose. I was so pleased at his flash connection with our joint past that I waved away the black-coveralled ones and joined in the game.

"Pete, your dad's here and is yelling for you to return the candles."

The voice was a familiar deep bass from the radio. "Yo tell de Kingfish I'se stayin' here at de lodge till Sapphire come an git me."

I did my best to cope in the gravelly tenor of the partner, although I had never personally been a fan of that show.

"Now you come on outa dere, Brother; that place about to burn down."

Then I switched to my own voice.

"Come on, Pete, it's on fire."

As he scrambled out from under the camouflage netting, I took his arm and led him, apparently relapsed into his withdrawn state, through the gate while the tank crew watched and tapped their heads. On the way back through the grounds I tried to keep the train of thought open, but Pete was having none of it. I walked him quickly back to the loony wing, left him sitting on the bed with a sister watching him, and searched out Dr. Knowles to break the good news. I found him in his office where he was peering into the eyes of a strait-jacketed victim propped up in a chair. Knowles wasn't wearing his usual soiled smock, and for the first time I noticed his major's crowns. Apparently he was one of those who regarded himself as a civilian in uniform; everyone around the place always referred to him as "doctor."

"Look at this one. Casualty Clearing straps him down, checks his blood pressure, then sends him on to us."

I let him ramble and thought about the grisly traffic they had to move out of the Casualty Clearing Stations: Patch, sew, and bind, and get them out fast. I was about to leave when Doctor (or Major) Knowles raised his eyebrows and asked me a silent question.

"It's Thorpe, sir. I got him to say something. What should I do now?"

Dr. Knowles turned his head and snarled: "Go back to your ward and stay there. You're getting in over your head." He put down the little gadget with the searchlight in its end. "Sorry. Be careful, eh? He won't be here much longer. I finally got them to clear some space back at Neurological. We'll be loaded here in the next few days."

"What'll happen to him there?"

"If they can do something he'll have to stay in and take what's coming to him. If not, he goes home with an S-5 and a discharge."

When I saw the chaplain and told him about my shock treatment with Pete, he shook his head and muttered, "Poor soul," and gave me such a stare I wondered if he was referring to Pete or me.

"Your lead about starting with Military District Thirteen was useful," he went on. "They've traced a P.J. Thorpe with an M regimental number who joined up in April 1942, was posted to the Service Corps, took his training at Red Deer, came to the U.K. in October 1943, was at Farnborough. I expect more details from

Army HQ very shortly. The Provost people are interested now, think it could be a desertion case. Which isn't good. We still can't cable any next-of-kin, not till we're sure. No word yet from CMHQ on his fingerprints."

Now we had really opened up a can of worms. I was too restless to settle down for my post-lunch nap. The constant rumble from the passing traffic was getting on my nerves. A rare sun had bestowed a hint of warmth, and almost everyone who could move had gone outside to cluster around the gates and watch the parade they would thankfully pass up. The card tables were empty. Irritated at officialdom and myself, full of the good old Sayers' malice, I went and woke up Pete, who was stretched out face down on his bed, his arms straight at his sides, looking somehow as if he was propelling himself to the surface of some dark and opaque liquid.

"Good news, Pete. You're going home. Understand? You're going home." I shook him until he turned to sit up. I repeated the false message. "Come on. It's a great day out. Let's go and celebrate."

The paths were crowded, and I held onto his arm to prevent collisions with the stream of rather shaky pedestrians, all of them maimed in some way, mixed up with the work parties lugging in more medical supplies and equipment. The exhaust fumes from the traffic drifted over the walls of the convent as though we were testing a new poison gas. Overhead, our esteemed ally's air power made a shattering roar, flying in daylight formation as they did because their navigators, so the legend went, were not good enough for night operations.

The noise from the air and from the road caused something to slip inside my own rather tender skull, in the way two plates of the earth's crust rub together to make a tremor. I grabbed Pete by the lapels and pushed him up against the stone wall.

"Come on, Pete. Knock it off. You're going home now. It's all over for you, but I've got to go back. You understand that? I've got to go back and you're home free. Don't you want to go home and see your folks?"

Whether from my unpredictable brutality; or the thought

that he might be released from his cocoon back into that household where there was so much prayer and so little love; or the dawning realization that he would have to maintain his catatonia through the rigours of more examinations and tests by hard experts, and then keep it up so that he could be invalided into the tender care of his parents, walking the fine line of a border case harmless enough to stay at home without going into an actual institution — I don't know. The fact is that on that sunny wartime day, with engines thundering nearby, Pete Thorpe tried to tell me something. He did it by mimicry.

This time he was Charlie McCarthy.

"You do that again, so help me I'll mow you down." The voice was exact, high-pitched, and raucous. I didn't know how to duplicate the ventriloquist's bland tones, so I continued to yell over the passing uproar in my own voice.

"You're going home to your mom and dad," I shouted. "Can't you get that through your head?"

I stepped back when I heard the unmistakable voice of his own father, that bitter nasal whine issued through teeth always clenched in the smiling grimace of brotherly love for corrupt mankind, no matter what it had done to him. The words were clear and came in a torrent, and he seemed to be chewing as though during a meal around the table.

"Them and their airs. False righteousness and sinful pride. Contempt for others. Good works, pah! Him strutting around in the shadow of false teachers. They're bad blood, I tell you, bad blood. Worse than the unbelievers, swollen with the maggots of ambition."

I could see them. As youngsters we had been in the Thorpes' dining-room just once; it was when the old man, caught up in another one of his obsessions, had enticed us in from the street with the promise of lemonade and films. From somewhere he had obtained a silent black-and-white print of an anti-smoking film that featured a villainous character who taught his dog how to smoke and then the dog had died, coughing up chocolate syrup for blood. We had managed to keep a straight face, then went home and tried to teach our dogs how to smoke. There were some sick dogs on the street for the next few days because most of them ate the cigarettes we had doled out from some Turrets nickel packs to which we had contributed a couple of pennies each.

I don't know why I'm so sure that it was in the Thorpes' dining-room where Pete's father was holding forth; except that I couldn't visualize the monologue taking place anywhere else. With three projecting bay windows that faced the yellow wooden siding of the Roothes' place, the room was dark, with deep-brown stained woodwork and a round table in the middle, painted black, and high-backed wooden chairs with leatherette covers held down by rough metal studs. It was a suite right out of the Eaton's catalogue.

I could see Pete's father, eyes hooded in the gloom, saying his words softly, almost in a whisper, to his huge alien wife, who seldom spoke because of her funny accent, and to Pete, hunched, ashamed about yet another foreign dish his mother had cooked, the reason why their house smelled different from the others, setting them apart yet again.

Where was Diane? I felt she wasn't there.

As Pete whispered on — in a way he had become sort of a medium for his father — I began to sense that Diane had been banished to her tiny room at the back of the house. On he went, reviewing and sifting the transgressions, until I caught a passing phrase, rustling by quickly as a weed blows around in a dust-whirl, that mentioned "the rally at the grounds" and "him strutting around." By this time I was straining to pick up the sequence of words dribbling so softly from Pete.

No, it wasn't Pete any more.

He had passed over to somewhere else. But this had been the first clue. For it must have been Albert Roothe he was talking about. Then there was a watchful pause as though someone had left the room, perhaps Thorpe's wife returning to the kitchen. The voice dropped even lower so that I had to edge closer to hear.

Outlined against the bright-yellow siding of the house next door, where the muted sun somehow slipped its light into the narrow spaces, old man Thorpe now leaned forward to confide something to his only son.

"I am now going to tell you something which you may or may not completely understand, and I who have kept you all these years, safe, healthy, and in a household the Lord knows I have tried to keep in faith against the corruption all around us, and tolerant of our own temptations: I know about your crystal set, you know. Stop your cringing. There's no injury coming to you, only to me. I am going to admit to you that I have failed and ask your forgiveness.

"Yesterday, Saturday, when you all went to that picnic and rally, against what I knew in my heart you should have been doing, a weakening on my part that I let you all go, an inner voice, possibly that of the Lord, but, if not, for a sinner like myself a real sense of dread, gave me the jitters. All that day I stayed in the house with the shades drawn to meditate and pray that you, your mother, and Diane would not be led into false ways by this so-called prophet (or saviour) who gathered around him ambitious men like Albert Roothe.

"All day I remained here and prayed for all of you, that you would come back to me whole in spirit, and not with your eyes afire with the prospect of a hope that could only lead you to the hell of bitterness and disillusion. It must have been towards evening when I arose to go to the kitchen and have the sandwiches that your mother had left for me in the icebox. The house was so empty, so silent; without all of you around, I began to notice the drip, drip, of the overflow from the melting ice, down the spigot into the pan under the icebox. Afterwards, I wondered if it was a sign; the dripping water seemed to speak to me of a baptism, but not in the usual way, a message I couldn't grasp. So I took the pan out to the back door to throw the water onto the grass.

"And when the water had gone from the pan, I happened to look up, and there, along the lane, I saw your sister and the boy slipping into the barn. I don't know how long I stood there with that empty pan, like a prospector who has washed for gold and finds only vile and stinking slime. All of my being told me to go there and drag them out, but a guiding hand seemed to touch me and hold me back. I seemed to realize that my final test had come, and instead of doing what any father should have done, I went back into the house, ashamed that I had drawn back, yet awaiting a further sign.

"I didn't eat. I didn't know what to do. To think that she had come away from that frantic mob over town with the brother of one of theirs to go into that barn and.... I wondered if I was running a fever. I filled the basin with icy water and dipped my head into it. Then, still wet, I remember kneeling on the green tile of the gas fireplace, as if the mantel was an altar, and rubbing my head against the bricks until I thought they'd scraped through to the bone. My prayers went unanswered, and the rage of Satan was in me. The next thing I knew I was there in Diane's room, the devil forcing my trembling hands to tear her dresses into shreds. And I fell onto her fresh, odorous bed, and I must have fallen into blessed sleep until I heard the clump of feet on the front porch.

"There you were! I couldn't believe my eyes. Your mother remarked on the place being in darkness, and she was excited, almost forgetting her English, babbling on about the rally and how wonderful it had been. You slid past and went off to your room to your crystal set. I couldn't believe that Diane was with her. Had what I had seen out the back door been only a vision? I began to question my own sanity. So I asked.

"Your mother told me that Diane had not been with her, that she thought she'd been in the streetcar ahead, that she and the Roothe boy had been waiting for her at the stop to walk down the street with her. I turned on the hall light, and I could read her face (I can tell your mother's mind) and saw that she was not part of the conspiracy. So then I knew it wasn't so, that they had left the barn to stand at the streetcar stop, car after car going past, until the one came along with your mother and you on it. What had happened at the rally, the orgy of false hope, had so blinded her that she hadn't noticed they had slipped away, or maybe they told her they were going to sit in another part of the grandstand and they'd meet her later. She hadn't missed them! Do you understand now? Never mind. I didn't have any idea what to do.

"Over breakfast the next day I watched your mother as she silently mended Diane's clothing, looking up at me with reproach and awe at what I had done, yet not knowing why, nor why I had forbad your sister to sit among us at the same table and partake of the mercies of Grace. You didn't say anything, didn't ask. And I saw in your sister the flash of guilt, the sudden knowledge that I must have known or figured it out, and her green eyes filled up as I told her, calmly yet with authority, that she had to stay in her room until I said she could come out. If you've been wondering why all these things have been going on within your family, you are now much wiser, I hope — nor have I told your mother any of this; I don't expect to. Here we are then, and I've brought you into my confidence in the full knowledge that a son has the burden and the final joy of facing up to the world of true Christian responsibility and must gird himself, steel himself with an inner core of strength to contend with the works of the Evil One who is always around us, poking and testing. I asked for guidance before taking the step to include you in this struggle, which you now join. We must pray together in the search for a just resolution.

"All I want you to do is get the lad out alone for a talk so that I can set him straight. Surely you see the need for a God-fearing father to do that to protect his daughter who is your own sister. Look, we have to do something before she gets into trouble or worse. She must be brought back to us, and the boy must realize he can't have her.

"Son? Peter? It's only right, only fair to both of them before they do what they may regret for the rest of their lives. You understand? Now, here's what I want you to do. . . . "

The voice changed.

Now, Pete Thorpe, throwing gravel against the stone wall of a convent in this faraway land, became his own sister. Although it was bright daylight, I could feel he was crouching in the dark under that window to whisper in his sister's voice at the open screen, the tabs pushed up. There was a pause, and Pete's sister asked Babe to meet her at the barn right away.

Then Pete himself ran — I mean at that moment, not in the time past he was recreating in those voices. He ran by me in jumps, knocked aside a couple of ambulatory cases tottering on the gravel path, and headed towards the convent followed by orderlies who realized something was up. My conscience had erupted in black spots. For a moment I couldn't move. By the time I had reached Pete's ward, they had jabbed him with a sedative and he was sweaty and comatose on his bed, his eyes closed and his skin as bleached as a scrubbed parsnip. The nursing sister told me to get lost.

Back in my own stifling ward, alone in the room, I began to realize what his mimicry had been trying to convey. For his father he had done Di's voice under the window in the dark, and Babe had slipped out of the house next door to sneak along the moonlit alley into the hot, humid interior of Headley's barn, where he didn't meet Di but Pete's father. But that didn't resolve the question. Had Babe, after feeling that soft raspy voice shatter him with biblical condemnation, stayed alone, frightened beyond belief, to finger and play with the rope Pete's father had probably left draped across his shaking knees like the dry, scaly corpse of a rattler? Or had Babe found himself left alone, fiddling in despair with a piece of rope he found on the floor of the loft in the dark? Or had Pete's father —

I couldn't let it go.

The next morning, before he left us forever, I found Pete, glassy-eyed and sitting up in bed, drinking thin soup through a straw. The nursing sister was down at the other end of the ward, and I only had time for one last question.

"Pete, why?"

He bit a piece off the straw and spat it onto the grey blanket. For an instant the eyes focused and his own voice came through the inner turmoil.

"Jesus, sometimes you're dumb. You're supposed to be the smart one, you and your big smile and your good looks. All the girls playing dead for you, and you pick on Di, for chrissake. You didn't know, did you, Babe? He wanted her for himself. Why do you think he'd never go up to the Mercy Seat, why we ran around from church to church like that? He wasn't going to let you have her, or nobody else. And you let him, there in the dark in the barn, spook you, hypnotize you, about your sin? What a sucker you were, Babe. He didn't keep the flashlight on you, he kept it on himself so you had to stay fixed on the shine in those eyes.

"And what he must've done was hint there was a way to

repent, and maybe it just came to him, and he told you to stand on the box with the rope loosely around your neck and contemplate the blackness of hell and the prospect of death and he would leave you there to come down when you'd taken your own vows against lust and fornication. And, kind of dazed or scared, or just going along because there wasn't anything else you could do, you got up on the box. Then you saw him turn away and shine the flashlight along the boards to find the ladder, and when you saw him turning away, thinking it was all over, you must've said something. Probably a wisecrack. You couldn't let him get away with it, could you? You had to show him he hadn't gotten through. And before you could do anything about it, he had scuttled back from the ladder, his lungs whistling from the rage that overcame him. And then he kicked out the box.

"Maybe he waited for a moment or two and meant to take you down with nothing more than a bad burn around your neck, but it was all too fast, the weight of your solid bone snapping the rope and crushing your neck. All too fast. All too late. You fell for it — fell right into it."

"Not you again!" said the nursing sister. "You're to stay away from him. Hear?"

So that was it.

Now I could tell Dr. Knowles, explain what the real cause for Pete's sickness was: the key that might enable the others back at Neurological, or maybe others at Ponoka or Oliver, to restore him and never send him back to that other house where they had moved when the harassment by Billy Cawner had provided a suitable excuse. The doctors would know what to do when I told them. Or perhaps Knowles would ask me to keep going until I found more of the answer, maybe not so much for Pete's benefit as my own.

I would go to the chaplain and tell him there was no desertion from the army here, that Pete was someone who only wanted to escape from his identity so badly that he had found comfort and a home inside a stinking, gut-splattered tank.

Above all, I had to answer to myself. What to do with the legacy that Pete, in a last desperate attempt to ingratiate himself with our bunch, had left to me? What if I went to Albert and told him? — Albert, whose price for his own success had been the suppression of his grief over Babe, who had refused to ask the questions that might have revealed too much about himself and the ideal, moral world he was trying to create. For Albert had survived yet another death, that of Aberhart in 1943, and he had joined his heirs in the Cabinet among practical men who looked back on 1935 and made wry faces about their youthful hopes. No, not Albert, and not his parents, who savoured his good fortune as partial payment for what they had lost. My own folks? For what purpose? No, it was an awful thing better left shrouded. Someone just might go to the authorities, reopen the case, and send ripples of pain across the years, even to Diane, sweaty and earnest, in Africa.

Silently, I made atonement to Pete for the heedless brutality that had kept me nagging at him for my own curiosity and gratification. Pete, old pal, I said, I swear to you I will never breathe a word of this to anyone who was there in 1935. I decided to go and tell this to Pete, hoping he would understand, and that, after it was said, he would realize he was truly one of the gang. This might prove to be the trigger that would start him on the way to recovery.

But I did nothing, and by the next day it was too late.

That night, in a last-ditch attempt to mess up the steel tide rumbling down the road towards them, the enemy diverted the buzzbombs from the port-city targets and, possibly by reducing fuel loads, flattened out their trajectories for more immediate work. One of them sputtered into silence and, on stubby wings, wobbled out of the clear frosty night well short of the road. It ended up in a grove of poplars at the far end of the hospital.

The entire wing where Pete was located collapsed, and there was enough terror, damage, and confusion even down at our ward to cause some of us, although unhurt except for glass cuts and bruises, to go off our heads. We had been through too much, and this was the end.

So it happened that it was me who ended up in Number One Neurological for several months and was then sent home. I went back to the prairie with its dusty brown roads and blinding skies.

There, in its silence and purity, I slowly mended. I never went on with my education, but by 1948 was learning all the oil lingo about step-outs, options, and the checkerboard system. Soon after, I met my wife and was on my way to becoming a small-time conglomerate, too busy to worry or feel guilty about the past, until an old woman died in an armchair with an overdue library book on her lap.

Pete Thorpe disappeared forever—no body, no tags, no trace. I'm sure that he had been there raving in the convent garden and that it wasn't in my imagination. I sometimes wonder if he walked away from the rubble and has been wandering around Europe ever since, curling up at nights in a foetal clutch in some dank culvert.

That was a long time ago, though, and I'm all right now.